*Trap*

A Nicki Foster Mystery

Why is Paris burning? For money, a lot of it, more than you can possibly imagine. A serial arsonist killer is loose and American Interpol agent Nicki Foster fights to stop him. To stay alive, Nicki and Fire Captain Paul Denis race to solve a puzzle leading to an immense fortune. Lose the race and a flashover fire will burn them alive, leaving only an x-ray of them behind.

UN-TIED ARTISTS

Based in Silicon Valley, these authors write comic fiction, thrillers, mysteries and adventures. Un-Tied Artists donate proceeds from sales of their books to Doctors Without Borders.

In 1999, the Nobel Peace Prize was awarded to Doctors Without Borders for their work in relieving the suffering of underprivileged countries. Why a peace prize for doctors? Because terrorists find eager recruits among the despairing millions of this world, living in unthinkable conditions.

See more about Un-Tied Artists and their books at
**www.SiliconValleyNovel.com**

# Other books by Un-Tied Artists

*Satan's Touch* is a Cold War spy thriller, based on the author's real life experiences working for CIA. The novel is a tale of malice and greed, the fast-paced action of Ludlum spiced with the sinister logic of Le Carré. *Satan's Touch* is the story of a man trained by the KGB and still having its power behind him. Driven by twisted obsessions, he's determined to find something he was forced to abandon years ago.

*Everest is Hollow* is an adventure novel, featuring a teenage Indiana Jones-style archaeologist. His nickname is "Trouble." Together with his friends Nuru and Tattoo, Trouble climbs Mount Everest's difficult West Ridge. Trouble enters a cave and realizes Everest is hollow. He discovers an abandoned city, the key to a lost civilization built on treasures of the past.

The theme of *Wire* is Watergate meets *The Fugitive*. A spunky investigative reporter uncovers a conspiracy involving a Presidential candidate. She finds herself stalked by a pro hit man. She lives on the run, chased by an assassin code-named Elijah. His connections reach everywhere she goes for help, including the FBI.

Stir outrageous characters in a thick sauce of greed and you have the recipe for *Silicon Valley Game*. This is a humorous, naughty book that really dishes. Everyone searching Google is curious to peek inside lives caught in the Silicon Valley Game. What will they find? Answer - backstabbing, gossip and juicy scheming.

# Trap

A Nicki Foster Mystery

This book's story and characters are fictitious. The story is set in Paris, France, Lake Geneva, Switzerland and Los Angeles, CA USA. Some well known public agencies, locations and establishments are discussed. But the characters in this novel are entirely imaginary.

ISBN-13: 978-0-9817702-7-7
ISBN-10: 0-9817702-7-4

Published in the United States of America by Un-Tied Artists

# 1

# The First Burn

At three A.M. in the morning Paris was quiet, unaware of the tragedy that would happen in a few minutes. City Commissioner Alain Vernier stared at Paris through the windows of his 22<sup>nd</sup> floor office. His view was spectacular, especially at night. Paris was truly the city of light. Well-lit boulevards glittered like diamond necklaces and thousands of lamps outlined every joint in the Eiffel Tower's iron skeleton.

Vernier glanced at his $50,000 Patek Philippe wristwatch. He was Swiss and expected everything to follow his detailed plan. Alain Vernier was angry when seconds ticked past the exact mark of three A.M. and nothing happened. He peered intently at a dark speck in the distance where his destiny was in the hands of another person. Vernier hated delegating control over his life to anyone, even a top professional paid several million dollars per job.

At last it happened, almost five minutes late. Orange flame seared the night, a pinprick of brilliant light like the flash on a camera. The visual event was over so fast Vernier had trouble believing anything happened. He was reassured by a red glow marking the spot where a quick fire had occurred.

Vernier knew a police inspector would call in an hour and ask for instructions on how to deal with newspapers and television stations eager for a ghoulish story. The chief inspector would expect Vernier to be at home, asleep and he'd pretend to be there. That was the beauty of cell phones. Nobody really knew where you were.

City Commissioner Vernier leaned back in his custom-made executive chair and relaxed. He allowed himself a rare smile of satisfaction. Soon he wouldn't have to worry about doing favors for campaign donors. They'd be doing favors for him, whether they liked it or not. He wouldn't need wealthy patrons to build his power base. He'd be richer than any of them. Oh, there were risks, but in his position there were always risks.

He indulged himself in a snifter of hundred-year-old cognac until the police finally called him. Vernier let his cell phone chime again and again, as though he were forcing himself to awaken from a deep sleep. Finally, he answered the call. "Yes, what is it?"

Alain Vernier heard the timid voice of Chief Inspector Clement apologizing for waking up the City Commissioner. Clement explained details of a crime scene, a burned warehouse. He cleared his throat and asked a hesitant question. The media were demanding a press conference. What should he tell reporters?

Vernier waited a moment as though he were thinking, but his reply had been rehearsed for weeks, part of a deliberate plan. "Tell the press," he said, "that we are speeding up the investigation by having Interpol assist us."

"Interpol?" Chief Inspector Clement asked in disbelief, his pride stung. "I assure you we can handle anything – "

Vernier cut him off. "Chief Inspector, this warehouse fire was obviously the work of an arsonist, a top professional. A pro will not stay in France, waiting to be caught. By now, he is out of the country. We must take immediate steps to find the criminal. I don't want to wait two weeks before you look for this arsonist in other countries. I want Interpol on the case now. Do you understand me?"

"Of course, City Commissioner," was the choked reply. There was a long pause. Then Clement asked in a tight voice, "Is there anything else?"

"Yes." Vernier talked in a slow, malicious way. "Last year, you told me with great pride how you solved an old case. But I discovered all the clues were found by an Interpol agent, a young woman. You even sent a note praising her to Interpol Headquarters in Lyon. I want her on this case, since you think so highly of her. I believe she was – " Vernier paused, as though he was trying to recall her name.

"Nicki Foster," was the strained response from Chief Inspector Clement.

"Good, you remember her. Get this Foster out of bed. Have her look at the fire scene. Maybe she can get this case moving." Vernier said the last part with deliberate contempt. "Oh, and have the Fire Chief report to my office in an hour. I'll meet him there and present him with a little 'gift' for his incompetent training methods." Alain Vernier was rude, hanging up the phone on the Surete Chief Inspector.

Vernier wanted the insult to sting, wanted to make certain Chief Inspector Clement hated Nicki Foster and hoped she would fail. That, of course, was the whole idea. She was supposed to fail.

There was great satisfaction in humiliating Nicki Foster, ending her promising career. A year ago, Foster caused City Commissioner Vernier a lot of trouble by solving an old crime. He'd done a favor for a powerful lobbyist and made a problem go away. But that meddling American Interpol agent wrecked everything. She resurrected the case by finding carefully hidden clues. Vernier wanted revenge against Nicki Foster and he was getting it, starting this morning.

Vernier looked at the 24-carat gold clock on his desk, one of the rare antiques he collected. A modern digital mechanism had replaced the inner workings of the timepiece. The clock showed 4:38 A.M. By now the Surete were calling Nicki Foster, pushing her into Vernier's trap.

# 2

# Nicki Foster

I was snuggled in the fold-down bed of my Montmartre studio apartment, deep asleep, dreaming of Central Park in the crisp air and brilliant colors of Autumn, when my home town of New York City finally has weather fit for human beings. I was hoping the dream would take me into MOMA, the Museum of Modern Art, and I'd spend a pleasant moment floating into Rene Magritte's *The Human Condition*, a mischievous painting where you can't tell where the canvas ends and reality begins.

As usual I didn't get my wish. Instead, I woke to the annoying trilling of my phone, sounding like an alarm clock. I should have ignored it. Answering that call was a big mistake, the kind that twists your life inside out. But I lifted my head and fumbled for the telephone. I put the cool plastic handset against my ear and heard a scratchy voice asking for Nicki Foster of Interpol.

My mouth was dry. I ran my tongue around my parched mouth to find some saliva, so I could talk without sounding like I was in the hospital. Finally I croaked, "Yeah . . . this is Nicki. What's wrong?"

The answer shocked me. "Sorry. All right, I'll check the fire scene for you. I have to go now? It's the middle of the night." My room was black inside. It couldn't be time to get up. There wasn't a trace of light pushing through the sheers on the window. I looked around and couldn't see anything in the dark but green lettering of the clock telling me it was 4:38 A.M. "OK, I'll go right away." I sighed.

I threw the comforter around me and stumbled out of bed, wishing there was time for breakfast, at least a cup of instant coffee to warm my hands in the car. I glanced at the crumbs of last night's dinner, left on a paper plate. A life-long New Yorker, I wanted to be in Zabar's, devouring a bagel slathered with cream cheese and strawberry jam. I could almost smell the espresso and hear the steam hissing.

Instead, I grabbed clean panties and dragged them on my tired body. Pulling a thin sweater over my head, I got a fuzz in my mouth and plucked lint off my tongue, sputtering. I loved the sweater for its soft warmth, though it had a nasty habit of shedding all over me. A pair of casual wool slacks finished my outfit. I didn't need to wear a formal business suit, just something to keep me warm. I was walking through a burned warehouse, not a diplomatic gala, escorting the secret service.

I swirled a cap of mouthwash to rinse away any dragon breath and did a fast check in the mirror, roughing up my hair so it looked combed. My mind was still asleep, hardly grasping that I was going to work. I grabbed my leather jacket, wallet and car keys, then started out the door. Walking down the worn treads of my apartment stairs, I peeked through a stairway window for a glimpse of Montmartre's famed church, the Sacre Coeur. Its unique beehive domes poked above the rooftops. The day was just starting, with pink sunlight leaking over buildings. Dew steamed off Sacre Coeur's white domes in fine wisps.

I reached in my jacket and snapped a quick photo with my battered camera, a high school graduation present that should have been discarded years ago. But it still worked, so I kept it handy, using it to freeze beautiful images. I promised myself I'd one day paint those images, dragging my dusty easel to the apartment roof on a mythical Sunday morning to start my real life. In the meantime, my other "real life" was calling. I hustled downstairs to find the Interpol car I'd taken home last night, against regulations.

My path threaded among the most eccentric homes in Paris, with styles that were strange even in Montmartre, where bizarre is normal. I turned into a courtyard formed by a jumble of houses squeezed together. A miniature Tuscan villa leaned into a Swiss chalet, sharing a wall with a modernistic concrete box. In another block, I found the patrol car I'd driven home and wiped dew off its windshield.

The sun rose as I drove, brightening rooftops but turning streets into dark canyons where long shadows played over the sidewalks, sliding across streets and up storefronts. I fell in line with early commuters rolling down Montmartre's hills. Paris unfolded below me in a carpet of twinkling buildings and streaking headlights. I took a moment to fall in love with the city all over again.

Paris is a mood that touches everyone who stops at a sidewalk cafe and experiences how intimate each little nook of a huge, anonymous city can feel. Every block is its own world, with shops and restaurants that are tiny by American standards, barely larger than a bedroom. There's always a bistro anchoring the end of the block. Seven generations bought their tobacco here because their parents did. They lean their elbows on the same zinc bar to drink a beer at day's end, before climbing flights of stairs to a small flat they call home.

The city is a paradox of tradition and energy where you always feel something unexpected is going to happen. For me, the unexpected was about to happen, and I wouldn't like it. What came next wasn't a dream but a nightmare. A slide into hell was starting and soon I'd be scrambling for a way out, fighting for my life.

# 3

# Flashover

At 5:16 A.M. my unmarked Interpol sedan jiggled over potholed asphalt in an older section of Paris. I parked behind a delivery truck and opened the car door, stepping into a frigid dawn. Jamming cold hands in my jacket pockets, I walked toward the fire scene, my breath forming clouds in the icy morning air. All around me, water from a firefighting effort rushed downhill in thick streams, pouring into gutters and drains with a loud gurgling sound. The morning sun glistened on the thick pool of water, a flood spilling over sidewalks, painting them black with cinders. I was forced to jump from one island of ugly debris to another, making my way over fire hoses wrapped like thick spaghetti around a burned warehouse.

I glanced up and saw a firefighter approaching me, a silver fire captain's badge glinting on his coat. The black fireproof coat hung to his ankles, dragging against slick yellow boots. He looked about thirty and a long, difficult night showed in his tired walk and the soot on his face. The tightness in his eyes and the hard set of his jaw made him look tough, street smart yet there were kind eyes stranded on the hard face.

He walked over to me. "Good morning. I'm Paul Denis. You're Inspector Foster of Interpol?"

"Yes. But nobody calls me Inspector Foster. I go by Nicki." I gave him a warm smile in sympathy for his exhaustion.

Paul yanked off a thick Nomex fire glove, tucking it under an arm. He shook my hand and the skin on his fingers was coarse as sandpaper, calloused from dragging fire hoses the way a fisherman hauls lines. "Thanks for coming right away. The Paris police were here earlier. They said Interpol would look at the damage. Where do you want to start?"

"With the injured firefighters." I took out a notebook to capture details. "They're most important. Were they hurt inside the building?"

"They weren't injured, Nicki. They were killed. The entire crew died over there, by the fire truck." Paul Denis swept his hand toward a wrecked fire engine. The raw power of the firestorm had bent a seven ton vehicle into a horseshoe.

I was astonished to see fire helmets stuck in the truck's side like arrows shot in a target. Apparently the firefighters were blown into the truck, slammed backward by a blast of fire. Heat welded their helmets to the steel truck, bending tough safety hats into the shape of licking tongues. Six firefighters were still wearing those helmets when the hats melted, pouring burning plastic on their faces. Then the firestorm finished the job, incinerating ears and lips.

I couldn't pull my eyes off blackened flesh left on the chin strap of a helmet. I knew a person's face burned until only their jaw remained, seared to the leather strap. "God," I muttered. I realized my hands were tight fists and took a deep breath, prying my stiff fingers open. I dragged my eyes off the charred flesh and put them on Paul Denis.

"I pulled a jaw out of that helmet so the teeth can be ID'd by the coroner." His face tightened. "It's a sickening thing, you know?"

I could see the pain in his eyes. "You've been through a lot. Do you need a few minutes by yourself, before we go ahead?"

"No," Paul insisted. "This won't get any easier. Let's do it now."

"OK." I nodded in sympathy. "You found their heads, but what happened to their bodies?"

"We didn't find any bodies, Nicki." Paul Denis motioned to yellow splashes on the ground, like someone dumped paint cans in the alley. "The yellow was their boots." He pointed at sparkling white streaks, glistening in the street. "Here's reflective striping from their coats."

I said in astonishment, "The fire was so hot their bodies melted into the ground? Boots, coats, everything?"

"Yes. Splashes of color are all that's left of them. Here's proof." Paul picked up a crowbar lying on the ground. He used the tip of the steel bar to outline a human hand, ironed by the fire's heat until the hand was flat as a sheet of paper. The fingers were gray shadows like an x-ray of a hand, just bones fanning from the wrist joint. The curled fingers were grasping for a way out and it never happened. Instead the firefighters' last moments were tortured by savage pain as their skin burned off. I felt nauseous at how the crew died and took deep breaths to settle my stomach.

Paul Denis was studying me intently, a sympathetic look on his face. "You're all right?"

"Yeah. I'm OK. It hit me how they died." I asked Paul, "Did you know any of the crew?"

"I knew Fire Captain Charles Blanc." He looked sadly at yellow streaks marking the dead fire crew. "One time, Charles saved my life." Paul tossed the crowbar down in disgust and it hit the ground with a ringing sound. He slapped his hands gently against the heavy black firecoat. "Well, taking risks is what we're paid to do."

"Not these kind of risks," I said. "So this was some businessman torching his warehouse for insurance money?"

"Oh, it had to be arson. This fire was very unusual. The arsonist cooked the burn so hot it melted bodies into the ground. That rarely happens. It needs a flashover, a blast of intense heat that doesn't linger. A flashover does a quick melt. A long fire leaves ashes. To get a flashover, the arsonist needed an exotic chemical. This guy was a real pro."

Paul shifted his weight and looked down. He dragged a shoe in a tight circle, scraping at the alley with his boot. "This wasn't just an arson job by a top pro. Maybe it's paranoid of me, but I'm sure there's more to it."

I encouraged Paul, "OK, be paranoid. What else is on your mind?"

"The arsonist wanted to kill my firefighters and he did it exactly right, a perfect ambush. He caught us getting off the truck, when we were standing together. This was a trap, I can feel it. I think the arsonist was watching and called in a fire alarm, pretending to be a security guard. His timing was perfect. He waits for the crew to step off the truck, then ignites his torch. Bam, his flashover hits the firefighters and kills them."

"OK, this was a deliberate killing." The idea sickened me, but I went on with my job. "Any ideas why the arsonist wanted the fire crew dead?"

"No, I haven't a clue. Worse, I have a bad feeling it won't end here. We'll be hit again soon."

"I hope not." I let out a sigh and watched my breath fog in the cold morning air. "It takes a long time to catch a professional arsonist. Did you find anything that might speed up the investigation?"

He wagged his head in a no. "I'll cut a slice of the melted floor and send a sample to the lab. They can look for trace chemicals, find what accelerant the arsonist used. But it'll take days to sort out what happened here. Everything in that warehouse fused in the heat, mixing up the clues."

"Sorry," I sympathized. "Did you find containers that held the accelerant? Or fragments of the triggering device used to ignite the torch?"

"No and I doubt we will," Paul responded, kicking cinders out of his way.

"Why is that?" I wondered.

"Two reasons. First, this was a top pro. They have a lot of tricks for making certain no container or timer is left behind." Paul shrugged.

"And the other reason?"

"It was fifteen minutes before I got here with a backup team. That's enough time to remove any evidence. The arsonist probably wore a special suit, like they use for measurements inside volcanoes or Hollywood stunts. Wearing that suit, he could walk into the burning warehouse and carry away evidence."

"Too bad. I'm sorry." I pointed to the center of the warehouse, where the firestorm burned a shallow impression in the concrete floor. Steel beams were twisted by the firestorm with tremendous force. "Maybe there's a clue in the shape of things. I wish I could see this place from above, look down on it. I can get a helicopter this afternoon and take photos from the air."

Paul smiled. "Let's take the photos now." I had an uneasy feeling about what he was going to suggest. Before I could protest, Paul walked toward a half-block-long aerial ladder truck with its stabilizers spread out. "Come on," he shouted, waving at me to catch up with him.

I followed Paul up a chrome ladder. There was a catwalk running along the fire engine, a truck so long it needed two drivers. There was a second firefighter in a booth at the back of the vehicle. He steered the rear wheels and controlled the aerial ladder. Paul waved at the guy in the booth and got a thumbs up, meaning we were going to be lifted in the air.

I climbed on a small platform at the end of the aerial ladder and was jerked upward about three feet, startling me. The ladder swung upward, carrying me to second story balconies. Soon I was lifted me above the roofline of surrounding buildings.

"Keep your eyes on the horizon. It helps. And hold tight," Paul shouted. He was standing a few steps below me.

"Sure," I said, trying to sound calm. I clamped my hands on the white railing in front of me as the ladder kept rising. The blue steel of the Pompidou Center became visible in the distance and I had a pretty nice view of Paris. I was beginning to like the experience when the easy part ended.

Suddenly I felt like I was on a thrill ride in an amusement park, but without the safety features. I shot forward as ladder sections extended. At the same time, I swirled around, twisting over the warehouse. The illusion of safety from having a huge fire engine under me was gone. I was floating sixty feet off the ground, my shoes on a thin steel plank, wind rushing up my pant legs. When we stopped moving, I was pushed into the railing with a shallow grunt.

"You're over the warehouse. You can look down now," Paul announced.

"Great." I hoped I'd spoken the word without revealing my anxiety. I took a deep breath and glanced down. Sixty feet below was the burned-out shell of the building. The warehouse roof was gone and tall brick walls were shortened to a charred hedge. Inside the hedge, blackened steel pillars looked like a crop burned in a grass fire, rows of dead stalks waiting to fall in the wind. The arson had been incredibly hot, baking the cement floor into colored glass, like artist's ceramic glazed in a kiln. Any contents stored in the warehouse were gone, turned into colored splotches scattered across the glassy floor. I stared at the hot cement floor and was fascinated by swirls of colored glass running under me.

I could see a path where the firestorm cut through the warehouse, slamming things out of its way. Heat flamed out the loading dock and hit six firefighters chest high, tearing off their heads. A half dozen heads strapped to helmets were shot into a fire engine like arrows and the seven ton truck was bent in a "U." Six headless bodies were pressed with enormous force into the pavement. The blast of heat flattened the bodies, ironing their stretched torsos on the asphalt. The shapes of a half dozen dead firefighters were etched on the pavement below me.

I put aside the grisly image and shouted over a cold, snapping wind. "We need a picture of this. The path of the fire is a good clue."

"You got it," Paul yelled back. "There's a pair of arson investigation cameras in the fire engine. I'll be right back with them – unless you'd care to come along." He grinned.

"Naw, that's OK," I said, playing along with the joke. "I'll wait here and enjoy the view."

"Suit yourself." Paul put his boots outside the ladder rails. He slid downward, using gloved hands as a drag to slow his fall.

A few cold minutes later, Paul bounced upward with amazing speed, two cameras slung around his neck. He gave me a camera and draped the strap over my head. "Standard point and shoot. Autofocus, autoexposure. Have fun."

I wanted the pictures badly enough to take my hands off the railing. I clicked a few shots, timing my photos to lulls in the wind. Then I asked Paul, "What's the other camera for?"

"It takes infrared pictures instead of normal photographs. Catches hot spots. One of those hot spots is always where the blaze started, so we know where the fire originated."

"Cool," I said, getting into it. I framed a shot with the infrared camera and a gust of wind shocked me back to reality. I was a long way off the ground with no safety net. I braced a little more carefully with my legs and took some photographs.

"What now?" I asked.

"Back to earth." Paul twisted around and signaled that we wanted to descend.

The ride down was faster and more disorienting than the ride up. I was relieved to hear the aerial ladder snap into catches atop the fire truck. A minute later, I stepped off the fire engine into a wet street where fire crews were rolling up hoses. City of Paris street cleaners were pushing trash with large green brooms, clearing the boulevard for traffic.

Paul held up the cameras. "I'll load the images on my computer today."

"Great. I'd like to see the photos. So far, it's our only clue."

Paul Denis walked back to the Interpol car with me. The work day was starting and I found my car wedged between delivery trucks carrying beer to a local deli. I reached in my jacket and pulled out the car keys, dangling from a wood block stained by the oils of many hands. There was a board lined with these wooden keychains at the Interpol office, where I'd checked out the car. Normally I hopped a taxi or took the Metro. Paris traffic was even more congested than downtown Manhattan.

I opened the car door, angling my body in the driver's seat. My pants clung to the cheap vinyl that comes standard with every government vehicle. Paul Denis shut the door, surprising me with his gentle touch. I rolled the window down and started the car, letting it idle.

Paul was staring at the fire scene with sadness, his cheeks smudged with soot. He took off his bright blue fire hat and the helmet looked almost like a child's toy in his large hand. We waited each other out, Paul drumming his fingers on the car top and me tapping the steering wheel. I didn't know what to say so I didn't say anything.

An ambulance pulled away from the fire scene and turned on its siren. Paul frowned and shouted over the deafening warble. "I'll call you later, when I get the pictures uploaded." He waved and headed toward the charred warehouse. Paul Denis glided along the street, his rubber boots squishing through shallow puddles.

I watched Paul and the man-to-woman, first time you meet electricity lingered inside me with a pleasant warmth. But it didn't last long. My life wasn't destined for that kind of happiness. I drove away slowly, haunted by Paul's belief the firefighters were murdered in a deliberate ambush. It was hard for me to imagine someone being so malicious, burning people alive just to get rid of a building. Yet this really wasn't my case. It belonged to the Paris police, the Surete. Technically, I was just assisting them. Still, I wanted to do something to help Paul Denis and a half dozen firefighters who weren't going home to their families.

Driving to the Interpol office, I wasn't able to appreciate the Paris I adored. My tires rumbled over cobblestone streets where every block squeezed a dozen quaint shops with family apartments above. Each street corner held a tobacconist shop or cafe, the heart of its neighborhood society. I was passing the same cafes where Van Gogh and Picasso ate when they painted here. The cobalt blue shopfronts seemed to come from their paintings, but the charming spell was lost on me. I kept seeing the bodies of dead firefighters melted on asphalt like spilled paint.

I flashed on that ugly image several times before I curled off Boulevard St. Germain, spiraling down the ramp to Interpol's underground parking. The garage's exhaust fumes smelled like perfume compared to arson smells lingering inside my car. For once I was actually glad to park and step into the gloom of the old basement.

I rode the slow elevator upward, staring through its open cage at cleaning crews running floor polishers. I didn't see how they could stand that monotonous whining, day after day. The noise was deafening. At the third floor, my shoes squeaked along a waxed hallway until I got to the last office. I touched the door marked "Interpol" and felt surprisingly edgy. The tension wouldn't go away. Anxiety stuck to me like I'd brushed against a spider web and the web was clinging on my jacket. I had to force myself to open the door and step inside.

# 4

# Interpol

The Interpol office is normally loud and frantic like a stock exchange with people yelling, pagers beeping and cell phones distracting everyone. But my workplace was strangely silent at this early morning hour. The quiet haunted me and I felt unsafe in a place that should be my own. I had a feeling something bad was going to happen this morning, on top of the warehouse fire. I hesitated, then hit a bank of switches. The office lights blinked on, revealing a crowded room without an ounce of privacy.

There were no individual cubicles where you have some personal space, a thin fabric wall taped with your snapshots. Instead, twenty desks were crammed in a bullpen, the desks shoved together to save space. Their plain wood showed years of abuse in chipped edges and missing drawer handles. All the desks had the same metal lamp squatting on them, looking like a round Martian flying saucer from a 1950s sci-fi movie. I walked behind a row of flying saucers and sat at my desk, pulling out my computer.

Before I could flip open the laptop, my partner walked in the office and slid in his swivel chair. Pierre Corday had the look of a basset hound, with bags under his eyes and sagging cheeks. Gray was sprinkled in the oily curls of his brown hair. In his late forties, he looked safe, fatherly, an accountant type but that was deceptive. Corday always watched for his own interests, calculating what was in a situation for him. Anyone else was on their own. He wasn't a bad guy, just cautious, always looking out for himself.

Pierre took a careful sip from his morning cappuccino and ran a hand across his face, wiping away a milk foam mustache. He cleaned his fingers with an old rag. The gummy rag had been hanging from a drawer handle on his desk for three years and I'd never seen him wash it. I doubted I ever would. He placed the cappuccino in the center of his desk blotter, turning the cup in little steps like he had to get the position just right or it would wreck his whole day. For a messy guy, Corday was a perfectionist about some things. It was an interesting contradiction.

Nothing escaped Corday's observation, though he tried to look ignorant of everything. Pierre feigned a calculated look of surprise at my presence, even though I was sure he'd seen me from the beginning. "Oh, good morning, Nicki. Why are you at work so early? You come in around eight, usually."

I shrugged. "The Paris cops got me out of bed to look at a warehouse fire."

A little bell rang in Pierre's eyes. He gave me a wary look. "Strange. You aren't with the Paris police. You're an Interpol investigator. Why call you?"

"Why not call me? I've helped on several cases. Last year, I gave them insights into an old, unsolved crime and they made an arrest."

Pierre waved a hand in the air. "I don't buy that. The Paris cops never call Interpol until it's too late. They don't want us getting credit for solving one of their crimes. Why don't you help me instead? Crank up your luck on one of my cases." Some days provoking me was his thing in life.

"It could be I have more going for me than luck, Pierre. I might have a touch of skill, huh?"

"Life is luck for all of us. I meant no insult, Nicki." Corday waited a moment, then muttered, "I should've called in sick. Today has a bad feel, somehow. We should get out of here, Nicki. Go to the track. We don't bet. We just watch the ponies run." He cocked an eye to see if I was buying.

I gently told him, "Sorry, Pierre. I can't blow off the day and go to the track."

Corday looked away, lost in thought. A hint of sadness crept into his features. He talked very softly. "I wish you'd change your mind."

Before I could reply, his desk phone rang in a long, irritating buzz. Pierre jerked the phone to his ear and spoke in a strained voice. "Interpol, Corday speaking. Yes, I will hurry. I know who you are." He squeezed the telephone and his face tensed. "One moment. I'll get her." Pierre acted like the phone was a messy diaper. He held the receiver away from his body, stretching the cord tight. His eyes locked on me. "It's for you, Nicki."

I took the phone from him. Uncomfortable in the heat of Corday's stare, I turned away for the illusion of privacy. "This is Nicki Foster. Yes, I'll be there. Right away."

I spoke my last words to the dialtone because they hung up while I was still talking. I was summoned to a meeting with the City Commissioner of Paris, a job similar to the mayor of New York City. I put the phone down, feeling a little suspicious at this sudden invitation.

Pierre gave me a nasty smile. "You're going to love Alain Vernier, our new City Commissioner. He's a real sweetheart."

"You have to come too, Pierre." I watched Corday's smile fade.

"Shit," he swore. "Why do they want me?"

"They don't want you feeling left out," I joked.

"Damn." He couldn't escape. Corday got up and straightened his sportscoat, but straightening that old coat didn't help much.

Pierre snapped, "Come on already. We are late. Let's take the stairs. The elevator's temperamental. We can't afford to get stuck, eh?"

I sighed. "Sure, fine." I was surprised Corday didn't want to use the elevator. He never walked when he could ride. But today Pierre skipped down the worn staircase, moving very quickly for an out of shape guy.

Trailing Corday down the steps, I rushed through the front doors and found myself blocked by restless schoolchildren jamming the sidewalk. I slid between kids in blue uniforms with backpacks and jaywalked into intense street traffic on Boulevard St. Germain. Dodging angry commuters, I made my way to safety at an art deco lamppost on the sidewalk.

A half minute later, I stood in a huge lobby where marble coated the floor and walls, gleaming stone surfaces reflecting each other like mirrors. I stepped inside the polished brass of an elevator and stood there like a department store mannequin as the doors shut. The box jiggled upward and I watched floor numbers roll in the control panel, six tumbling into eleven. Eventually twenty-two bounced up and the elevator doors parted. I started walking on inch-thick carpet, soft as a fur coat. Each step sank in the deep rug, pulling on my shoes like a wet beach at low tide.

Ahead of me, the City Commissioner's secretary was sitting at a huge red desk, an island in the sea of light blue carpet. His desk shined like it had just been delivered from the showroom, smelling of lemon oil polish. The gleaming desk held only a thin laptop computer in a silver titanium case. The secretary's looks were stolen from investment bankers on Wall Street, complete with a plaid bow tie matching his plaid suspenders. Gold cufflinks pinned the white cuffs of his starched blue shirt. In keeping with the power and money look of the clothes, his hair was combed back, making a devil's Vee out of a receding hairline. A "hands-free" phone bud was plugged in one ear with the cord trailing inside his shirt collar. The secretary sat with hands folded, glaring at me.

I tried a smile on him, but the smile never had a chance.

The secretary spoke in an icy, sarcastic voice. "Commissioner Vernier's been waiting for you. You're late."

"We'll go right in, OK? That way we won't be any later." I returned the secretary's stare, walking slowly past him.

Pierre Corday grabbed my arm and whispered, "You're hopeless."

I wriggled my arm free. "He was a jerk. Cut me some slack, Pierre. I won't be that way with Vernier."

Pierre rolled his eyes. "First impressions are forever, you know?"

"Don't worry. I'll zip my lip in front of Vernier." I drew a pinched thumb and forefinger across my lips like I was zipping them shut. "You know anything about Vernier? Has he got a rep'?"

"Yes, Vernier has a reputation, Nicki. His reputation is not for kindness. Vernier is supposedly quite wealthy and I believe it. He has a penthouse on the Avenue Foch. But I don't know how much he really has because I haven't found where Vernier keeps his money, much less how he got it. He came from nowhere and doesn't belong to any of the power cliques. The City Commissioner has risen to an unusual level of powers. Many say that Vernier plays on both sides of the law, Nicki, so be very careful."

"Wonderful," I sighed. I was having a marvelous day. My day got even better when I walked into City Commissioner Vernier's office. Even with massive furniture, bookcases and a fireplace, there was enough empty space to lose a grand piano. In a world of small cubicles, Vernier's extravagant square footage was a sign of his power as City Commissioner.

Vernier's power bought him an awesome view of Paris. Floor to ceiling windows showcased the Eiffel Tower, an iron skeleton curving to wide metal legs straddling a green park. In the distance, the Seine River was a blue ribbon wrapping around the Eiffel Tower. At my feet was the domed cathedral holding Napoleon's tomb, but I felt like Napoleon was alive and I was in his office.

My eyes flicked to a short man standing in front of the plate glass windows, hands clasped behind him. City Commissioner Vernier was wearing a double-breasted blue suit with faint silver pinstripes. His red tie matched a silk handkerchief carefully folded in the chest pocket of his suit coat. A few threads of black hair streaked across the full moon of his bald head. The pale skin of his round face was pulled tight over a heavy layer of fat and a double chin sagged under his jaw.

Abruptly, Vernier sat in his executive chair, folding his hands on thick Spanish leather lining the desktop. He flexed his fingers and sunlight glinted on ten immaculately manicured fingernails. All that neatness made my skin crawl. Vernier's eyes were heavily lidded when he began talking and a bit of slyness crept into his voice. "Inspector Foster, you've spoken with Fire Captain Paul Denis. You are familiar with the case."

I answered simply. "Yes. I met Paul Denis at the burned warehouse this morning."

I looked around and realized something was wrong. Corday and I were the only people in Vernier's office. The Paris cops were supposedly in charge of this case and they should be in this meeting. I didn't have time to ask why the police weren't here before the City Commissioner spoke again.

Vernier talked in a tight, controlled voice. "Inspector Foster, I'm making you lead investigator on this warehouse fire. I've coordinated your assignment with Interpol headquarters." He paused a moment to enjoy the shock effect of his words.

His face was bland, but his eyes held a malicious smirk, just a hint of gloating at dumping this case on me. He lifted his hands off the desk in a vague wave, dismissing me. "That is all."

I was startled by Vernier making me lead investigator on the case, yet I forced myself to look calm and sound positive. "I'm flattered, but usually the fire department investigates arsons. Why isn't the Fire Chief in this meeting?"

I watched an unpleasant smile crease Vernier's inflated face. "I dismissed the Fire Chief this morning for incompetence. His firefighters should not get killed in a simple warehouse arson."

I swallowed my surprise at the Fire Chief losing his job and stayed focused on the issue. "I expected the fire department and the Paris police to be in this meeting. Their absence doesn't make sense to me."

"It does not need to make sense to you," Vernier replied coldly. "It only needs to make sense to me." He rose from his massive desk and the eyes staring at me were cold hard pebbles. "The Paris police told me you are competent, Inspector Foster. They indicated you solved crimes others failed to understand. Did they overestimate you? Perhaps they made a mistake and I should ask your superior to assign a better person to the Paris Interpol office. If you like your job, solve this case promptly."

He moved around his desk and stood near the massive entrance doors. The cathedral doors were twelve feet high, fanned open, framing his desk. Vernier spoke with chilling calm. "You have a great deal to do Inspector Foster and you can't do it in here. You can't solve this arson in my office."

I wanted to ask more questions but Pierre grabbed my arm, urging me to leave. I walked with him through the cathedral doors. We moved in silence across the plush light blue carpet, making the long trip from Vernier's office to his secretary's desk.

With each step, I could feel the look on the secretary's face burning into me. He sat there smugly in his crisp Yves St. Laurent shirt, with a sleek perfection only money and power can buy. Vernier and his secretary could be that perfect because they didn't live in the real world. They had people like me to run their errands, do their work and take any blame.

The secretary flashed an arrogant smile with sharp bright teeth. "The City Commissioner gets daily progress reports." The secretary pointed to a form orphaned on his empty desk.

I swept the report form off the desk and walked stiffly to the elevator, where a twisted image of myself glistened in the polished brass panels. I knew what the City Commissioner was doing. He was making me a political scapegoat like the Fire Chief.

I'd get the blame and lose my job if the crime wasn't solved fast enough. Vernier demanded the warehouse arson be solved immediately and no one could do it. That flashover fire was so hot that every clue melted in the ground like the bodies of those firefighters. A lump of ice formed in my stomach. Something weird was going on here.

The elevator doors slid open and a delivery service messenger ran his bicycle into my leg. He charged around me without a word of apology. I was having a wonderful day. I brushed the bicycle tire mark off my slacks and punched the down button.

When the elevator doors opened on the ground floor, I paraded with Corday through the sterile marble lobby, grateful to be leaving Commissioner Vernier's building. I waited for the traffic light to change, leaning against a lightpole in disgust. Corday had survived twenty years of politics at Interpol and maybe he had an idea that would help me. I looked for Pierre and didn't see him anywhere, so I walked around a green street kiosk racked with the latest French magazines. I found Corday thumbing a soccer daily, chatting on his cell phone.

He peered over his newspaper and saw me glaring at him. Pierre guiltily ended his phone call and jammed the newspaper back in the rack, crumpling the pages. He lamely explained, "The French National Team played an exhibition match yesterday, you know?" It was a poor excuse and he knew it.

"You could care what happens to me, huh, Pierre? I am your partner, you know. Something funny's going on here. I'm being set up to fail. There's no fire department and no Paris cops assigned to this crime, yet Vernier says the warehouse arson's important. You can't solve a pro arson job fast without a lot of resources."

A little embarrassment showed on Corday's face and he looked down, examining his scuffed loafers. "Nicki, we should talk. There are things

I need to tell you. I have some important information to give you. Let's have a drink. I'll buy, eh?"

Before I could answer, Corday slid between slow walkers and glided along the street, showing his fading athletic grace. He was heading toward an elegant sidewalk cafe frequented by wealthy businessmen and their lovers. A dark green awning flaunted the cafe's prestigious name in gold script letters. This particular sidewalk cafe was once the hangout of a penniless Ernest Hemingway, before he was a published author. But today Hemingway's favorite cafe is a chic, sophisticated bistro.

Corday normally took me to a cheap neighborhood bar for drinks, a place with stained tablecloths, stale nuts and warm tap beer. Pierre choosing an expensive bistro made me suspicious. I assumed he must have bad news to give me, somehow linked to Vernier making me lead investigator on the warehouse arson.

I caught up with Corday at the cafe's front door. The usual cynical Pierre was gone, replaced by someone I'd never met before. I was startled by how sad and detached he looked.

Corday paused near the cafe's mascot, a carved wooden figure, and rubbed the statue's tummy. He commented sadly, "For luck." Pierre gave me a hard stare. "You should rub his belly too, Nicki. You need all the luck you can get."

Corday acted like he was leading me into a strange new world I'd never seen. I had the feeling I wasn't going to like it.

# 5

# Strange World

Pierre Corday's eyes drifted along the boulevard and he stalled. "It's easier to talk after a drink." Corday sipped from his beer and clinked the glass back on the table. He said with artificial sympathy, "Your arson case is a real bitch."

I nodded, wondering why Corday was suddenly interested in my arson case when he'd been ducking it all morning. I sensed he wanted to tell me something and it wasn't good news. I picked up my snifter of green liqueur and the alcohol burned down my throat, taking the edge off my mood.

Corday dragged a crushed pack of cigarettes from his sportscoat and teased one out. He stuck the filter tip in a tobacco stained corner of his mouth and lit up. He held the cigarette in front of him and stared at smoke curling upward in a hazy question mark. "Years ago I worked for the Paris police, before I joined Interpol. I remember a certain case. It was a murder. Just a prostitute, nobody rich or powerful. But she had two kids. I met them." His voice had a strange edge to it.

I stared into the green pool left in my glass. "How's your prostitute case related to my arson?"

He flicked the ash off his cigarette and talked bitterly. "I wasn't supposed to solve the crime. They didn't want me to find who killed the prostitute."

I was holding a breadstick and put it down. I didn't like where this was going. "You're telling me not to solve this warehouse fire. I'm not supposed to catch the arsonist."

Pierre didn't answer me. Corday took a drag on his cigarette and let out a long, slow trickle of smoke.

"OK, bottom line, Pierre. Did you find who killed the prostitute? You solved the crime anyway, even though someone threatened you, right?"

Pierre cocked his head and his eyes had a melancholy look. He ground his cigarette in the ashtray, staring at the bent stub. "Well, not exactly."

"Did you arrest the killer?" I pressed.

"No. My partner left to make the arrest and we couldn't find him for a week. Then I got my partner's fingers in the mail. They looked like mangled shrimp. The coroner said my partner was tortured. The fingers were torn out of his hand with pliers – while he was still alive."

"I don't believe this. You can't be for real."

Pierre was sober now, like he hadn't drunk a beer at all. The flush was gone from his face. "I was idealistic like you, Nicki. But I learned power wins over idealism. There's a lot of power in the world. There are people with even more juice than City Commissioner Vernier. Maybe one of them wants this arson to fade away. They trade favors with the City Commissioner. Then you get the case, Nicki, and you get no help – no fire chief, no police support. It smells the same way my prostitute case did. It stinks."

"Six firefighters died, Pierre."

Corday talked in a soft, fatherly voice. "The dead firefighters aren't your fault, Nicki. You can't bring them back. Here's my advice. Don't try to solve this warehouse arson."

Irritated, I asked, "Why not?"

"Vernier will crush you and arrange the investigation the way he wants. Vernier can do it. You saw his office. You know the power he's got." Pierre jabbed a finger at me. "I warned you what happened to my old partner. Leave the case alone and you'll be all right."

Corday took out a new cigarette. He thumbed the lighter and cupped a hand around the flame, shielding it against a gusting wind. Pierre took a drag and smoke lingered in his mouth while he carefully pushed words out. "You don't have to worry about solving this crime. You won't get that far. You'll be fired before you get close to the arsonist."

"How will they know I'm getting close?" I asked, but I already knew the answer. My hand was resting on Vernier's report form, keeping the paper from blowing away in the wind. I lifted my hand and the wrinkled paper stuck to me, glued by stress.

Pierre tapped the form. "You'll tell them you're getting close to the arsonist in your daily report. It was the same for me. They told me this dead prostitute case was hot and they wanted to track my progress. Bullshit. They used a daily report to make certain I wasn't getting close. It's how they're tracking you, Nicki."

I slammed the empty liqueur glass on Vernier's report form. I didn't want to touch the paper anymore.

A gust of wind danced the shadows of tree limbs across Pierre's face. Corday couldn't look at me when he said, "Don't try to solve this arson. Putter along, go through the motions and Vernier will leave you alone."

"Oh yeah, right, Pierre. Vernier isn't going to leave me alone. This fire's high profile with the media. There's a lot of pressure to solve the crime. I have to make progress or Vernier will get me fired for incompetence. I lose either way, sitting around or working the case. I'm screwed."

Pierre gave me a brief sympathetic look. "Yes, you got a shitty deal. But I learned on that prostitute case. It was better to quit the Surete and work for Interpol. There's always another job somewhere. Think it over, Nicki."

He picked up a thin matchbox and stared at a drawing of the cafe's Chinese merchant statue on the lid. Pierre idly tumbled the matchbox, then pressed it on the table with a finger. He looked along the boulevard, his eyes drifting toward some vague horizon. To my amazement, Corday ignored a long legged blonde in a plastic miniskirt and clingy sweater at the next table. She was reading *Match* through violet tinted sunglasses as skimpy as the miniskirt. Usually, the heat of Pierre's stares embarrassed me around a babe like her, but this time he hadn't even noticed her. I coughed discretely, worried about Corday.

Pierre came back from his fog. His eyes darted to his watch and he pretended to be shocked at the time. "I told my wife I'd get a new toaster. Ours croaked this morning." Pierre imitated plucking a slice of bread from a hot toaster and wagged his hand, like he'd burned his fingertips.

"You're leaving to buy a toaster after telling me not to solve this arson case. Wonderful."

"You have a long career ahead and there are lots of criminals to catch, my friend. What's one criminal more or less?" Corday pulled a battered leather wallet from his pants pocket and carelessly tossed a few bills on the table.

I stared at the money he'd casually thrown on the marble table. I put his empty beer glass on the cash so wind wouldn't blow the bills away. Corday paying for drinks was a first and it emphasized how much Pierre really believed what he told me. I felt sick inside.

He patted me on the back and promised in a silky voice, "Don't worry. I'm going to help you." Ignoring my glare, Corday walked to the edge of the street. Shielding his eyes with a hand, he peered into traffic, a blur of motor scooters and delivery vans whizzing along Boulevard St. Germain. Pierre waved at a police car approaching the cafe. A cop in the passenger seat tapped his buddy's arm and their patrol car swerved toward us. They pulled to the curb, disc brakes shrieking.

Corday yanked the car door open and slouched on the torn vinyl of the back seat. He looked at me and smiled. "Don't worry, Nicki. In the old days, I had dirt on everyone. I could squeeze back when they stepped on me. I'll find some dirt on this prick Vernier and get him off your back."

"Yeah, right," I said with all the cynicism I felt at the moment.

Corday gave me his hurt, puppy dog look. How dare I not believe him. When I didn't buy it, he slammed the car door.

The cop car bolted into traffic and I watched Pierre lean over the front seat, chatting up his buddies. The patrol car vanished in the chaos of Paris traffic and I never felt so alone in my life. For all his words, I knew Pierre wasn't going to help me. Corday wasn't on my side. He was watching out for himself.

I knew Pierre didn't like his role in this mess. I remembered the strange way he acted this morning. Pierre wanted to leave the office and go to the horse races. Corday was trying to get away from Vernier and take me with him. When it didn't work, Pierre reluctantly warned me to lay off the warehouse arson case, enduring his role as Vernier's messenger.

I had good reasons for believing Corday was in Vernier's pocket. I flashed on the call ordering me to the City Commissioner's office. The call didn't ring on my extension. Vernier phoned Pierre at his desk. After the meeting, Vernier called Pierre on his cell phone, reminding Corday to take me out for a drink – and give me a warning. My partner didn't worry about going to an expensive bistro since the bill was on his tab with Vernier. I was sure the City Commissioner owned my partner and I felt sick.

I stretched my hands in front of me and imagined Pierre unwrapping a small box and looking inside. There was bloody flesh, stringy tendons, crushed nails – and my fingers. The gore was sickening. I came back to reality. Tiny raindrops were misting my hands like fog sinking over a city and dampening sidewalks. A fine rain was sifting down, sweeping away the sunlight and making it unpleasant to sit outside.

The mist turned to freezing drizzle and I decided to leave, pushing my chair backwards, screeching it over rough gray stone. The miniskirted blonde next to me didn't like the rain either. She folded her magazine in a slick plastic bag, colored a shade of lavender that went with her yellow skirt. The blonde left her table, joining the herd of pedestrians clogging the sidewalks. I followed her, walking toward my office.

My mind tumbled ideas, looking for a careful next step in the arson case. I quickly realized that I couldn't tell a safe idea from a dangerous one. Everything I did was risky. I wasn't the hero type and I didn't want to do something that got me killed, yet I couldn't abandon six dead firefighters either. I was so distracted I didn't notice anything along the boulevard until I saw my office building and walked up its familiar salt and pepper granite steps.

The lobby's beveled glass door swung closed behind me and the mechanical surf of Paris traffic vanished, leaving me in silence. Yellow light from a porcelain bowl lamp ran up a flight of stairs and I followed the lamp's dull glow up the staircase, my footsteps echoing off a copper ceiling.

Inside the office, the air was heavy with cigarettes and black coffee, the ritual of agents pumping themselves up to face another day. I walked past rows of desks and pulled out my chair. Too antsy to sit down, I ran a hand along the back of my neck, feeling all the kinks in my muscles from stress and the day was just starting. I slid the bottom drawer out, studying a nearly empty box of Russ & Daughters chocolate with lust.

I'd nursed the box of exquisite cocoa-dusted truffles all month, saving them for times when I wanted to escape and today I really needed an escape. I picked a truffle from its delicately ridged paper cup, sliding perfection in my mouth. Intense chocolate dissolved on my tongue and I had some solace in life. I licked a finger and chased cocoa dust in the chocolate truffle box, thinking about what I could do on this arson case. Maybe a jolt of caffeine would jump start my brain.

I started for the coffee pot, but my stomach ran into a hand holding a small box, thrust toward me. I stared at the little box, feeling a strange uneasiness about it. Then I ran my eyes up a shirtsleeve and put them on the face of Jacques Benet. He'd just joined the office and got tagged with minor errands, like picking up the mail.

Benet's soft peach-fuzz face dimpled in a smile. "This just came for you, Nicki."

"It did," I said flatly. "Who sent it? There's no address label."

"Came by bicycle messenger. Said it was urgent you get the box. Must have to do with that arson case you got assigned this morning." Benet gave me a look of admiration. "Tough job," he added. "I'm not surprised you got it, Nicki, after the way you helped the Surete on those other crimes. Makes sense they asked for you again."

It was amazing how fast gossip ran around the Interpol office. I get a case assignment and everyone knows about it in five minutes. "Thanks for the compliment."

"Sure, anytime." He wandered into the maze of desks. I watched Benet squeeze between jammed chairs and agents hunched over their telephones, punching buttons to replay voicemail messages. Then I stared at the small white carton in my hand.

I did what everybody does with a gift box. I shook it and it rattled. I didn't like the sound. It reminded me of a snake I'd met earlier, City Commissioner Vernier. Opening the box in the public area didn't feel right, so I went in the break room. My gaze drifted to a window, picking up a vaguely familiar shape in the street. I saw the messenger who'd run his bicycle into me at Vernier's office.

He caught my stare and lifted his helmet in acknowledgement, letting me know he'd delivered the box. An arrogant smirk flowed across his face like a quick, slashing knife. Then he was on the bike, disappearing into Paris traffic. I struggled to see the color of his tight-fitting nylon shirt and spandex tights but it was impossible to spot him through the crowd. I vividly remembered a dense black shadow of beard and his ugly attitude.

I was struck by how beautifully Vernier choreographed this whole thing. The bicycle messenger running his tire into me at the elevator was no mistake. The collision was planned so I'd remember the guy and know this "darling little gift box" was from the City Commissioner. The delivery of the carton was done very cleverly. The connection to Vernier could never be proven, yet I knew it came directly from him. This was personal, a "love note" from Alain Vernier to Nicki Foster.

I was so wired I was shaking from the rush. Angry, I slammed the box on the sink counter. I pulled a scissors from a pencil can, tipping it over and spraying colored pencils across the counter. Some rolled off and clattered on the floor. I didn't care about the mess. I'd clean it up later. I dragged the scissors tip along brown tape sealing the box until its flaps popped up.

I held my breath and looked inside. I was shocked, but I guess that's just human when you're looking at a person's amputated fingers. They were a woman's fingers, narrow and tapered like mine. None of them had been cut off with a scalpel. They were pulled out of the hand, just like Corday's partner on the prostitute murder case. The fingers were yanked from their sockets with pliers, leaving a gory trail of cartilage and ripped flesh.

Chilling touches had been added to the bizarre ensemble. Painted nails on the crushed fingers exactly matched the shade of nail polish sitting in my bathroom cabinet. In case I missed the connection to the warehouse arson, a "hint" was crazy-glued to the fingers. A burnt match was jammed between a thumb and forefinger like a dead woman was holding the extinguished flame. A note in the box identified the morgue refrigerator holding a mutilated body, a homeless person with missing fingers. Vernier was flaunting his power to hide evidence and be ahead of me at every step in this case.

Even the press didn't bother Vernier. His solution for that problem was clear – feed me to the media as a scapegoat when I didn't solve the crime. The initial stall was a press conference saying Interpol was assigned the arson to accelerate the investigation. The next press conference would announce my assignment to Siberia, without a coat. Maybe I'd get a slight rescue, a clean re-assignment to Marseille, where I could join the futile effort to halt drug smuggling. I'd become yet another Interpol agent abused by the power drug money brings to the criminal underworld.

Alain Vernier wanted me intimidated, a mouse sitting at her desk, waiting to be shunted aside. But I wasn't intimidated. Oh sure, I was hit by it all and I'm no hero. Only anger, not glory, shoved the stupid box closed and got me moving again. I slammed the fingers in a bio-hazard evidence refrigerator but it was pointless to keep them. They weren't traceable to the City Commissioner and Vernier was certainly cunning enough to have someone steal the box. There was no point in trying to hide the carton in my studio apartment. It had been searched to find the color of my fingernail polish and could easily be broken into again.

I needed to clear my head, get some fresh air, so I left the office and punched the elevator button. I almost took a walk, but I changed my mind and went to the garage instead. Then I drove to the closest firehouse and made inquiries. Understandably, Paul Denis went home after being up all night. I knew he was exhausted but I called him anyway, hoping I wasn't waking him up.

For once I was in luck and Paul was surprisingly perky. Best of all, he already had the images ready. He was planning to send them to me by e-mail. I stalled him by lying that my e-mail server was down, hit by a computer virus. I was worried Vernier might be able to tap my e-mail, so I got Paul's home address in Belleville. The directions he gave me were certainly unusual, but it didn't matter. Paul Denis was holding the only clues I had in this case and I wanted to look at them.

# 6

# Aerial View

I turned into the neighborhood where Paul Denis lived, driving past blocks of row houses with their stoops touching the curb. It reminded me of the less affluent areas of Brooklyn where new immigrants live, melting into the underclass that makes a city run. They stay alive by doing jobs the average American would never touch, earning pitiful wages. The lucky ones start in a rickety tenement, save every nickel and work their way into a decent flat. A few move into the really nice areas of Brooklyn and buy a townhouse.

I rounded a curve and hit a streak of tiny cafes with gaudy neon signs for Moroccan couscous, Chinese takeout and Italian ravioli. Elderly pensioners were clustered at the sidewalk tables, paired across a chessboard or sharing a newspaper. Their watery red eyes were fixed on a distant horizon, not a far away place so much as a lost time, when they had a full life ahead of them.

Unemployed younger men didn't mix with the pensioners, preferring their own generation. Their faces were sullen, coming to life only when they tossed dice out of a cup to see who paid for the beer. My patrol car slid in front of them and I could feel their eyes staring at my back. The stares leveled at me varied in hostility, from cold indifference to searing malice.

Following Paul's directions, I turned down a little alley, a narrow passage leading to the delivery entrance for the local hospital. It felt like bricks were going to scrape my cheek. I heard a snick as the driver's side mirror clipped a drainpipe.

At the end of the alley I popped into a square jammed with cars. The only empty place to park was a loading dock cluttered with small ambulance vans for the hospital. I put the patrol car in reverse, grinding backwards. Eventually the car pillowed against a bumper of old tires, slithering along the loading dock like a giant caterpillar.

I shut the car off and ran my eyes around the little square. There was a smaller building clamped between the hospital's wings. The ground floor of the building had dirty windows protected by rusted steel mesh. I squinted at a faded sign that read Machine Shop & Iron Toolworks. I imagined the inside as reeking of oil, with metal scraps piled on the floor. It didn't make a good impression, but I walked to a dented metal door and knocked anyway.

The heavy steel plate swung back. I saw Paul Denis in a t-shirt and workout pants, his hair wet from the shower, a damp towel draped over his shoulders.

"You're up to having a visitor?" I asked tentatively.

"Sure, come in."

I took a half step over the metal threshold and looked up, expecting to see paint flaking off iron girders and a tin roof. Instead, the machine shop was like a refinished loft in the SoHo area of New York. Sunlight drifted through skylights above the open rafters. Track lights laid a rosy glow on sandblasted brick walls and a lacquered wooden floor. It was impressive, even with paint cans stacked in a corner.

I stood there in amazement until my eyes finally swept back to Paul. He had his arms folded over his chest and was rocking on his heels, looking at me with an impish smile. "Well, it's not as bad as you thought. It won't bite you. Come in."

I took a few steps inside. The only furniture was a wooden carousel horse he was refinishing. Paint remover had stripped the horse bald, leaving speckles of color buried in the wood grain. Soon the carved horse would come to life again in glossy colors, the crimson, cobalt blue and ivory I saw on paint cans stacked nearby. I went over to the carousel horse and petted its mane.

Paul left me by the horse and moved into the kitchen where a used restaurant stove awaited installation. A big red auction tag was still wired to the stove's hood. Paul stuck his head in a refrigerator and pulled out a half-empty bottle of white wine. Before I could stop him, he'd poured a glass and was about to start another.

"No thanks, Paul. I have to drive."

"Well, how about some Vittel?" He held up a liter bottle of mineral water.

"Great." I leaned on the carousel horse and felt it give slightly under my weight. The unpainted saddle was cool and smooth beneath my forearms. I watched Paul fill a serving plate with slices of apple, baguette and some brie cheese.

Paul brought his wine glass up and gestured at the far wall, where brick had been knocked out and replaced by French doors. Outside the doors was an empty lot. The area was surrounded by industrial buildings, their walls a blight of graffiti. But Paul planted ivy and it was growing over the walls, hiding some of the ugly sore. The ground near the kitchen was furrowed in neat garden ridges. Herbs and leafy vegetables jostled each other for sunlight as they popped out of the soil. The remainder of the lot was pockmarked with weeds.

"I like your vegetable garden. What will you do with the rest of the land?"

"Oh, I have great dreams."

"Like what?" I prodded.

Paul hesitated. He studied his wine glass for a moment, then stuck the glass out as a pointer. "You see over there? On that side, I'd put a wildflower garden. I have a vision of it billowing in the wind, all the colors in beautiful, harmonic chaos."

"Sounds poetic."

"Making a poetic speech is easier than digging all those weeds." Paul laughed. "But if I get the ambition, I'll do it. I'd like to put in sunflowers."

"Sunflowers are your favorite?"

"No. That empty space there is reserved for my favorite, the foxglove plant. It has little bell-shaped flowers speckled with colors. The heart medication digitalis is made from foxglove."

"How did you learn so much about flowers?"

"Reading books." He pointed at the library loft he was building. "It's all in books. I didn't read until ten years ago. I've much to make up for."

"Didn't read? How can that be?"

"We were too poor." He sighed. "I didn't go to school much. I went out and scrounged. The cops called it shoplifting. They didn't like my idea of Robin Hood." Paul smiled.

"No," I agreed. "Cops don't see theft from the rich as a charitable contribution, that's for sure. They have no sense of humor. So how did you decide to go straight?"

Paul Denis shrugged. "Well, that's a very long story. I need to be somewhat drunk to tell it well." He looked a little shy. He cocked his head and changed the subject. "What part of America are you from, Nicki?"

"New York, Manhattan to be exact."

Paul asked me, "You grew up in New York City?"

"Yeah, pretty much. My family moved there when I was three. My dad teaches musicology at Julliard. My mom's head nurse for the cardiac ward at New York's Weill Cornell Medical Center."

Paul wagged a hand to show how impressed he was. "So brains run in the family. You have brothers and sisters?"

"One of each. My sister's an accountant. I don't think she's done anything exciting since the sixth grade, when a boy looked up her dress."

Paul laughed. "That boy was very advanced. I didn't try looking up dresses until I was fourteen. What about your brother?"

I said impishly, "I have no idea when he started looking up dresses."

Paul hurried to explain, "No, no, Nicki, I meant what does he do now, eh? For a living, not with the girls."

"My brother? He works at the Fulton Fish Market during the day, plays gigs at night in a Reggae band."

"Well, then, your parents must be very proud of you, working for Interpol. Yes?"

I laughed. "No way. Are you kidding? I'm the black sheep of the family. I didn't become a doctor or have a grandkid, and I live too far away for frequent visits." There was a moment of awkward silence and it was my turn to change the subject. I nodded at a kitchen prep table that served as his desk. A set of glossy photos was stacked beside his computer. "So, you printed the pictures."

"Yes. They came out well, especially since you had to take them in a gusting wind. The images are surprisingly crisp." Paul gestured for me to take a look at the photographs.

I stepped to the prep table and shuffled prints to get oriented, then looked at the computer screen. The display showed a normal visual image next to an infrared version of the same area. I pointed at the images. "So what do you make of these?"

"I just started working on the computer when you knocked. There's a useful pattern that shows better in the infrared, but it's hard to tell where you are in the building." He scrolled with the mouse.

"I've got a disc in my briefcase that might help." I pulled out a CD. "We can use this Interpol software to register the visual and infrared versions, line things up so we can toggle from one to the other. It's easier to know where you are in the building that way."

"Go to it." Paul moved aside.

I loaded the software disc and got the program installed. "We need registration points, at least six places on each photo that we know are the same things."

"How about the roof support beams?" Paul suggested. "They show as a regular pattern, so it's easy to spot them."

"OK." On the visual picture, I clicked on beams in two rows running along the warehouse, matching each beam with its infrared image. Then I clicked Run and the cursor turned into an hourglass. "Takes about a minute to rubbersheet one picture into the other. I told the program to leave the visual intact and distort the infrared."

"Makes sense. Doesn't matter if the heat picture gets warped. We can't track it easily anyway." Paul offered the plate of snacks to me and I took an apple. "Cheese?" he urged.

"Not yet. In a moment. I'll take some as a treat if we make progress, give myself a reward." The hourglass cursor went back to an arrow.

"OK," Paul said. "Let me use that mouse for a second. I'll show you where I think the fire began. It started there. On visual, you see a saucer area scooped out of the concrete, but a round hot spot on the infrared. The fire moved. You can see a streak of heat across the floor and then the whole ball of flame piled against the far wall. When the torch shot out and killed the fire crew, there must have been some reaction, a momentum exchange."

"I see what you mean, the blast outward shoved the incendiary material inward. Physics. Action causes reaction, like a rifle recoiling when a bullet is fired." I chewed some apple and thought it over.

"Exactly." Paul tried a different analogy. "It's like the plume from a rocket. Hot gases go out the tailpipe and the missile jumps into the sky."

"You've given me an idea. I need to check on something." I dropped the apple, too excited to eat. "You've got a Web connection on this machine?"

"Internet? Sure. What are you going to do?" he asked curiously.

"Connect to Interpol's database." I pulled a little plastic gadget from my briefcase. "This is my secure ID token. With this thing, I can log into the Interpol database when I travel. I can't get into the really sensitive areas of the Interpol database on the road, but I don't need that access right now." I hit a few more keystrokes and said, "There's the report I needed."

"It says 'Vladivostok.' How does that Russian seaport relate to my warehouse arson?"

"Vladivostok is the biggest Russian naval base, comparable to Pearl Harbor for the United States," I answered. "Two years ago there was a real panic when five submarine launched ballistic missiles were stolen. There would still be a white hot alert except no warheads were on the rockets. Better yet, the missiles were found within 48 hours, complete with guidance systems. The rockets were intact except for one thing. Want to guess what it was?"

Paul gave me a sad laugh. "Their fuel. You're telling me this arsonist used rocket fuel to torch the warehouse."

"Looks that way, doesn't it? Except I don't get how he did it. That was a special kind of fuel that burns hotter than anything used in rockets today. It came from the Cold War. This special 'hypergolic' fuel shot missiles faster at their targets, made it harder to detect an attack. But the fuel was unstable and eventually abandoned."

"Let's see if we can find evidence he used that hypergolic fuel." Paul ran an edge detection program on the visual image, outlining the fire's path along the warehouse. It also highlighted two lozenge-shaped areas. "I think these areas were fuel bladders. He used a pair of thick rubber aviation bladders to hold the rocket fuel. Thrust from the burning rocket fuel shoved the bladders across the warehouse until they hit the far wall. Then they burst and threw even more fuel on the inferno. I was in the French Army when we participated in Desert

Storm as a NATO partner. Remote fueling depots use huge rubber bladders to refill helicopter gunships."

"But there weren't any bladders inside the warehouse when we walked through. You think he dragged them out during that fifteen minute gap before your team arrived?" I asked.

"No, Nicki, I don't. Rubber burns very well and he was smart to use it. If you hadn't suggested these aerial views, we'd never have thought twice about the presence of rubber in a warehouse. Trace rubber found in the warehouse just makes us think tires were stored there."

He paused for a moment. "Five missiles were stolen and bled for their fuel. Only one missile's fuel was used at this warehouse, so four remain. Are there any leads that might help us find the remaining rocket fuel?"

I sighed. "No, there aren't any existing leads. This whole case was dropped because the only thing missing was the fuel. It wasn't thought to pose a real danger. Nobody uses this type of propellant anymore. Hypergolic fuel is very tricky stuff."

"How was the arsonist able to bring this rocket fuel into France? Maybe we can trace the path."

"Probably on a container ship, got unloaded at a port and trucked somewhere. There's no easy way of tracing an individual shipment. Thousands of sealed containers are put on trucks and railroad cars every day. But there is some hope. Information about these missiles is kept in a more secure area of the main database. I can't get into that security level from your computer. I'd have to visit our headquarters in Lyon."

Paul rubbed his chin. "I'll send out an alert tomorrow. In 48 hours, every fire station in Europe will be a lot more cautious in responding to alarms. We'll change our tactics, be less aggressive when we arrive at a fire scene. Lives may still be lost." He looked discouraged.

"Ouch. I'm sorry. I'll think about this tonight, see if I can come up with a way to trace the rubber fuel bladders. Tomorrow, I'll go to our headquarters campus in Lyon and search the database."

He looked a little better, but still dejected. "I laid out a grid like an archeologist on a dig and took core samples of the warehouse floor. So we have a map of the fire. But the techs say it will be three days before they have lab results. What can you do in the meantime?"

"Well, even without clues, I still have a suspect, the same person you always consider in an arson."

"You mean the owner of that warehouse. When a commercial property gets arsoned, it's usually because the business is going under, failing. The owner hires an arsonist, hoping fire insurance money will cover his debts."

"Sure. So I'm going to find who owned that arsoned warehouse."

"How do you track this person down?" Paul looked better, knowing something useful would get done today.

"In the United States, property owners are kept on file at the county courthouse. But it isn't that easy in Paris. Real estate titles are a scrambled mess that started in the French Revolution, when Paris was taken from the aristocracy. Properties were shuffled like a deck of cards. It's happened many times since."

Paul nodded. "Yes, I had quite a problem buying this machine shop. I waited almost three months for the title to clear."

"I'll bet. A lot of problems date from the 1950s, when socialist politics added a legal tangle to the puzzle. But I know Diane St. Remy, head of the Paris Archives. I think she'll help me." I smiled. "It won't take three months. With Diane's help, I'll find the owner in an hour." I got up to leave.

Paul accompanied me to the door of his home. We reluctantly said our good-byes and I walked alone to the patrol car. Rain was sprinkling the windshield, turning clear glass into foggy gauze. I put the wipers on intermittent and they cleaned an arc in front of me. The rain turned to noisy splatters so I cranked the wipers to full. I watched the rubber blades play metronome, ticking back and forth, while I considered my options.

I briefly thought about calling Diane St. Remy and decided to visit her, drive to the Paris Archives and talk to her in person. She'd feel stroked when I paid her some attention. Diane was a real porcupine, but she could find documents in the Archives that others took months to locate – if she was on your side.

# 7

# The Paris Archives

The Paris Archives are on the largest island in the Seine River. To get there, I had to drive through clogged traffic on the Pont St. Michel, a stone bridge linking the core of Paris to the island. When I pulled on the parking brake, rain hit the windshield like I was in a car wash. A storm was rolling across the city, bending trees in strong gusts. Fighting the storm, I got out of the car and headed for a wooden carriage door in a little stone garage. This shed once housed the royal coach and now sheltered the entrance to the Paris Archives. I dragged open the door against the storm's embrace and cold wind shoved me inside, blowing wet leaves around a room the size of a large walk-in closet. I jammed the door closed, then leaned my soaked umbrella in a corner, leaving a puddle on the tile floor.

The shed was lit by an antique river lantern. In its yellowish light, I peered anxiously down a staircase, watching spiral stairs twist downward and disappear in a black hole. This dark well was an old mine shaft, the entrance to an abandoned limestone quarry holding the Paris Archives. I held a cold metal railing for balance and started down, moving carefully from one narrow step to the next. The farther I went, the darker it got and I felt like Alice falling down the rabbit hole into Wonderland, dropping into a strange world. At the bottom of the mine shaft, I walked into a huge cave, a vast man-made underground cavern. Its high walls were scarred by the marks of chisels where miners tunneled under the Seine River, risking death to earn their living.

The river's unrelenting flow pressed against the roof of the cavern. Tons of water rushed above my head, leaking into the cave with a persistent dripping. This slow trickling mottled the sandy limestone walls in black streaks. Darkened walls vanished on all sides of me, making the cave look endless and that was close to the truth.

This cave led to an underground city two stories below Paris, a sunken world called the Catacombs, a network of tunnels joining abandoned mines, aqueducts and filthy sewers. For centuries, fugitives hid in this bizarre underworld beneath the ancient core of central Paris. To escape the police, hunted criminals lived inside the Catacombs like Jean Valjean did in *Les Miserables*, the Victor Hugo novel made into a Broadway stage production. French Resistance fighters inhabited the Catacombs during World War II, hiding important documents in this ancient limestone quarry. Quietly, the history of Paris was taken from government buildings and moved into the cavern to prevent destruction by the Nazis. Decades later, the Paris Archives were still here.

In front of me, acres of storage racks were spread with thousands of documents spilling over shelves – green cloth ledgers, loose sheaves of paper tied in ribbon and thick leather bound volumes heaped on each other. Adding to the chaos of paper, stacks of cartons leaned against the end of every row. All the cartons were labeled in the same tight, precise handwriting. It was an elegant old-fashioned style I'd seen every time I visited the Archives to do research. When I submitted questions, they were answered in notes written by Diane St. Remy, head of the Paris Archives. Diane's familiar handwriting was on hundreds of cardboard boxes in front of me, heaps of boxes nearly blocking every aisle. She was the only person who knew this immense jumble of paper by heart and the best person to research who owned the arsoned warehouse.

To find Diane, I had to wind through a maze of shelves, eventually reaching a large iron door for the office area. The iron door was actually a waterproof ship's hatch, used to keep people safe in the office area. There was always a risk the limestone quarry might flood from a cave-in, letting the Seine River pour tons of water into the cavern. The metal hatch was installed so many years ago that its iron plates bubbled with rust from the dampness of the cave. With a struggle, I pulled the rusting antique door open and stepped into a cramped hallway. I was no longer beneath the Seine River and was now walking underground on the island where I'd parked my car. The trench-like hallway ran for only a short distance before ending in Diane St. Remy's office.

I leaned against the open office door and watched Diane. She was totally focused on work, perched stiffly on the edge of a chair, her spine arched in tension. Nearsighted, Diane was pressing her face against a computer screen, her gray eyes magnified by oversize reading glasses. When she caught my reflection in the glass computer screen, an arrogant look flashed across St. Remy's face. The look vanished in a cold mask.

Diane spoke in an icy voice. "So you've come to visit me again, Nicki. You must need a favor." She took off her glasses, letting the spectacles drop against her chest, held by a cord. Her gray eyes were brightly lit, watching me intently. Diane sat there in prickly silence, a blue vein pulsing under the transparent skin of a hand.

I didn't say anything. Diane was a real porcupine and I had to earn her respect or get trampled. Neither of us wanted to break the silence. It was like a business negotiation. The first one to talk loses.

At last Diane grudgingly spoke. "All right, come in Nicki." She raised an arm stiffly, pointing her pale hand at a round table with four leather chairs.

I walked to the little table and sat on the rich leather of an executive conference chair. My hands were in the pockets of my raincoat, fingers shuffling a familiar litter of gum wrappers and used Kleenex. I became aware that Diane's office had changed radically. On past visits, I'd seen her old metal desk jammed against dented filing cabinets that belonged in a landfill. Her sagging bookshelves used to be layered in paper, stacks of folders leaning against each other for support. Now wooden cabinets with richly grained doors hid Diane's clutter of documents. Diane's office was elegantly decorated in lush rosewood furniture.

New furnishings weren't the only change in the room. Diane was no longer dressed like a forgotten city bureaucrat. She was wearing a gray pinstripe business suit, accented with a gold rosebud stickpin on her jacket lapel. Diane was trying to look younger, more attractive to men.

Her brown hair had a red highlight and her cheeks were rosy in a full load of makeup, an attempt to soften her image. Unfortunately, Diane still looked cold and logical like the computer she was using.

Diane stood and walked around her desk, bending over a low cabinet near me. "I was about to make tea for my staff meeting. I'll have to go ahead with preparations while we talk."

Diane standing so close to me was uncomfortable and I instinctively moved my chair away. "Sure, go right ahead with the tea." I watched her closely. Diane's eyes warned me something was coming and I was about to get put in my place, the standard intimidation game Diane St. Remy always played when I visited her office.

She slid open a thin door and pulled an elegant teapot from her cabinet, flaunting its looks like an auctioneer displaying a richly jeweled Faberge egg. Then she presented a matching set of cups, saucers and sugar bowl with a dazzling cream pitcher as the finale. I guessed her new tea set cost what I paid in rent and I didn't mean what I paid each month. I meant what I paid for the entire year.

Diane St. Remy's eyes flashed over my face, catching my astonishment. "My tea service was handcrafted by Neva Careme. I commissioned her two months ago. Do you know Careme?" Diane caressed a pearl inlaid in the delicate teapot.

I tried to take the edge off Diane's arrogance with humor. "No, I wouldn't know Neva Careme. A handcrafted tea set hasn't figured in a major crime lately." Ironic humor was wasted on Diane, but it loosened me up. I got to be myself for a moment. I didn't want to hurt her feelings and make her even more antagonistic so I added, "It's a beautiful tea service."

Diane smiled and made a ritual of putting out the cups, like her staff was having high tea with a Duchess. Diane was the Duchess, of course.

I sat in silence until it was painfully obvious I should say something. It wasn't easy to find a safe topic that would interest her. There'd been some gossip about the Archives being reorganized. "I heard the Paris Archives was changing its role. Will you be moving some responsibilities to other city departments?"

Diane laughed sarcastically. "Of course not. My role is expanding, not shrinking. City Commissioner Vernier is only changing my department's name. He's the first City Commissioner to realize how valuable I am. It's about time. I've spent fifteen years working underground in these Archives. You don't know what it's like working for nothing in a pit. Everyone in Paris depends on my Archives and no one's ever given a damn about me except Alain Vernier."

"Really?" I asked, startled by a connection between Diane and the City Commissioner.

Diane bragged, "Alain Vernier agreed to upgrade my department. I'm putting the city's records on a new computer system. Don't get the wrong idea, dear. I'm not a slave to the computer. I have an American software consultant, Taylor Hansen. He does all the work. And he's cute." A smirk danced on Diane's face.

"Cute" wasn't normally in Diane's vocabulary. I translated "cute" to mean Taylor Hansen wore a good suit, a techno-geek trying hard to be sexy. I imagined Diane sneaking glances at him while they shared long technical articles, reading aloud to each other. Maybe Diane was wearing makeup because she was dating Taylor Hansen.

Sensing my curiosity, Diane grew uneasy and fingered the lid of her teapot. "We aren't going out or anything. Taylor hangs around after hours and we talk."

"Talk?" I asked. I gave Diane a skeptical look and for once I got to her.

"Yes, we talk. I don't remember the topics."

"Sure," I said. "Uh huh." I smiled knowingly.

Diane tried to ignore my attitude and couldn't. She became defensive. "We talk about the system Taylor's installing and how I want the computer to work."

The computer gave me an opening to bring up the arson case. I leaned toward Diane and eased into the topic. "You know, Diane, maybe your new computer system could help solve a crime. There was a warehouse fire this morning that killed six firefighters, an obvious case of arson."

Diane cut me off. "Yes, I heard about it on the news while I was dressing this morning. I knew you wanted a favor. You need me to look up the owner of that warehouse, don't you? Sorry, I can't help you." Her voice was so detached it was like Diane had left the room.

I pressed her. "Maybe the warehouse is already in your computer. You might have loaded the records for that part of the city. It's worth a try."

"I've checked and the warehouse isn't listed." She was firm, crossing her arms. Her eyes sparkled with satisfaction. "Now you'll have to excuse me. My staff meeting is starting."

"This won't go away Diane. Six people died."

She ignored me and fussed with her tea cups. I'd never seen her act this way. There was a quiet smile of satisfaction on Diane's lips.

"OK," I said, "Have it your way for now. But I'll be back. I'm not giving up on this one. It's too important." There was no point in fighting with Diane, so I moved away from her office, walking along the corridor that led to the limestone cavern. I was walking underground in a trench-like hallway and it felt like hiking in a narrow canyon.

Light drifted hazily down the canyon, shining through newly installed French doors. The doors opened on a freshly planted garden where sprinklers softly misted plants. Moisture fogged the French doors and water droplets trickled down the glass panes in rain streaks. The beautiful little garden was more evidence of City Commissioner Vernier spending money in the Archives.

I couldn't get new office furniture and a garden, but I could find Taylor Hansen, Diane's consultant friend. Maybe he'd look up the warehouse owner in his computer. I figured Hansen must be working in Diane's conference room. The meeting area was really a small cave dug hundreds of years ago when miners explored for more limestone. None was found and the cave was abandoned, leaving behind a hollowed-out chamber, a little grotto. Stepping through the rusted iron door into the limestone quarry, I spotted the sunken grotto. I walked down creaking wooden stairs to the rough stone floor of the conference room.

Unlike Diane's expensive office, the conference area furnishings were crude. Lighting was simple, long fluorescent tubes clamped in cheap metal garage fixtures. The unshielded bulbs flooded the area with harsh light, forcing me to put a hand up to protect my eyes from the glare. I stopped in front of a battered folding table and looked around. A man was leaning over a computer display and I saw his name on an ID badge clipped to his belt. He was Taylor Hansen, my best hope for finding the warehouse owner.

I'd assumed Hansen would be an aging techno-geek, an expert on computers and naive about life. I was wrong. He was a tall man in his thirties with a slim waist. A blue silk shirt was tucked in the narrow waistband of wool slacks. The expensive slacks were tailored in a perfect fit and the pants cuffs broke exactly over his tasseled loafers. His shirt sleeves were rolled up, showing tanned forearms. I understood why Diane St. Remy upgraded her appearance, wearing heavy makeup and expensive clothes. The answer was Taylor Hansen. I understood even better when Hansen turned around.

Taylor was handsome, with sculpted hair and magazine cover looks. His hair was slicked back and his teeth were almost too perfect to be real. He looked at me and his thick lips twisted in an unpleasant smile. The smile said he was always one step ahead and this time wouldn't be any different. "Yes?" he asked.

I said flatly, "I'm Nicki Foster, with Interpol." I put out my hand and his shake was soft, cautiously measured. It gave me the feeling Taylor Hansen played life like a chess game, thinking through each move, toying with his opponent.

Hansen spoke, dragging out his words like carefully placed steps. "You're with Interpol, the International Police?"

"None other," I replied. I flipped a quick smile at Hansen but my smile glanced off him. I took a business card from my pocket and laid the card on the table.

Taylor waved his hand. "That's not necessary, Inspector. I believe you." His eyebrows went up slightly. "How can I help you?"

"I need to check ownership on a property."

"You have the property's address?" He let his words hang in the air like a half built bridge and I sensed he didn't want the bridge finished.

I smoothed a Post-It on the table. I left the Post-It orphaned on the table and dragged my hand away slowly, feeling the cold folding table on my fingertips.

Taylor squinted at the street address. "This is in the Les Halles area. I don't know. I'll try." Taylor struck a pose, leaning over a computer in the corner. He typed a few keystrokes and shook his head. "Nope, there's nothing in the system."

I stole a look at the computer and all I saw was a blank screen, no words, nothing. Hansen had erased everything. I asked, "Are you certain that address isn't in your system?"

"We haven't gotten to that area yet."

I pressed him. "How long before you get to that neighborhood?"

Hansen shrugged lazily. "You'd have to ask Diane. She sets the priorities." He spread his hands, emphasizing his helplessness.

I decided to stare at him and wait. Sometimes that worked for me. People couldn't take the tension.

Taylor coughed. He looked bored, but I could feel a simmering curiosity in him. "You're working on a case?"

"I'm working on an arson." I pushed the crumpled Post-It toward him and watched Hansen, studying his reaction.

He looked at me with real interest for the first time. "I think I read about this on the Internet. A whole fire crew was lost."

"Yes. This is the warehouse arson where six firefighters died." I hoped to tweezer some help from him, but Hansen just smirked. He'd made a connection in his own mind and he wasn't going to share the idea. I'd told him enough to set his own plans in motion and he didn't need me anymore. I could tell by how superior he acted.

Taylor crossed his arms and talked without conviction. "I hope you find whoever did it."

"Yeah? I'm certainly trying to get 'em."

Hansen flashed a smile. The grin faded so quickly I wasn't certain the smile was ever there. He said, "Good luck on your case." I knew he didn't mean it.

"Right." I said it flatly, letting Hansen know he hadn't gotten to me. There was no point in staying around this guy. I walked up the creaky wooden steps and into the huge limestone quarry. There was nothing more I could do here.

But my visit wasn't a total failure. I'd learned the Archives were tied to Vernier, somehow involved in his plans. Diane and Taylor were willing to thwart me on an investigation where people had been murdered. They could've handed me false leads and let me waste a few days chasing around. But they didn't bother. Instead, Diane and Taylor made no attempt to mislead me. I concluded events were going to happen so fast it didn't matter what they said to me. Vernier's next step was already in motion and would happen before anyone could stop it. That wasn't a pretty thought.

I wandered through the document storage area and went up the coiled staircase, climbing its narrow iron steps to the cramped lobby. It was nice to see my umbrella leaning in the corner, waiting for me. The old, battered thing felt like my only friend in this crazy world. I nearly kissed the umbrella as I picked it up.

When I pushed the carriage door open, the storm was still rolling over Paris, its strong wind pressing the door against me. I buttoned my raincoat and fought the umbrella open, sprinting to the car. I fell into the car, happy to be out of the Archives, not caring that I was dripping wet and the windows were fogging on the inside. I started the car and waited for the heater to clear the windows while rain drummed the windshield in thick noisy drops. Finally, I could peer through an arch at the bottom of the windshield. I kicked the fan on high, blasting heat, evaporating the gray haze in front of me.

When I pulled away from the curb, I didn't go very far. Paris traffic was at its peak and my car crawled along the riverfront. In front of me, the Seine River flowed around the pointed nose of the island and swept under the famed Pont Neuf Bridge. The only good thing about being stuck in traffic was having the chance to study the bridge's richly detailed streetlamps, topped in glass bowls glowing orange. I wished I'd lived in Paris a hundred years ago when the cast iron lamps were gaslights, lit each night by a singing lamplighter. Above the bridge, I watched clouds tumble against each other, tinted blue and red and gold, like a Dutch Masters landscape painting. The sky began clearing and the sun poked bright fingers through holes in the billowing clouds.

I longed to relax, forget the damned arson for a while, just mellow out. I knew a great cheese shop near Montmartre's open air food market. I'd binge, buy some Fontainebleau cheese and fresh strawberries. At home, I'd curl in my chair with Sunday's *New York Times*. For a moment, it felt like I had a normal life again, but I knew that idea was a silly illusion. In truth, I was in for a long, sleepless night.

# 8

# Rush

The stress of the warehouse arson case got to me, as I thought it would. I tossed restlessly in the fold down bed of my tiny Montmartre studio apartment until dawn turned my window curtains pink. I'd just slipped into deep sleep when Pierre Corday pounded on my door. The thin wood bent like it would snap, hammered by his angry fist. Corday growled, "Foster, wake up." His fist smashed my door again.

Sleep clung to me like an ugly hangover. My head felt stuffed with wool and my dry tongue stuck to the roof of my mouth. I rubbed my face. "Hang on, Pierre," I said in a soft, depressed voice. "I'm coming."

Corday sagged heavily against the thin door. His lighter snicked and cigarette smoke leaked into my room. Wonderful, I thought. Another perfect start to another perfect day. I propped an eye open and bright daylight was pushing through my sheer drapes, bruising my eyes with glare. The little traveler's clock by the bed blinked 6:16 A.M. Normally, I felt better at six in the morning but I hadn't slept all night.

I grabbed my orange velour robe from a hook on the bathroom door and wrapped the robe around me. Crabwalking between my fold down bed and the wall, I headed for the door. I tore the chain across its holder, letting it fall with a little thunk. The chain swung back and forth like the pendulum on a grandfather clock, ticking across the wood. I stared at Pierre Corday in bewilderment.

He demanded, "Get dressed, Foster. We've got to go."

"Lighten up, Pierre, will you? Come inside. How about putting out your cigarette?" I headed for my shower, leaving the door open for Corday.

Pierre dropped his cigarette on the hallway floor and ground the stub with a twist of his shoe. "Skip the shower, Nicki." Pierre shoved an apricot tart in his mouth. Some of the pastry stuck to his upper lip and part fell on my floor. Neat was not Pierre's style.

I glared at him. A few crumbs on the floor didn't wreck my college dorm decor scheme, but it was the principle of the thing. Principle got me as far as it always did, nowhere. I bent over and used a Kleenex to sweep up his mess, holding my robe tightly closed. Corday was beginning to look me over a little too closely. I shut the bathroom door when I dressed.

"This better be important," I complained, grunting on tight jeans. "I have a lot of things to do today. There isn't time for distractions." I didn't trust Pierre enough to mention my plan to visit Interpol headquarters in Lyon. "Whose emergency is this, Vernier's?"

"No." Corday shouted at me like I was in another building. "Paul Denis tried to call you. He couldn't get through and called me instead. Believe me, I wouldn't have answered, but Severine picked up. My bitch of a wife could've told them I was out. But, no. Severine said hold on and I'll get him for you. I was hooked."

"You got a call from Paul Denis?" I was astounded. Then it hit me. There'd been another arson. "Did anyone get hurt?" I peeked around the door to look at Pierre.

Corday was irritated. "I don't know how many people were hurt, Nicki. I was told it's bad and we have to go right away. Fire Captain Denis is there, waiting for you. He will know more. Me? I'm just your chauffeur. This isn't my case, you know."

"Thanks, partner." I said it with obvious sarcasm, annoyed by Corday's attitude. I dragged a sweatshirt over my head and stepped out of the bathroom. Then I scooped up my keys and wallet, grabbed my leather jacket from the chair and turned off the light. I glanced longingly at the bed and felt a natural human urge to crawl under the covers, pretend I'd never heard about these arsons. Instead, I locked the door and followed Pierre along the walkway and down the stairs.

We jogged through the apartment building's courtyard, lined with plants that never saw enough sun, never tasted enough rain to be anything but dusty runts. The apartment's open court narrowed to a covered entry, jammed with bicycles, early morning light twinkling on their handlebars. I barely had time to smell the cool air before Pierre and I bounced in his patrol car from opposite sides, slamming the doors.

He popped the clutch and lurched into the street, driving with the aggression of a Boston cabby, scaring me half to death. Corday jabbed the brake pedal, nearly sending my face into the windshield.

"What's gotten into you? Pierre, can't you slow down?"

Corday was bitter. "Paul Denis shouldn't have called me." Pierre slapped the car into second gear and shot into a gap in the traffic, whipping my head backwards.

I tried sympathy, hoping Corday would mellow his attack dog driving style. "Sorry. How'd Paul get your home phone?"

"I'm sure that asshole Vernier gave my number to Fire Captain Denis." Corday slapped the steering wheel in anger. "I'm cursed. I will never retire with a pension." Pierre sucked in his cheeks like he'd swallowed lemon juice, his eyes rolling heavenward. "It is bad, this thing. We have to find a way out."

"Now it's we, huh?" I got a little satisfaction from Corday realizing he was my partner, a fact he'd conveniently forgotten in this arson case. "So you figure Vernier will dump these arsons on you – after he fires me as his scapegoat."

Corday knew I was right. He ignored me, glaring at traffic like he could melt cars out of his way with rage. The moment I was gone, Corday was Vernier's next victim. Pierre tore the steering wheel in a sharp turn, pushing me into the center console.

"Hey, Pierre, you should keep me alive if you don't want this case dumped on your head. How about slowing down?" I grabbed a handle above the window for support in Pierre's next tire squealing move.

Corday lurched to a stop behind a wall of trucks waiting at a light. Their diesel fumes leaked through car vents, churning my empty stomach toward nausea. The stoplight changed and Pierre shot ahead, threading his patrol car between trucks, letting the warbling siren and pulsing strobe lights melt traffic out of our way.

I tried a different tactic to calm Pierre. "After the cafe, you went schmoozing with your Surete buddies. You were going to get some dirt on Vernier to back him off."

"Schmoozing!" Corday was offended. "You act like I'm some door to door salesman, hitting on lonely housewives."

"Sorry," I apologized. "Research," I corrected myself, trying not to choke on the word research. "You checked your contacts in the Surete. Did you find anything on Alain Vernier?"

Pierre turned to look at me. "Vernier's got a lot of juice, Nicki. He can crush you. You should remember that."

"Wonderful," I sighed. "But did you find anything on Vernier?"

"No," Pierre said in a tired, irritated voice. He grabbed the steering wheel tighter and white showed on his knuckles from the angry grip.

There was no point in asking more questions since Pierre wasn't going to answer them. I stared out the windshield, watching a blur of apartment buildings roll past. We were in the Menilmontant neighborhood of Paris, an area dating from the 1950s, a new ring built around the old Paris to house baby boom families. The streets were canyons walled by featureless apartment towers rising ten stories, leaving sidewalks and playgrounds in perpetual shadow. Menilmontant was block after block of high-rise apartment clusters. The repetition of concrete walls numbed my mind and I was lulled into a fantasy there was no second arson, nothing had happened.

Then a sick feeling hit me as fire smells pushed through the car vents. I knew something horrible was coming. Pierre slowed the car and pointed at a ghastly scene. The arsonist hadn't burned a warehouse this time. He'd leveled an entire apartment complex, leaving only a jumble of cement pillars tossed into a cratered hole. Where ten stories of concrete should fill the block, there was nothing but curtains of smoke and ash drifting in the air, lingering ghosts of a hell that happened here.

Streams of water trickled out of the ruins, wetting pavement in an oily shine. The street was filled with hot debris where water hissed against smoldering lumps of seat cushions, heaps of clothing and charred books. Around me were the remnants of families – children's toys and lifetime mementos, coats and kitchen tables, one Rossignol ski still good, the other melted into a pretzel. I was stunned.

Ambulances waited everywhere, their strobe lights spinning urgency into the chaos. Rescue workers crawled over debris and small tractors shoveled rubble out of the way, their growling engines blending with bursts of static from police radios.

Pierre drove in the middle of the rescue effort and stopped. With a click of the door handle, I stepped into the terrible odor of burnt human flesh. The awful smell coated my throat and nose, causing my eyes to water, blurring my vision. I swiped a hand over my eyes and blinked to clear my sight. In front of me, uneven rows of stretchers were spread across the glistening sheen of wet pavement. Dead bodies lay on these stretchers, draped with wool blankets dotted in red crosses.

I saw a paramedic kneel in oily water and gingerly lift a long black object. Despite her tenderness, the object fell apart and I was horrified to realize she was moving the remains of a child's arm. The paramedic lifted a blanket to gently put the arm with the rest of a charred corpse, barely recognizable as a human being. I sagged against the car, sickened by the image of the burnt child.

Next to me, Pierre Corday leaned his butt against the car, his face pale. He rubbed anxious hands on his trouser legs and complained bitterly, "Why did you drag me into this case?"

I snapped back, "I didn't drag you in, Pierre. You were already in this thing and you know it. From the very beginning, Vernier fingered you as the next fall guy. This case gets dumped on your head after I'm sunseted. You've got to help me or the heat gets turned on you."

Corday gave me a sly look and his eyes brightened. "Maybe the two fires aren't connected. Perhaps the warehouse and this apartment building have nothing to do with each other."

"Fat chance." I pointed at the foundation of the apartment building, glazed like a ceramic bowl. "You see that melted concrete, all glassy and smooth?"

"So what? It means nothing."

"The hell it doesn't." I jabbed a finger at the glossy concrete. "The warehouse floor looked exactly like that, Pierre, melted into glass. This is the arsonist's signature, his way of doing business. It's the same guy."

"You don't know that, Nicki." But Corday didn't mean it. He knew I was right. The same arsonist committed both crimes, the warehouse and this apartment complex.

"You're trying to squirm out of this thing and you can't."

"No," he corrected me in a calm voice. "I am getting out of this thing."

I suddenly felt cold, despite hot, steamy air all around me. "What are you going to do?"

Pierre couldn't look at me. "Something with big bucks is going down, huge bucks. I have to stay out of the way, Nicki. I'm taking my family out of France. I want them safe." He swallowed hard. "I'll be back in a few days."

"Then leave me the car keys. One of your Surete buddies can take you home." I held out my hand.

Corday dragged car keys from his pocket and slid them in my palm. "Fine. I'll grab a ride with one of the gendarmes." Pierre stared at me. "You can't stop this, Nicki."

"I can try." I didn't feel anywhere near as brave as I sounded. I stuck the car keys in my pocket so Pierre couldn't hear the keys shaking in my hand.

"You're crazy to keep working this case," Pierre warned me.

I answered him by pointing at rows of stretchers. "Look at those burned kids. How can you see them and leave?"

"I can't do anything for these dead ones, but I can protect my family, Nicki. You don't understand. You don't have children, yet." Corday hunched his shoulders.

I gave up. "So go save your family."

"Well," Pierre said awkwardly. "OK, then. I'll see you after this is over." Corday shuffled off in his slightly bowlegged stride, his scuffed brown loafers sloshing in water coating the street. He slid through a knot of workers in hard hats and vanished behind a curtain of dusty smoke. I kept watching the spot where he disappeared, expecting Corday to walk back through and apologize to me. He didn't of course.

Despite hundreds of people working frantically all around me, I felt alone and abandoned. I stood there wondering how I could possibly stop this arsonist. Would Paul Denis be any help? I was sure he'd been here all night organizing the firefighting and rescue efforts. Maybe Paul found a clue in the rubble since this blaze wasn't completely devastating like the warehouse arson. There was only one way to find out, talk to him.

# 9

# Questions

I was caught in the middle of a frantic search for survivors. Teams of rescue workers were breaking huge concrete beams with jackhammers, sounding like a bizarre orchestra of prehistoric instruments. Where a body was found, more delicate tools were used and diamond saws screamed as they sliced through fallen pillars, pumping the noise to rock concert level. I was deafened when a crane swung overhead in a screeching pivot. Then a bulldozer dropped blocks of concrete, backed up and scraped another load into its bucket, billowing dust in the already foul air. I walked around the debris, anxious to find Fire Captain Paul Denis.

Picking my way through the remnants of shattered lives, I stepped over graphite tennis racquets melted into question marks and a small TV morphed into a figure eight. I was surrounded by images of loss, charred bodies on stretchers and blistered family photo albums.

I saw a makeshift first aid station, just a hand-lettered sign propped against boxes of supplies. A knot of anxious medical workers checked their watches, worried that each passing minute made finding survivors less likely. In the center of the first aid station, a doctor used surgical cutters to slice away the torn shirt sleeve of a firefighter, revealing a deep cut on his arm. It took me a moment to recognize a tired Paul Denis, layered in dirt from searching the ruins for survivors.

A male nurse cleared a syringe of air bubbles, squirting a dribble of tetanus serum. Paul winced in anticipation and turned his head away, unable to watch the long needle run under his skin. Injections were among my least favorite things so I couldn't bear to watch the plunger slowly ooze into the hypodermic. I sank into an empty canvas chair near the first aid station, waiting for the doctor to finish with Paul's arm.

Eventually Paul Denis started walking toward me, stepping through a tangle of canvas fire hoses. He shook his head to clear hair out of his eyes and I was shocked at how much Paul changed since last night. Rage and depression seemed to age him five years in a few hours.

Still, he managed a wan smile and said, "Good to have you here, Nicki."

"Thanks." I looked at his bandage. "How's your arm?"

"Not serious. I had a cut and they wrapped me like some Egyptian mummy. I'll take these off soon." He picked at the bandages, his dirty fingers scratching at the white gauze wrapping.

"I'm glad it wasn't serious." I leaned forward in the canvas chair. "Are you up to answering some questions?"

"Sure, I'm fine. Go ahead." His radio squawked and Paul Denis turned down the sound, reaching around his belt to thumb the volume wheel on the unit.

"In looking for survivors, did you find any clues? Like where the fire started or an incendiary device."

"I was too busy to look for clues, but I've got a witness who wants to talk with you."

"Really," I said eagerly. "Someone who lived in the apartment house?"

"No, a fire captain. His team was first to respond. When they got here, Fire Captain Marc Dubois was badly hurt. Paramedics are taking him to the hospital. If we hurry, you can catch him."

"I'm going." I popped out of the chair and walked alongside Paul Denis, my feet sloshing in water from leaks in high pressure fire hoses. The tangled spaghetti of canvas hoses from the five alarm fire was unbelievable. I was sure it would take a day to unravel the mess. We cut through a curtain of smoke and I realized almost every emergency vehicle in Paris was here, more than a hundred ambulances clustered together, their blue strobe lights spinning violently. Running to ambulances for supplies, rescue workers bumped past me, muttering apologies but not slowing down.

Near the ambulances, paramedics were crowded around a fire captain sitting on a pile of rubble, five clean blue uniforms surrounding a dusty, sagging man. His firecoat was splotched with gray ash, powder covering his face like a mask. Dull eyes peered from the ashen mask, seeming not to realize we were approaching him. When we got close, Paul Denis knelt down, making eye contact with Fire Captain Marc Dubois. "Marc, you wanted to meet Inspector Foster of Interpol, tell her what happened. Well, here she is."

I waited, squatting so Marc Dubois wouldn't have to stand, shifting my body to be more comfortable. Marc angled his head to look up and his eyes were glazed by emotional shock and blood loss. Antibiotic paste clotted a gashed cheek held together with clamps. An emergency cast on his arm was tucked under his firecoat and a medical tag showed morphine had been given for pain.

I tried to be low key and sympathetic. "I'm sorry, Marc. What happened?"

The morphine made it tough for Marc to talk. At first his mouth moved but words didn't come out. Finally, he whispered, "When we got here, the top stories were in flames."

"Yes," I encouraged him, "the upper floors were burning …"

Marc gave a tiny nod. "The top floor was in flames and we wanted to rescue people. I put the biggest truck next to the building and started elevating the aerial ladder. I shot a protective spray to dampen fires on the upper floors. You understand?"

"Yes, you shot a fan of water, like you're spraying a lawn," I replied. "The soft spray cuts down heat. Spraying water slows the spread of fire and keeps people from being burned. You were buying time to get people out."

"Exactly. My firefighters were very motivated, you know. They started up the aerial ladder before it finished extending. Climbing a moving ladder is very tricky. You can get hurt, but we had no choice. We were out of time."

"Sure." I imagined firefighters charging up a swaying ladder. It was hard enough when I took aerial photos at the warehouse, standing motionless while the ladder turned in a circle and motors pushed ladder sections out. It made my palms clammy to think about running up a ladder sixty feet in the air while you swing around and shoot even higher. "So you got to the top and rescued people."

"We tried. A couple were burning, their clothes on fire. Jeanette yelled at them to wait because she wanted to get closer, but the couple jumped anyway and missed the ladder. There wasn't a thing I could do. I watched them fall to the street. Their heads smashed on the pavement and I'll never forget the popping sound." Marc continued in a depressed voice. "All I could do was cover them with a tarp. I knew it didn't matter for them but I felt better."

Hit by the image of a burning couple splattering on the pavement, I rocked on my heels, momentarily losing my balance. I steadied myself by putting one knee on the ground. "Why couldn't people use the stairs to leave?"

"The stairs were on fire and we couldn't put the flames out. The arsonist used some exotic chemical. His fire laughed at our water. The heat was terrible and my crew had to get out of the building." Marc looked stunned. "Then the whole damn thing blew up. There were no warning signs, no telltale glow in the ground floor windows or smoke venting from cracks in the walls. The apartment building lifted up and exploded, smashing our largest truck like a toy. There's what happened to the aerial ladder." He pointed at a hundred feet of metal steps blown across the street.

The heavy steel ladder was a twisted wreck. Dead firefighters were jammed inside, hanging like limp dolls, crushed by the ladder's metal cage. I saw neon blue flame as welders worked to cut loose mangled bodies. I recognized one of the dead men as the firefighter who controlled the aerial ladder when I took pictures at the warehouse. Never again would he sit in the little control booth at the back and drive the rear wheels or swing the huge ladder into action.

It took me a few seconds to recover. Then I asked, "Did you see a sheet of flame under the apartment house, like it was being pushed upward, thrust up like a rocket?"

"I think so." Marc nodded his head. "The ground shuddered, the whole building lifted up, then it melted and disappeared in that hole." Fire Captain Dubois pointed the apartment house foundation, now a crater shaped like a funnel and coated in melted glass.

I stood and turned to Paul. "The arsonist used rocket fuel again, enough to lift this huge building like some missile. That's why Marc couldn't put out the fire. A single stream of water just evaporates into steam against that kind of heat."

Guilt was cutting Paul Denis like a knife. "It's my fault they got killed. I sent off an e-mail last night, warning everyone. But I should have done more."

I shook my head. "It wasn't your fault. The arsonist gave them no choice. They had to risk their lives, getting close with the truck ,or they couldn't save anyone on the top stories. They tried to rescue people instead of protecting themselves. It's what you would have done."

I couldn't do anything else for Paul so I turned back to Marc. "Thank you. We've got the basics. Is there anything else? Something you saw that might help us?"

Marc shrugged. "No. I was knocked out by the blast. When I came around, bodies were scattered everywhere. I was too hurt to walk. I crawled to the second truck and radioed for backup. This arsonist has to be stopped." Marc's eyes rested on my face, pleading for help.

I wanted to comfort Marc but there wasn't anything I could say. There was no quick way to stop the arsonist. I gently urged Marc, "Take care of your wounds. I'll talk to you later, at the hospital."

A paramedic elbowed past me. "Come on, Marc. There's nothing more you can do here. Let's get you into surgery."

Paul reassured him. "It's OK to leave. I'll take care of the cleanup."

The paramedic helped Marc wobble to his feet, his coat buckles jingling. I watched them stagger to a waiting ambulance where Marc collapsed on a stretcher. Paramedics covered him with a blanket, then slammed the ambulance doors. In a minute, the ambulance rolled away, growing smaller and smaller, its wailing siren fading.

Paul Denis jammed his gloves in a coat pocket. "When we find this arsonist, I'm going to kill him, burn him alive."

"First we have to catch the arsonist and there are no clues. It'll be days before lab techies tell us something from this mess."

"Nicki, you can't wait days to catch this maniac." Paul was angry and frustrated. "The killing must be stopped now."

"Paul, I don't need more pressure. I need evidence."

"Sorry," he apologized. "I didn't mean to dump on you."

"Forget it." I shrugged. "There probably hasn't been time to get an aerial view of that crater and see how many fuel bladders were used."

"You're trying to count how many rockets he has left?" Paul asked.

"Yeah. Two bladders at the warehouse means he used only one of the five missiles, unfortunately. This 'hypergolic' fuel is stored in pairs, two kinds of propellant. Spraying a little of each propellant into a nozzle pushes a huge missile and its warhead over 8,000 miles. Mix both fuel tanks together at once and you get a volcano. That's why the warehouse roof disappeared and this apartment house melted into its foundation."

"How many rockets got used here?" Paul wondered. "Two, maybe three? I don't think he used more. Just enough to melt the entire foundation and first floor, so the whole thing collapses."

I agreed. "There's four down and one to go. Even knowing he's got only one left doesn't help much. We need more clues to find him. When you searched the wreckage did you see anything?"

"Not really." Paul Denis rubbed his chin. "Maybe I have a lead for you, Nicki. The phone company records all emergency calls. I asked them to trace the call for this fire. By now, they should know where the call originated. Maybe that information will do you some good."

"Sure. I'll check it out." I saw a burnt teddy bear lying on the ground and picked it up. I put the toy on a low wall, hoping its owner could reclaim a treasured possession.

Paul Denis handed me a slip of pale green paper. "This is my cell phone number. Feel free to call me." He tapped the mobile phone clipped to his turnout pants. "I'll squeeze the lab guys, get them to move a little faster. I know all their damn tests are chemistry and chemistry only goes so fast. But a shove might help them. Maybe they'll have some early results."

"I hope so." We stood there awkwardly.

"Well, I'll talk to you later. Good luck."

"Thanks," was my tired reply. There was nothing else I could do here, so I turned and walked away.

In a few steps, I ran into the haunting sight of fifty small trucks parked in even rows. Coroner's vans were now on the scene loading bodies for the morgue. Every time a stretcher was lifted into a truck, burnt flesh flaked off and clung to the wet pavement. I looked inside a coroner's van and saw stretchers racked like bakery pans with white name tags hung on them. The tags were all blank and there weren't going to be any names written on those tags for a long time, if ever. Faces and fingerprints were burned away and most bodies didn't even have teeth left for identification by dental records.

Sickened by what I saw, I got to the Interpol car and stood there, staring at the car keys. I could drive away from the fire scene, but there was no leaving this job. The smell and feel of the dead would stay with me, no matter where I went.

# 10

# Voice

I pulled away from the fire scene and hit a wall of traffic, rubberneckers gawking at the rescue effort through their car windows. I tried to roll off the clogged boulevard to a side street. I left a gap to change lanes but a pushy motor scooter cut in, squeezing ahead of me. Frustrated, I turned on the siren, waking up the couple on the scooter and they darted out of my way. I swung to a less crowded avenue and started moving across the grid of Paris, heading for the phone company's main switching complex. I wanted to listen to a recording of the 911 call for the apartment house fire.

In Paris, the phone company's central switching complex is near the Louvre, France's grand museum. Morning commute traffic always gridlocks at the Louvre, making it one of the worst congestion points in the city. Everyone living on one side of the Seine River goes to work on the other, so no one goes anywhere. They all sit in their cars waiting to creep across some ancient, narrow bridge and I sat with them, anxiously tapping fingers on the steering wheel. To keep myself awake after a sleepless night, I hummed a French song. I didn't dare sing. I sing the way a shredder treats paper, destroying the song.

I gave up humming an Edith Piaf tune and stared at the Louvre Museum, one of my favorite places. I spent the free hours I rarely had in the Louvre. Inside, the museum felt alive and vibrant, filled with light flowing over beautiful treasures. But outside the building was grim, its classical stone walls blackened by pollution, making the museum look more like a prison than an art palace.

In contrast to the Louvre's classical stone walls, a glass pyramid was stuck in the courtyard, tilted at a weird angle like a crash-landed spacecraft. Window washers were using rock climbing techniques to crawl up the glass pyramid and scrub its triangular windows. The huge glass diamond was actually a new entrance to the museum, built to handle crowds from fleets of tour buses. A Metro stop dedicated to the Louvre also pumped several thousand tourists daily into the grand art palace.

I crawled past the Louvre in annoying starts and stops, looking for the phone company. Their bland concrete building was hard to spot behind a flashy pyramid and a sprawling museum. I almost had to endure another loop around the Louvre in commute traffic when I spotted the phone company and darted into their parking lot. With every space occupied, I wedged my car between shrubs in the true spirit of Paris drivers, who jam their vehicles everywhere, including tiny gaps normally taken by a bicycle.

I squeezed from the car and walked toward a 1930s Modernist cube building. The only bit of glamor on the bland architecture was an art deco door. The colored glass entrance looked like a Tiffany lamp shade. I swung through the beautiful door and looked around. Everything in the lobby was an antique except the receptionist, who was barely out of high school. The only makeup on her pale face was a thin streak of lipstick. She was dressed more for a rock concert than the French national phone company. The receptionist wore tight leather, a black biker's jacket over black toreador's pants. Leather wasn't my style. Leather clings to you, showing way too much of your body line. You have to be model thin with that look. I learn I'm not model thin every time I try on a new dress.

The receptionist wore massive Doc Martin boots and crossed one leg over the other. She bobbed a heavy shoe up and down like an oil derrick, studying me. "Can I help you?"

"Yes." I flashed my Interpol ID. "You know where they tape emergency calls?"

"No. I've only worked here a month, but I'll call someone who knows. Have a seat." She pointed to a waiting area where gummy residue from a thousand restless palms soiled the metal arms of a chair. I took one look and decided to stand.

I loitered by a worn table with a plastic fern, its dusty fronds spread across a stack of magazines. Bending over their torn covers, I shuffled glossy pages, looking for escape in a Godiva chocolate ad. I found only articles describing what women want from men in bed. I peeked at what I was supposed to want and felt out of it as usual.

The receptionist put her phone down and waved to me. "Take the elevator to the basement. Someone down there records emergency calls."

"Thanks," I said. I bent my path around the receptionist's small plastic desk, heading toward an elevator in the brief hallway. I hit a metal button with a down arrow and the doors quivered, then shrugged open. All I could do was stand in the box and run my eyes over its drab interior, tapping my foot impatiently. I sank downward until the elevator doors opened and dull gray racks of equipment hit me in the face.

I squeezed through a maze of equipment stacked floor to ceiling, sliding my body along narrow canyons of gray racks. It felt suffocating, like being packed in a subway car at rush hour in New York City, not the environment for a mild claustrophobic like me who didn't like closets and small elevators. Finally, I stood in an open space and my chest relaxed from being tight as a wrung towel.

Nearby, a technician was sticking a thin metal rod in circuit cards, probing the electronics. His shiny bald head reflected fluorescent lights like a waxed floor. A cigarette dangled in his mouth, sprinkling ash on his shirt. The technician saw me and brushed the flecks of cigarette ash off his chest. He pushed librarian glasses up his nose with a calloused finger and gave me a curious stare. "Yes, mademoiselle?"

"I'm working on an arson case, an apartment complex that burned this morning. I'd like to listen to the call for that fire."

"Ah, you want Fredo," the technician replied. "He records emergency calls."

The technician gestured at a gray industrial desk decorated with butt shots of girls in thong bikinis. The only innocent decoration was a lonely Asterix doll, a plastic model of the little Viking cartoon character the French love so much.

A teenage boy sat in a canvas director's chair with the nickname Fredo stenciled on it. He was deliberately wearing his jeans rolled up, showing white socks and loafers in a 1950s look recycled as vogue in Paris. His sock hop look featured a denim jacket with colorful patches from all over the world, including one patch from the New York Yankees. Fredo couldn't be all bad, I thought. Then I remembered what I was like as a teenager and I cringed.

Fredo swung around and took off a set of headphones, exposing ears thick and lumpy like his nose. He had a 1950's rock and roll hairdo, an Elvis pompadour, complete with a greasy lock curled on his forehead. Fredo checked me out with a quick top-to-bottom scan to see if I was worth a real looking over. I flunked and his eyes went back to my face. An ugly question mark danced in his eyes.

I tried to sound pleasant, hoping to improve his mood. "I'm Inspector Foster of Interpol."

"Oh, that's nice," he replied smugly. "I'm Fredo of the phone company." He chewed gum in an exaggerated motion, moving his thick lips a lot. Fredo crossed his arms and sat there staring, waiting me out.

I broke the silence, trying kindness to thaw him. I talked softly. "I heard you kept recordings of phone calls to the fire department. I'd like to listen to a call made early this morning, reporting an apartment house fire in Menilmontant."

"Yeah, I have that call." Fredo sneered and plucked a micro CD from the console in front of him. "I thought someone from the police would come by, once they woke up." He flipped the CD carelessly in his hand. Dropping the micro CD could scratch the disc and a precious clue would be lost.

I scowled at him. "You might treat that disc with a little more respect. I was at the fire scene this morning and a lot of families got hurt. The fire department lost a crew."

Fredo thawed. "Oh, I'm sorry." He put the CD flat on his desk, under a pair of curled fingers.

"Can you play the call for me?" I asked, adding, "It would save time." I tried giving Fredo a smile and it worked about as well as my smiles did when I asked for a raise.

"Yeah, I guess I can play the call for you." He snapped the micro CD in his console, then shoved headphones over his shoulder without turning around. He ordered me, "Use these. You can hear better with a headset than speakers." He rolled a cabinet back, almost running over my feet. He caught me jumping away and smirked.

I ignored his attitude and put on the headset. "How do I know which call it is?"

"Don't worry. I queued the CD to that call. You'll hear a really old lady after the time code beep." He pointed at buttons on the console. "This one is play and this is rewind. It's easy to use. Even your generation can do it." He talked like I was a hundred years old.

I tried humor. "This case is aging me fast, Fredo, but I've got a few years before I hit a hundred." Fredo broke a smile, but immediately swallowed the grin, not wanting to give me any satisfaction.

I forgot him and focused on the emergency phone call. I hit play and listened to a time code beep, followed by a moment of static. Then I heard a high pitched voice with a tremble of age, an old woman saying her apartment house was on fire. The dispatcher asked her to repeat the address and the old lady stuttered. It sounded believable, like someone really panicked, yet there was something wrong.

I backed up the CD, heard the call again, then listened to the voice a third time. When I let myself feel the voice, ice water trickled down my spine. I knew I was listening to the arsonist, not a panicked old lady. The voice of the arsonist haunted me the way stench from burnt corpses clung to my nostrils. I was stunned. "Where'd this call originate?"

"From a phone inside the burning apartment building." Fredo crossed his arms.

I pressed him. "What floor, what apartment exactly?"

"Third floor, number 313." Fredo sneered again. "You think I wouldn't know that, Inspector?"

I ignored his sarcasm. "You're sure it was the third floor, not the top floor?"

"I told you it was the third floor, apartment 313." Fredo was annoyed.

There was too much at stake to let Fredo's moods stop me. Still, I didn't want to hurt his feelings. I hinted, "What about that mechanical sound in the old lady's voice. Not quite a woman talking, is it?"

"Yeah, I heard that. No big deal." Fredo looked smug. "I asked our technicians. They said the apartment's junction box was probably hot from the fire. Heat makes a piezoelectric effect that distorts the signal. The tinniness in her voice is from that effect. I hope I wasn't too technical for you, Inspector." He twisted his face in sarcasm.

"No, I got it. Oh, just one thing, Fredo. The fire started on the top floors of the building. The junction box in the basement wasn't hot. No piezoelectric effect. Sorry." It felt nice to jab him for a change.

I ignored Fredo's sullen glare and played the CD again, focusing on the frightened old lady's plea for help. "You sure this call was made from inside the building?"

"Yes, I'm sure. I traced the phone number through records department to its owner." Fredo was angry, balling his fingers in tight fists.

"Suppose you had the right equipment. Maybe you could make the call come from apartment 313 when you were really somewhere else. Can you do that?"

"I don't think so, Inspector." Fredo folded his arms and his surly mouth took on a really ugly look. "It's an old lady calling, not some nut case." A flush spread across his face and his hands tensed on a pen.

There was too much at stake here to back off, but I tried to soften the argument. "Maybe the arsonist disguised his voice to sound like an old lady. There are electronic devices that change your voice. I've seen them in practical joke catalogs. Perhaps the arsonist used one of those devices."

Fredo didn't answer me. He bent the pen in his hand and lurched out of the chair, stomping away in angry footsteps.

I couldn't let him go like that. I remembered how my parents hurt my feelings when I was a teenager and then ignored me, treating me like I didn't matter. I walked after Fredo and found him sitting on the floor sulking, with his knees drawn up to his chin.

He snapped, "What do you want?"

I knelt on one knee. "Fredo, I didn't mean to put you down. I'm sorry I came off that way." He thawed a bit and I went on. "I think the arsonist faked his call. It didn't come from inside the apartment house.

I want to find the spot where the arsonist actually made his phone call."

"What good will that do you?"

I shrugged. "Maybe I'll get lucky and find the arsonist's signature, a personal touch he left out of ego. It's a long shot, but I don't have anything better to go on. Will you help me? I need someone who knows the phone system really well."

"Yeah," he mumbled. Fredo rubbed his legs and looked at the floor tiles. He thought it over and his face relaxed. "There's this lineman who works the area." Fredo looked at me. "The lineman's real smart, you know."

"Yeah? Good. We need a smart guy. This lineman teach you a lot of things?"

"Some," he grudgingly admitted. Fredo shrugged. "So you want to talk to this guy?"

"You bet," I agreed, standing up.

"The lineman's not here. He spends all day in the field. I'll have to page him."

"That's OK." I smiled at Fredo and got a nice smile in return. I put out my hand to help him stand up.

He waved off my help. "Nah, that's all right, Inspector Foster." Fredo rolled to his feet and dusted the butt of his pants.

"Call me Nicki."

"Yeah, OK – Nicki." He gave me a shy smile. We were friends now. I followed Fredo to his desk.

It took a while for Fredo to track down the telephone lineman. I went out and got some breakfast, but couldn't taste anything I ate. I used Fredo's phone to play my voicemail three times, listening to the same empty messages. I almost took up smoking. Finally, the lineman arrived and Fredo was right. The lineman immediately understood what I wanted to do. It only took five minutes for him to trace maps of the area, identifying where the arsonist could've made a wiretap.

Reaching in my pocket, I pulled out the slip of paper with Paul's cell phone number. I asked him to meet me at an address about a quarter mile from the Menilmontant fire. I left the phone company and headed for where the arsonist made his wiretap. I was excited and afraid at the same time. Maybe I finally had a clue.

# 11

# Wiretap

I parked close to an abandoned building with a phone company junction box on the roof. When I got out of my patrol car, a light wind was blowing, carrying ugly smells from the fire. I zipped up my jacket, shielding myself from the cold breeze, and looked down a narrow alley, just a thin opening between old industrial lofts. Squatters had moved into the lofts, screening upstairs windows with plastic trash bags. On the ground floor, windows were boarded over with sheets of plywood. The plywood was pasted with layers of handbills and posters, peeling to reveal faded advertisements underneath. Wind and rain had shredded awnings and ruined old business signs, completing the alley's neglected look, a one block ghost town in the heart of a bustling city.

Water trickled along the alley, wandering through charcoal colored paving stones and forming a large, dirty puddle at my feet. I rolled a loose paving stone in its hole with a splash of dirty water and waited for Paul Denis to arrive. Eventually, a soft crunching noise sifted along the narrow alley from tires rolling over cobblestones.

I watched a brown van wedge in the alley's thin canyon, then move closer and closer to me. I felt like a target standing there and was relieved to see Paul get out, wriggle a key from a jeans pocket and lock the van's door. He was wearing a faded denim work shirt and the sleeves were too short, riding up his wrists. He waved hello.

Paul saw an old rubber ball lying in the alley and trapped it under a scuffed tan workboot, squeezing the scarred rubber ball flat. He lifted his shoe and let the ball ooze back into shape. "So you had some luck at the phone company."

"Yes," I said. "You were right about the 911 call. It turns out the arsonist made the call. He disguised his voice. I talked to an expert at the phone company. The arsonist may have done a wiretap on a junction box in this alley."

Paul Denis used his fingers to comb his hair. It was peppered in soot from the rescue effort. "Why didn't the arsonist just use a cellular phone? Tapping a junction box is complicated."

"The arsonist didn't want you on your guard, looking for an ambush. An anonymous tipster on a cell phone is suspicious. Better to fake calling from inside the burning apartment building. He wanted to seem like a victim, trapped and frightened. He made the call by doing a wiretap in this alley. That way the phone company can't tell his fake call from a real one. The junction box circuits here trace to that apartment building."

"OK, let's play arsonist. I open this junction box and see thousands of wires. How would I know which wire to pick?" Paul shrugged.

"A phone company lineman told me the wires are tagged. The arsonist just reads the labels."

"Sounds logical. Where's this junction box?"

"Over there." I shielded my eyes and pointed to a large metal box outlined against the blue sky. Thick black cables came into the junction box from all directions of the compass.

He asked, "How do we get a closer look?"

"We go on the roof. The phone company gave me a key to the building. It's an abandoned print shop."

"OK, let's check it out."

I went over to the heavily braced door. A huge painted sign slanted across the door, reading "Typo et Lithographie." In its day the sign was impressive, drawn in elaborate lettering with a shimmer of gilt backdrop. But the lettering was now faded to a shadow and the gilt backdrop was just glittering speckles in the grain of the wood. I pulled a key from my pocket and used it in the padlock, opening the green painted door with a screech of rusted hinges. Behind the door, a flight of stairs was hidden in the shadows of the dark building.

I took a cautious step up the dark staircase, then a second, my footsteps echoing in the empty stairwell. The old stairs under me felt like sponges and I was worried one of them would break. The higher I went, the darker it got until I bumped against a door at the top and it swung back, venting bright sunlight into my eyes, nearly blinding me with glare.

I stepped on a black tar roof where a row of skylights ran along the center like a miniature greenhouse, its glass turned milky gray from years of dirt. All over the roof black vent pipes angled up, looking like an abstract sculpture garden of stick figures. I started weaving through the maze of vent pipes to reach the junction box, my footsteps springing on the soft give of the old roof. Then I stopped, feeling uncomfortable.

Paul gave me a questioning look, sensing my apprehension.

"You feel it?" I asked him.

His eyes scattered along the roof and came back to me. "I know what you mean. It doesn't feel right. Do you think we should leave?"

"No, this is the freshest clue we've got. Let's take a quick look around." I kept going across sticky tar, moving toward the shiny metal box I'd seen from the alley. My fingers held a small key they'd given me at the phone company. "That's strange. They gave me a key for the junction box, but I don't see any lock."

Paul Denis knelt on the roof and picked up a shattered padlock. "It was sliced off with bolt cutters. When they jumped on the bolt cutters to get extra leverage, it made that slight dent in the roof." His fingers traced a groove in the tar. He straightened up and dusted his hands on the front of his jeans.

"Maybe there's more evidence inside the junction box." Opening the doors, I snapped them in catches that kept wind from blowing the doors shut in my face. Inside, beige plastic bridges held bundles of wires, each strand tagged with a label printed in ball point ink.

I said, "Here are the lines from apartment 313 where the emergency call was supposedly made. The phone company lineman explained it to me. The arsonist used a portable phone clipped on this circuit."

Paul bent to examine the wires, turning his head for a better view. "You're right, Nicki. You can tell a phone was clipped on the wires.

Bright scratches from the clips haven't had time to oxidize and become dull. This was done very recently."

"Then it must have been the arsonist. The phone company lineman said no one's worked on this junction box in months."

Paul wrapped his hand around a thick rubber cable running in the direction of the burned apartment house. "This bundle of telephone wires goes from the apartment building to the junction box. The arsonist followed the cable, spotted the junction box on this roof and decided to use it for his wiretap."

My eyes ran along the wire bundle to the arsoned apartment complex a quarter mile away. The long arm of a construction crane hung over the ruins, a funnel-shaped hole I recognized as the scar of this morning's fire.

I suggested, "The arsonist stood here and called in the alarm. Then he waited for the fire trucks to arrive. When they parked close to the building, he triggered the explosion killing the firefighters. It must've been hard to catch the right moment to set off the blast. You'd have to know exactly what was happening and it's a long way to that apartment building. How did he see what was going on?"

Paul outlined faint chalk marks on the roof with a finger. "I think these chalk X's were for registering a telescope, focusing it on the apartment house. And there are these orange marks on the wall, Nicki." His finger traced orange scrape marks on a low stucco wall running around the roof.

I bent over to see what he was talking about. "What made the scrape marks?"

"These orange scars are from a fiberglass crane clamped on the wall. The arsonist used a portable crane to haul his telescope on the roof. We have little cranes like that, for freeing injured people from a car crash."

I nodded in agreement. "Yeah, it fits." When I leaned against the wall, rough grit pressed into my hands, trickling on the rooftop like sand draining in an hourglass. I stared at the industrial crane in the distance, listening to the chatter of jackhammers from a search for bodies in the rubble of the arsoned building. "The arsonist just stood here and watched people die. This guy is sick."

"Yes," Paul agreed. "Unfortunately he's also smart. He'll be hard to catch."

"True," I sighed, feeling very stressed. My technique for releasing stress was taking long, slow breaths, filling my lungs and letting the air out gradually through my nose. Breathing with an even rhythm refocused me, the mental fog cleared and I became aware something was wrong. I felt I was being watched, not a clear idea, just a strong hunch that I was in serious trouble.

I surveyed the flat roof and saw only dark tar flaked with a dandruff of gray pebbles. Then my eyes drifted to a nearby building and I saw a man outlined against the dark glass of an upstairs window. He caught my stare and melted away, vanishing so quickly I almost thought he was a ghost.

But now I knew someone was watching me. Standing on the open rooftop offered little protection from anyone trying to harm me. I had to find out who was there and why. I moved to get a better look and was shocked to see an observation team with a telescopic lens snapping pictures of me through a dormer window. City Commissioner Vernier must be having undercover cops follow me to learn everything I did on these arsons.

It was important Vernier's team didn't know I spotted them, so I could mislead them. I forced myself to turn away, tearing my eyes off the long telescopic lens. I looked at Paul Denis standing next to me on the rooftop, unaware of Vernier's surveillance team. He knew nothing of my frantic thoughts and was still trying to find clues to the arsonist.

Paul suggested, "You can have lab techs go over this roof. They'll spot anything we missed."

I had to be very careful what I told Paul since Vernier's surveillance team might be using a long distance microphone, picking up our conversation. I cautiously said, "I don't want lab techs going over this roof, Paul."

"Why not?" he asked in astonishment. "They'll comb the area, find every shred of evidence. You can call on my cell phone, get a lab crew here in minutes." He flipped his phone open and held it out to me.

I refused to look at his phone, knowing I was being photographed and probably videotaped. The safe thing to do was stare at my Nike Air athletic shoes and not say a word. I could feel my jaw tighten as I looked at my feet, wishing I could be glaring at Vernier's observation team. Frustrated, I jammed my fingers in the tight pockets of my jeans.

Paul's hand faded to his side and he clipped the telephone on his belt. He gave me a peculiar stare.

I took a deep breath and shrugged my butt off the wall, looking at Paul Denis with sadness. Then I turned my back on the ever-watching cameras and whispered quietly, "There's a lot I need to tell you and I can't say it here."

We climbed down the narrow staircase and walked a few blocks, looking for a safe place to resume our conversation. I saw a thin street curving between buildings and it looked like a great place to lose anyone following me. I turned in the narrow street, ducking under a laundry line filled with bed sheets. Linen on the clotheslines blocked any view of us walking along the alley and Vernier's surveillance team would go past, not knowing I'd gone in here.

It wasn't obvious this place even existed, a tiny lane built in a time when oxcarts, not cars, roamed the streets of Paris. The homes around me were very old, part of the original ancient city. Building walls were made from rough hewn timbers glued with coarse mortar and there were almost no windows. The homes were built at a time when glass was rare, mostly used for stained glass in churches. Scarce materials and crude techniques made for small buildings, cramped as phone booths but five stories tall. The thin buildings leaned against each other, stiffened with a plaster of raw cement like a cast on a broken leg. Stairways climbed as steeply as ladders and there was hardly space for a bedroom on each floor. Students were the only people renting the cramped one-room flats and even with no possessions they were forced to hang bicycles through the window of their tiny room.

At the end of the street, I found a quaint bistro with outdoor tables. The patio area was screened by elegant Japanese pine trees, their arms drooping like weeping willows. The pines grew in huge clay pots lined with carnations, their blooms a chorus of red bow ties adding vivid color to a gray, overcast day. I picked a table bathed in a rectangle of sunlight and dragged a wicker chair backwards, screeching it over flat paving stones. More tired in mood than body, I sat in a woven bamboo chair, sagging against its brown cushions.

Under other circumstances I would be charmed at finding such a cozy spot hidden in the midst of Paris, but at the moment I was too stressed to appreciate my surroundings. I had a lot of things to share with Paul Denis and I could see he was very unhappy.

Paul had an arm bent stiffly behind his cafe chair. "I don't see why we had to leave all of a sudden. We proved the arsonist was on that roof. Why not call the Surete crime lab and wait 'til they've examined the area? They're sure to find more clues, Nicki." He picked at the seam of his jeans in nervous energy.

"We couldn't do any more on that roof. It's too dangerous. We were under surveillance. I spotted a crew photographing me. They were probably eavesdropping on our conversation with a long-distance microphone. That's why I wanted to come here, where it's safer to talk." I looked along the alley and it seemed that we weren't followed.

He spun a pack of matches through his fingers and put them down. "Nicki, I don't mean to be unsympathetic. I know you're under a lot of pressure. But I think you're paranoid."

"Paranoid? I'm just trying to stay alive, Paul."

"And I'm trying to keep the fire department alive." He made an obvious effort to calm himself, flexing his hands. "All right, so who has you under surveillance?"

"OK, I'll tell you, but you aren't going to believe me."

"Try me." Paul Denis leaned over the table, pressing me with his body language.

This conversation wasn't going the way I'd hoped. I stalled by toying with a menu du jour, a printed list of today's specials slipped into a plastic sleeve. Reluctantly I explained, "I'm being tailed by undercover cops on orders from City Commissioner Vernier."

"Vernier?" Paul was startled. He started to laugh and checked himself. "Look, Vernier canned the head of the fire department over this thing, for incompetence. The City Commissioner is having you watched because he wants fast progress. He isn't doing it to harass you."

Paul Denis played with an ashtray like he used to smoke and was considering starting again. "Think about it this way. In the fire department, we have your boss ride along with you for your annual evaluation. You know, for your performance rating. Vernier is doing the same thing, but he can't do it himself. So he sends a surveillance team to watch you, make sure you're going all out to find this arsonist."

I rolled my eyes. "Paul, this isn't being done to make certain I solve the crimes. It's the opposite. Vernier is making sure I don't solve them. He doesn't want these arsons investigated. I was told that in no uncertain terms. Right after Vernier made me lead investigator – and gave me no resources."

Paul Denis surprised me. Instead of being angry, he was alert and focused. "You were told not to find the arsonist. When did that happen?"

"After I got assigned the case. My partner, Pierre Corday, took me out for a drink. Corday warned me somebody doesn't want these arsons solved. Try to solve the crimes and City Commissioner Vernier will crush me, then he'll fix things the way he wants."

"Are you sure?" Paul Denis didn't sound skeptical. He just wanted some proof.

I exhaled a sad laugh. "Oh, I'm sure. Corday told me a story about how his first partner didn't listen to a warning like this. The guy was tortured. His fingers were pulled out of his hands while he was alive. Then I went back to the office and a bicycle messenger delivered a box. I'd briefly seen this bike delivery guy in Vernier's office. He made a point of running his bike into my leg so I'd remember him and know he worked with Vernier."

Paul's eyes narrowed to slits. He was looking down at the table but I could tell that he was listening very intently. "What was in the box?"

"Exactly what you think. A woman's fingers, torn out of their sockets. There were some nice touches. The nails were done with polish from the bathroom cabinet of my apartment. A thumb and forefinger were glued together holding a burnt match, in case I was having a stupid attack and missed the connection to these fires." I waited a moment to let it sink in. "Still think I'm crazy? Paranoid, as you put it."

Paul waved his hands in disgust, but not at me. "Of course not. I apologize. It all makes perfect sense. The fire chief Vernier dismissed was also our top arson investigator. I agree. We're being screwed. You have any idea why?"

"No," was my simple reply and it was the truth.

"Damn, there must be something we can do." He checked his watch and frowned. "I'm supposed to be at the main firehouse in fifteen minutes for a conference. I can't skip it. I called the meeting to warn everyone that we have to change tactics when we roll to a fire, stay away from the building, disperse our trucks. It'll take hours to iron out the details. Maybe tomorrow I can go on that roof and look for more clues." Then Paul laughed at himself. "Won't be any clues there tomorrow, will there?"

"Not one. That roof will be so clean you can eat on it. The junction box will be sanitized and locked. Those orange wall scrapes will be stuccoed over." I sighed. "Well, you better get to your meeting.

There's no point waiting around here." I pushed my chair back to get up and was startled by my pager vibrating against my hip.

"That's weird." I jerked the pager off my belt and dropped the quivering plastic box on the table. Great, I thought, all I need is another demand on me. Annoyed, I hit the big key on the front of the pager like I was smashing an ugly bug. I spun it around to read the message.

Paul gave me a curious look. "So, um, who wants you?" he asked, trying to sound casual and failing. "Is it Vernier?"

"No, it's not." I looked at Paul in surprise. "I got paged by Taylor Hansen."

Paul Denis leaned over the table. "What does this Hansen guy want?"

"I don't know. He left me a voicemail. I have to call and play his message. Whatever he wants, I don't like it. Hansen's tied to these arsons somehow."

"How did you meet him, this Taylor Hansen?" Paul Denis sounded worried.

"I met Hansen in the Paris Archives when I was researching the owner of the arsoned warehouse. Taylor Hansen's an American computer consultant working on a new system for property titles."

"Did he help you find the warehouse owner?" Paul asked curiously.

"No." I shook my head. "Taylor was a waste of time. And I had no luck with Diane St. Remy, who runs the Archives. They wouldn't help me."

"Do you know why?"

"Not really. I know Taylor and Diane are tied to the City Commissioner. Vernier's spending money very freely in the Archives. The place is normally rundown and neglected." Feeling puzzled, I ran a hand along my chin. "Can I borrow your phone? The battery on my cell died."

"Certainly," Paul said, handing over his mobile phone. "You want some privacy? I can go for a walk."

"No, it's OK. I'm just playing my voicemail." I punched buttons on the phone to go through prompts and I was amazed to hear Taylor Hansen asking me out to dinner. When I first met the guy, he was in a rush to get rid of me, yet now he wanted me to dine with him at an expensive restaurant. Hansen must want something from me or he wouldn't have picked such an elegant place to have dinner. Ordinarily, I'd decline his invitation, but this might be the break I needed in this case.

I replayed Hansen's message to get the restaurant address. I looked in my coat pocket for a pen and was startled to see a couple approaching the cafe. The man walked tight hipped, hands in his pockets. He was wearing a black sweater tied around his neck, the sweater arms hanging down his gray dress shirt like a big, sloppy tie. The woman wore an all white jumpsuit including white shoes. A brown paisley scarf large enough for a sofa cover was draped over her shoulders. There was something vaguely familiar about her and I knew this wasn't the first time I'd seen her.

With a jolt, I recognized the woman as the miniskirted blonde sitting next to me at the sidewalk cafe. When Corday took me out for a drink, the blonde sat next to us reading a magazine and listening as Corday talked to me. She heard Corday warn me about his ex-partner being tortured, losing his fingers. The woman had tailed me from the very beginning. Vernier ordered her to eavesdrop on my conversation with Corday. The City Commissioner was making certain Pierre told me to lay off the arson case. Vernier also wanted to know how I reacted to Corday's threats. The blonde woman was part of the surveillance team I'd seen from the rooftop. They searched the area, finally locating me.

The blonde stopped and eyed the cafe, chatting with her partner about having a drink, trying to look casual. They walked past the area where I was sitting and I sighed in relief, but it didn't last. Their drifting past the cafe was just an act and they decided to stay, pulling up chairs only a table away from me.

I caught a glimpse of the man's hand and my body went cold. There was a funnel-like object in the man's palm and a wire ran up his sleeve. I wasn't an expert on electronic bugs, but I assumed he had a long distance microphone for eavesdropping. I asked Paul, "You got a pen and paper to write something?"

"Maybe." Paul Denis checked his pockets.

I searched my jacket and found an assortment of objects trapped in the coat pockets. I pulled out a scrap of paper and a pencil stub, then wrote my apartment phone number down, adding a brief note about Taylor Hansen asking me to dinner. I warned Paul Denis the couple sitting nearby were spying on us, that they'd taken pictures of us on the rooftop. I pushed the message across the table to him.

Paul read my note and a flash of anger darted across his eyes as he glanced at the couple.

"We'll talk later," I suggested.

"Sure." He jammed the slip of paper in his shirt pocket, then grabbed his cell phone off the table and clipped it on his belt again. "See you soon, Nicki."

"You bet," I agreed.

Paul Denis got up and the scraping of his chair echoed along the alley, a rusty screech that was completely out of place with the lovely surroundings. He wandered off slowly, pretending he didn't have a care in the world, hands in his pockets, scanning the area like a tourist on holiday.

When he vanished around a corner, I felt the cold shadows of the street creep under my jacket. I was alone, just me against the pair of undercover cops. I watched confusion flicker across the cops' faces as they debated, follow Paul Denis or stick with me. They stuck with me. I was the priority target. How nice, I thought. Getting free of two cops would be very tough, yet I had to get rid of them or they'd follow me to the dinner with Taylor Hansen.

I needed a diversion. I decided to order a meal and ditch out after the food arrived, saying I was going to the bathroom. I didn't know if it would work but I flagged a waiter and ordered double espresso with a basket of pommes frites, French fries. Waiting for my order to arrive, I tried to look casual, staring at everything but the cops, my eyes running over the cafe in triplicate.

The cafe was marked by an antique sign with an outline of a horse-drawn coach unloading passengers. Two centuries ago, this cafe was an inn and passenger coaches reaching the outskirts of Paris stopped here for the night. Then Paris expanded, swallowing the countryside and bringing this area into the heart of the city. The cafe was at the end of a narrow lane barely wide enough for a scooter and a pedestrian to pass each other. Originally, the lane was a muddy Roman footpath, then became a cobblestone road for oxcarts and finally a little alley between hostels built in the time of Shakespeare.

Half the alley sank away in deep shadows, but sunlight swept the alley's other side, glancing off stone walls. The sunlit walls were decorated with colorful banners on brass poles like a Medieval castle. Gold, red and purple banners wiggled in a light breeze, announcing a dozen unique restaurants hidden in this alley. Parisians came here to eat dinner, but tourists would never find this hidden spot and its parade of chalkboard menus. Dense with elegant handwriting in blue, red and yellow chalk, the slate menus marked tiny restaurants the size of a bedroom. Tables were packed against the walls with barely enough room for waiters to float plates on their fingertips.

When my waiter arrived with the basket of pommes frites, I thanked him and asked directions to the bathroom. Keeping my eyes off the cops, I took a sip of espresso and jammed a few fries in my face. The crisp fries tasted wonderful, but I was too nervous to eat any more food. I slipped some bills under the basket to pay for everything. Then I blotted my mouth with a napkin and forced myself to walk slowly toward the cafe.

I stopped in the cafe's entrance, casually examining bright images of hovering birds hand-painted on the door frame. Walking inside the restaurant, I was masked from the cops by hydrangea bushes with clusters of large pink flowers blooming along the cafe's windows. I watched the undercover cops closely through the glass and they were getting more anxious by the moment. The blonde woman said something and the guy nodded, glancing nervously at the cafe. I stepped back, using the dark interior of the restaurant to avoid being seen. I had only seconds before the woman came inside and searched for me.

It was hard to see in the dim lighting but I bumped my way into the kitchen and out its back door. I bent a jagged path down the street, dodging around stacks of boxes and dumpsters until I reached my patrol car. I never got a car started and into traffic so fast in my life. Looking in the rearview mirror, I saw both undercover cops standing in the kitchen doorway, furious with me. What those two would tell Vernier was their problem and I didn't care what they said. My problem was Taylor Hansen.

It was my impression that Hansen was playing his own game, not just coasting along as Vernier's puppet. Instead, Taylor Hansen was a wildcard running loose in Vernier's plans and dangerous to everyone, including me.

# 12

# Wildcard

After ditching the surveillance team, I drove home, changed into my best dress and headed for dinner with Taylor Hansen. The walk from my studio apartment to the restaurant was only three blocks, but I was walking into a different world, the domain of the rich. I could see the change immediately in expensive homes lining the street. Perfect lacquer paint shimmered on front doors as owners tried to outdo each other with sculpted door handles and elegant brass knockers.

My feet ached from wobbling over rounded cobblestones in three inch spike heels. To give my sore ankles a rest, I stopped and looked at the restaurant. It was large by European standards, occupying an entire white stone building. Flower boxes with purple and yellow pansies lined balconies, forming a hanging garden. Vivid blue awnings were embellished with gold script spelling the restaurant's name, Olivier's. I reached for Olivier's frosted glass door and it opened magically, pulled by a white gloved hand. The doorman bowed respectfully and gave me a gracious smile of welcome. I stepped across the threshold, entering a world where rich power brokers cut deals over a dinner that cost a month of my salary, especially when they ordered a rare wine.

The entry had a glossy black bar running the length of the room. Glass shelves behind the bar held sparkling Venetian goblets and crystal decanters with silver pouring spouts, backlit with soft lighting to emphasize their delicate lines. I walked along red leather stools facing the bar, picked one on impulse and sat down for a drink. The bartender finished polishing a glass and came over to me. He was wearing a black tuxedo jacket and heavily starched white shirt with ebony studs, his neck wrapped in a stiff collar and thin bow tie. His clothes were elegant enough to mistake him for a guest, except for a gold name badge reading "Jean."

Jean planted his hands on the bar and leaned toward me, setting his head at an angle. "Mademoiselle would like a vodka martini, am I right?"

I shook my head. "Nope, not much on martinis. You know how to make a Tasmanian Devil?"

"Oh, yes indeed. Orange juice, grenadine and vodka." He reached under the bar to get a Collins glass. "You are American, surely."

"Yes. New Yorker to be exact." I pushed a heavy glass ashtray out of my way and realized the ashtray was Steuben leaded crystal.

Jean began mixing ingredients for a Tasmanian Devil. "I was in New York on holiday once. Ah, New York City," he sighed. "It is much like Paris. This is your first time in our restaurant, yes?"

"Well, yes, it is my first time," I laughed. Jean's banter was relaxing me a little. "Does it show that badly or are you a superb judge of character?"

"I would like to think I am a good judge of character. It goes with being a bartender to know people." Jean put a little wafer under the tall, narrow Collins glass and slid the drink toward me. There were no other customers and he loitered, putting his hands on the bar. "You are waiting for a friend to join you?" he asked.

"Not exactly a friend," I said hesitantly. "I'm waiting for a computer consultant named Taylor Hansen. Does that name sound familiar?"

"Ah, yes. Monsieur Hansen dined with us last week." A mischievous look twinkled in Jean's eye. "Monsieur Hansen, he is always with a beautiful woman."

"Beautiful like me?" I laughed. "Well that was certainly a flattering way to answer my question." I lifted the cocktail glass in a toast. "Thank you." I took a sip of the Tasmanian Devil and the alcohol felt nice sliding down my throat. Jean winked at me and drifted away to serve newly arrived customers.

I sampled my drink and watched the restaurant fill up as the fashionable dining hour approached. When I thought about Hansen, my stomach tightened. He was a wildcard out on his own, playing some dangerous game and I didn't like the idea of dealing with him. I liked it less with every minute that passed as I waited for Hansen to arrive. I checked my watch, figuring he wouldn't be on time and I was right. I sipped the cocktail for twelve long minutes before the doorman ushered in Taylor Hansen.

Taylor stood in the little entry room like a model posing for an advertisement, a calfskin trench coat draped over his right arm. He held his chin lifted above a black silk turtleneck and the pose exploited his looks, a soft handsomeness. Taylor was dressed in several thousand dollars worth of casual tweed that fit perfectly, custom made by some Jermyn Street tailor in London.

Hansen wearing tweed to Olivier's was a form of reverse snobbery. In its own way, the elegant casual tweed was more pretentious than the sable furs being tossed casually to the coat checker. Dressing down for

Olivier's was a way of showing Hansen took this place for granted, that there were even grander places in his life. Hansen surveyed the room disdainfully. He spotted me and beamed a floodlight smile.

The overkill of his smile was so painful I wished I'd gone for a second Tasmanian Devil. I drained my cocktail glass and looked at the ice wistfully. I wished the glass could magically refill itself so I could have another drink before Hansen crossed the room.

Taylor bent his path through elegantly dressed people clogging the small bar and posed himself on the empty stool next to me, sticking out a hand. His handshake was firm, but guarded. Hansen said charmingly, "Hello, Nicki. Thanks for coming. Sorry I was a bit late. Hope you weren't waiting too long."

"No," I lied. "I just got here." I shielded my empty cocktail from Hansen, pushing the Collins glass behind my arm. "Did you work late?" I asked.

"No, just traffic. It never lets up." Hansen stretched his neck to look around the room.

"Tell me about it," I agreed cynically, playing with the ashtray.

"That's right. I suppose you drive in Paris traffic all day long," Taylor said with artificial sympathy.

My forced dialogue with Taylor was broken by the coat checker approaching, looking cute and a bit sexy in her maid's uniform. She put out a hand in a suggestive pose and asked, "May I take monsieur's coat?"

Taylor smiled. "Ah, sure." He draped his calfskin coat over her arm and she gave him an inviting smile, then did a suggestive turn. Taylor's eyes followed her butt swiveling away in a tightly wrapped black skirt. I could feel Hansen's eyes unwrapping the skirt.

I didn't like being snubbed by Hansen. He was taking me to dinner and he could pay attention to me, even if it was all a farce. I interrupted Taylor's fascination with the coat checker by asking, "Where're you from, Taylor?"

Taylor kept his eyes on the coat checker's tight fitting skirt. He responded dully, "Los Angeles." Hansen remembered I was there and spun around on the stool. He leaned against the bar and turned on his floodlight smile. Hansen said charmingly, "You're lucky, Nicki, living in Paris. There are too many great places here for all the evenings of a lifetime. Last night, I dined at Le Grand Véfour."

"Ah, you poor boy," I deadpanned, "you forced yourself to endure one of the finest restaurants in the world – and its prices."

"Well, the prices are a bit stiff." A conceited smile leaked through Taylor's forced humility. Ever the self-obsessed butterfly, Hansen scanned the room to see who was noticing him and check for celebrities. His "see and be seen" ritual went on for a while. Finally Taylor raised an arm to catch the maitre d's attention. Hansen curled a finger like he was summoning a taxi cab, as though he were the only important person in the room.

The maitre d' was immune to Hansen's rude treatment and waited a calculated minute before disdainfully sauntering over to us. He talked in a cold, flat voice. "Ah, good evening Monsieur Hansen. Nice to have you with us again."

The maitre d' turned in my direction and spoke warmly, "You must be Inspector Foster of Interpol. Welcome to Olivier's. I'm honored to have an Interpol inspector. This is your first visit?"

"True," I responded, "but I'm certain it won't be my last visit." Taylor must have told the maitre d' about me when he made dinner reservations. I was surprised and a bit pleased at the personal attention. I was also suspicious, wondering what price I was expected to pay for this dinner.

"This way, please," the maitre d' announced, sweeping an arm toward the dining area.

We entered the central dining salon and it was dazzling like the hall of mirrors at Versailles Palace. Mirrors reflected images of diners, waiters, tables and floral arrangements in a kaleidoscope. Ornate cut glass chandeliers hung from the ceiling, where a wreath of royal blue lilies was painted. Lilies were the emblem of French Kings, a reminder that these dining salons were once open only to royalty. One of the first restaurants in Paris, Olivier's originally served only the aristocracy, those born to nobility. Three hundred years ago, even the wealthiest merchant wasn't allowed to dine here, much less myself.

Today, I was in the private Paris of the rich, and the rich were draped in tailor made tuxedoes, wear only once designer dresses and expensive jewelry. The effect was overwhelming luxury, made even more luxurious by displays of brilliantly colored flowers. Large arrangements of delphinium blossoms, marigolds, roses and tulips shielded diners, making each table a private alcove. In a Paris overcrowded for centuries, this was a lavish use of space. Without floral displays, the salons could have been packed with twice the guests.

Our table was in a lovely alcove sheltered by bouquets, almost hidden. In the table's center was a small lamp with a fluted brass stem and fringed shade, its glow pushing soft yellow light on a delicately patterned linen tablecloth. We were seated with a flourish by the waiters assigned to us as the opening act of the performance at Olivier's. Dining in a fine Parisian restaurant wasn't just about the food and wine. It was personal spectacle, theater with you at center stage in the spotlight, the play unfolding around you.

The lead waiter handed me a huge menu on a stiff gold board, with tassels dangling off the binding. After introducing himself, he glided away and subordinate waiters brought courtesy appetizers of hard boiled quail eggs sitting on pastry buttons filled with pate. I let an appetizer melt on my tongue, savoring heavenly flavors like nothing I'd experienced before.

My rapture was broken by the wine steward hovering pretentiously between Taylor and me. The sommelier wore the key to the wine cellar dangling from an ornate chain around his neck. He was a tall man with long, thin hands. His extended fingers made the wine list look small as he handed a copy to Taylor and me. The wine steward talked in a tight, puckered voice. "Would you care for a bottle of wine tonight, or perhaps champagne?"

I put my copy of the wine list on the table and said politely, "I defer to you, Taylor."

"Well," Hansen murmured. He rubbed his chin and flipped pages in a leather bound book. "Hmm. I'll splurge. Maybe I can convert you to Bordeaux cabernet, Nicki." Taylor announced pretentiously, "I'll have the Margaux '61."

Startled, the wine steward recovered, talking in a polite but firm voice. "Is Monsieur certain he wants that particular wine? We have many excellent cabernets in our cellar. Margaux '61 is, how shall I say it?"

"I'm fully aware what a bottle of 1961 Margaux premier cru costs." Hansen was smug. He looked arrogantly at the steward and slipped a platinum credit card from his coat. "I'm good for it. You'll see. Call and check me out." Taylor held his wine list to be taken away. Hansen leaned back and put an arm behind his chair, looking expansive.

The wine Hansen ordered would have been a serious purchase for any gourmet. Marked up in the restaurant, the bottle of rare cabernet was costing almost my weekly salary. I said, "You must make pretty good money at the consulting game, Taylor."

"Well, the pay is decent. But I'm not rich. You know what I mean?" Hansen blotted his mouth in an affected manner, not feminine, just overly perfected.

Hansen's false humility put me off. "Seems to me you're rich, since you can afford to eat here and Le Grand Véfour often."

He laughed and looked around the room, comparing himself to others in the salon, searching for a good example in the crowd. I felt Taylor drifting far away from me. Abruptly his attention flashed back to the present. He put his elbows on the table, leaning toward me. His eyes gleamed even in the low light. Taylor's stare had such intensity I suspected he was high on cocaine. He talked in a low husky voice. "You can never be rich enough."

A madness danced briefly in Hansen's eyes until Taylor caught me staring at him. There was a moment of awkwardness and Hansen broke off visual contact with me, jerking his head in a nervous twitch. Hansen extended an arm in a detached, mechanical way. It felt like I was watching a robot as he picked a bread from an elegant basket. Taylor lifted the dome of a sterling silver dish and carved a sliver of butter with total focus, then spread the chilled butter in perfect swaths across his bread. Hansen's eyes were so intense it seemed his eyes were driving the knife across the bread, not his hands.

I watched Taylor's finger ballet in fascination, struck by Hansen's manic behavior. I'll always remember little beads of water on the chilled slab of butter, water droplets condensing from the cold of crushed ice under the silver dish.

Hansen finished painting butter on his slice of bread and stopped, his hands and face frozen. He gradually thawed, looking disoriented, like he'd forgotten where he was. There was a hint of fear in his eyes. Hansen's behavior was almost a psychotic break, like there were two Taylor Hansens.

I used a soothing voice, trying to bring him back to reality. "Taylor, why did you invite me here tonight?"

Hansen was disoriented by my question, but he quickly recovered. He replied smoothly, "I simply wanted to know you better. You're an unusual woman. I don't meet an Interpol inspector every day."

"Funny. I have the feeling you want something from me." I pressed Hansen, hoping to learn what this lavish evening was really about.

Taylor was his glib self again. "I want nothing from you beyond your companionship, I assure you. We're friends, right?" Taylor leaned over, putting his elbows on the table, pouring on all his sexy charm. "You never know, though, where friendships can lead."

"Where's this friendship supposed to lead, Taylor?" The normal answer is friendship leads to more intimate things, an upscale way of asking me to screw him. There wasn't any penalty for saying no to sex with Hansen but I knew it wasn't going to be that easy. He didn't want sex. He wanted something else. "What do you want from me?"

Taylor's face was flushed, like he'd drunk several glasses of wine. "Well," Hansen said softly, "you've seen tonight what money brings to your life. I mean lots of money. There are levels above this, Nicki. You know that. You've seen how the rich live."

"Really, have I?"

His eyes narrowed to jabbing needles.

I tried to calm him. "Forget my weird sense of humor, Taylor. Go on with your proposal."

Hansen stared at me. "None of this tempts you?"

I leaned over and put my arms on the table, feeling cold marble press through the tablecloth. I talked in a low, husky voice. "Sure, I'm tempted. I just don't believe it's real. Nobody offers you money without wanting something in return."

"You're wrong, Nicki. This can be very easy for you." Hansen pushed his chair away from the table and crossed his legs. He adjusted his napkin to flow perfectly over the crease in his trousers, pinching the fine linen napkin in little, prissy snips. Taylor said, "I'm in a position to reward you. I brought you here tonight to prove I'm generous."

"Generosity appeals to me." I wanted to string Hansen along. "I hope your generosity doesn't require anything too risky. Jail isn't a nice place to spend your life."

Hansen talked quietly. "You have to commit a crime to go to jail. I don't need anything illegal. I just want a favor. You'll be well compensated."

"Then how do I earn your generous compensation?"

"Soon I'll need some information and you'll give it to me." Hansen toyed absentmindedly with the knife, smearing greasy butter on the delicate linen. He acted like the expensive tablecloth was his to ruin. Taylor stared hypnotically at the flattened yellow ball of greasy butter, a squished blob clogging the delicate filigree of the tablecloth.

I asked cautiously, "Am I the butter?"

Taylor exhaled a quick laugh. His vision caught the wine steward approaching our table, flanked by two waiters. Hansen shrugged, looking blandly apologetic at the interruption.

I returned his poker face and waited for the wine to be poured. Time moved slowly, measured in little events that prolonged the tension. With a flourish, the sommelier took the wine bottle from a wicker basket. Holding the bottle from its indented bottom only, he poured a small amount in Taylor's glass. The wine steward stood back, waiting for Taylor to sample the expensive cabernet and give his approval.

Hansen acted his part to the fullest. He went through the ritual of washing his mouth with wine to savor the bouquet. Hansen waited a dramatic moment and finally said, "Superb."

The steward bowed slightly, then completed Taylor's glass of wine and made a circuit around the table to my side. The sommelier again held the wine bottle from its very bottom, rounding his wrist to wrap off the pour. A drop spilled in my lap and a new napkin was immediately brought to me, neatly folded on a green Olivier's plate.

The fresh napkin was served with a flourish, clamped between silver tongs. It was another reminder of how the rich were pampered.

The wine steward drifted away, leaving our team of waiters behind. The lead waiter asked, "Would you care to order?"

There was a deadly pause as all eyes turned on me. Taylor looked at me questioningly and spoke in a condescending voice. "What are you going to have, Nicki?"

"Poulet of Bresse with morels in cream sauce and baby baked potatoes," I said, snapping the menu shut. I flicked the menu at a waiter, letting Hansen know I could hold my own with him.

Hansen talked in a lecturing voice. "I'm going to try your canette, female duckling topped in slivers of candied tangerine peel. Cabernet's a bit heavy for that, but you only go around once." He looked pleased with himself as he folded his menu shut.

The waiters melted away and we were alone again. Taylor was lost, savoring his rare wine and I waited for him to come back to reality. After he put his wine down, I said, "You wanted some information." I tried to sound casual.

Taylor smugly patted his lips with a napkin. "There's really no need to talk now. When I need something, I'll call you."

"Really. What makes you think I'll care?" I asked sarcastically. Taylor had become a weasel, dancing away, expecting me to chase him.

"Oh, you'll care," Taylor laughed arrogantly. "You'll remember tonight. You'll remember living like this."

I tried to pry him open by teasing him. "Maybe living like this isn't what my life's about, Taylor."

"Then you'd best enjoy tonight. There won't be another." Hansen ignored me and lost himself in his wine.

I waited for an opening to resume the conversation, but it never appeared. Food courses came and went, with enough chit chat to maintain an icy civility. At the end of the meal, desserts were presented on a wicker tray for our selection. I needed solace and I went for chocolate cake with frosting the texture of a velvet jungle night.

I kept watching Taylor for an opportunity to discuss the arson, but he sat in stony silence, eating an ile flottante, carving the floating island of poached meringue in slices and dipping each piece in a lake of crème anglaise. I waited, sliding chocolate on my tongue until the cake disappeared. In love with the flavor, I gently pressed moist crumbs in the fork and licked them off. When the desserts were cleared, I expected to leave, but Hansen surprised me by ordering a glass of port wine. I ordered decaf coffee and the waiter glided away.

My decaf coffee was served with a flourish like I ordered Dom Perignon champagne, the coffee poured from a Sterling silver carafe in an acrobatic motion. A waiter held out a tray of different sugars and I plucked a ball of rock candy with silver mini tongs. I stirred the sugar using a delicate silver coffee spoon, the size used for feeding infants in high chairs.

We sipped quietly, the silence growing more awkward with each moment that passed. Olivier's was emptying out and only a few tables were occupied in our salon. Nearby, an older couple laughed noisily with friends, overfed and inebriated. A forest of floral bouquets separated me from a business dinner that was winding up, some deal being concluded with lots of handshakes.

The maitre d' brought Taylor the bill, a simple handwritten chit presented on a golden platter. Waiters slid trays in front of Taylor and me, presenting an assortment of tiny pastries, petits fours and other delicacies. I fought against temptation and lost, indulging myself in a truffle dusted with dark cocoa. The truffle exploded chocolate in my mouth, flooding me with semi-sweet intensity.

Taylor signed the credit card receipt and stood. A waiter moved behind me, sliding my chair back as I rose. I walked out of the salons, feeling a little fuzzy from the heavy wine, chocolate and rich sauces mixing in my stomach. Hansen let the coat checker help him with his overcoat, flirting with her again while I stifled a yawn. I didn't care this time. The evening had fizzled for me.

I walked out of the restaurant and a blast of night air greeted me, the shock of damp cold waking me up. A Citroen cab glided to a stop in the dull yellow halo of a streetlight. The doorman opened the cab's back door and I expected Taylor Hansen to go through the motions of saying good night but I was wrong.

Without saying a word to me, Hansen slid in the cab. The Citroen sank on its hydraulic suspension, bobbing like a toy floating in a bathtub. Even the doorman was startled at Hansen's cold attitude, expecting Taylor would slide over and make room for me. The doorman stood there waiting and was surprised when Taylor pulled the door closed, acting like there was no one else in the world. The cab immediately started away, leaving me there. The doorman gave me a sympathetic look.

I shrugged philosophically. "Well, thanks for a marvelous evening. I'll always remember tonight."

The doorman returned my compliment with a shy reply. "Oh, it was nothing. We were honored to have you, Inspector Foster." He was concerned. "Shall I call you a cab, Inspector?"

"No," I said, "I live nearby and the walk'll do me good." I wanted to unwind from the stress of the evening and work off the heavy food.

"As you wish," the doorman replied tentatively.

I said goodnight and began walking away. The restaurant door closed behind me with a hushed click, then the outside light died and darkness flooded over me. I took another step and stopped, feeling a woman's certainty that she's being watched by a man. Instinctively, I flicked my head around and saw Taylor Hansen's cab stopped in the street. I was surprised to see his taxi lingering in the dark. Then I caught Taylor's eyes on me, staring at my reflection in the driver's mirror. I stared back and was startled to see Hansen looking depressed and frightened.

This was a different Taylor Hansen, a person I'd never seen before this moment, a total contradiction to the self-assured image he always projected. He looked lost and scared, not the smug man I'd watched all through dinner. Taylor's perfectly controlled world had crumbled somehow and his game plan was falling apart. He played life like a chess game, laying out all the moves in perfection, but this time it wasn't working.

Hansen noticed me looking at him and tapped the cabby on the shoulder. The taxi flowed downhill, turned a corner and disappeared behind a row of townhomes leading to Montmartre's old cemetery. The alcohol I'd drunk abruptly left me and I felt the night's cold stabbing my bare arms, poking icy fingers through the thin material of my dress.

I walked home from Olivier's at a fast pace despite wearing high heels. I was relieved to get inside my apartment building and hike its circular staircase, twisting upward past dingy landings to the fifth floor. At the top of the stairs, I made my way along the hallway, walking in a dim spray of light from a wall fixture coated with dried insects. Entering my studio apartment, I flicked on the light and leaned against the thin door, pressing it closed. I heard the reassuring click of the lock snicking in place and should have felt safe in my room, but I didn't. I was anxious, the way I'd been all the way home. I hugged my arms around my body, feeling cold despite the overheated room.

I'd always found solace in a view of Montmartre at night so I went to my window and lifted thin fabric tacked over the glass. Pinning the cloth up, I pressed my forehead against the window glass, letting cold sink into me. I looked into the empty street and saw something move in sly cautious steps. A stray dog slinked along, always finding the next shadow, keeping its tail curled against its butt. The cowering animal disappeared in an alley and my gaze jumped to the yellow moon sitting on the rooftops of townhomes.

A movement caught my eye and I looked at a townhome, startled to see lovers embracing openly in a bedroom window. I was ashamed to watch and too fascinated to turn away when he peeled her top back, pinning her arms, then kissed her naked breasts. I hated them for the life they had together while my life was twisted in these arson cases.

I spun around, feeling raw and thwarted. I vented by kicking a high heeled shoe across the room and it felt good, so I let fly with the other shoe. My high heels hit the floor with muffled thumps, sending dust motes tracing lazily upward, caught in a beam of moonlight. I stared at the spinning dust, hypnotized by its slow float suspended on the moonbeam.

Then the phone rang, trilling insistently and the buzzing noise tore at my nervous exhaustion. My hand went toward the phone and I paused, touching it with only a finger. Instinct told me something vicious had happened and I wanted no part of it. I rubbed my temple and listened to the telephone ring again in an irritating buzz. I took a hiccup of breath and snapped the phone up. "Yes. What is it?"

I was startled to hear Taylor Hansen's voice, sounding hollow and artificial. "Nicki, I'm glad you're there. It's Taylor. Sorry to bother you tonight, but something's happened. I need your help. Will you come over to my hotel? Now? It's, er, rather urgent. I need to see you." Hansen sounded fuzzy and muted like he was drinking again, on top of the wine he'd consumed at dinner.

I paced in a tight circle, wrapping the phone cord around me. "I don't know about going to your hotel, Taylor. There better be a good reason. What's up?"

Taylor pleaded. "We'll talk when you get here. Come over, please. I need your help."

I stalled, asking, "Where are you?" I trapped the phone against my shoulder and picked at a broken fingernail.

Taylor rushed his words out. "I'm staying at the Regis. It's the new hotel on Place Vendome." Hansen talked like a frightened boy asking his mother to pick him up at school. If Hansen was faking, it was an incredible act.

The fear in Taylor's voice gave me confidence. Maybe this was the break I needed. Or an ambush. I sighed. There was no way to know. I tapped a finger against the phone for a long moment. I said flatly, "I'll be there in fifteen minutes."

Hansen didn't say thanks or that's great, or anything. He just hung up. I listened to the dialtone buzz for a second and muttered sarcastically, "You're welcome, asshole." My hand drifted the phone into its cradle and I tried to make sense of Hansen calling me. It was crazy. I shook my head to clear my brain. I realized I'd agreed to visit the Regis, but I had no idea what was waiting for me in Hansen's hotel room. Getting help, some backup, was necessary and Paul Denis was the best choice.

He'd be willing to take a risk to solve these arsons. I found a scrap of paper with Paul's cell phone number and dialed.

I was wired and things happened in slow motion. It felt like I waited a day before Paul's number started ringing and there was an hour between rings. Finally, a recorded voice told me the party I'd dialed was unavailable. I left Paul an urgent message to call me and chopped the phone down. I grabbed my address book from the desk, peeling the book open to Corday and tried his number. I heard Corday's voice in my ear, sounding groggy from being woken in the middle of the night. Alarm bells jangled in my head.

Something was wrong. I remembered Corday telling me he was going to keep his kids safe by staying with relatives. He'd return to France in a few weeks, after these arsons blew over. Now, I'd found Pierre asleep in bed, not staying with relatives in another country. I couldn't trust Corday any more than I could trust City Commissioner Vernier.

I let the phone drop away from my ear, watching my hand slip the plastic handset in its cradle. No help from my Interpol partner, no Paul Denis either. I paced for a moment, tried Paul Denis a second time, and again a recorded voice told me to leave a message. I left another voicemail and put the phone back on the nightstand.

My options weren't pretty. Going alone to the Regis wasn't safe, but I had a chance to crack Hansen. He was vulnerable on the phone and that wouldn't last long so I found my high heels and dragged the tight shoes on my aching feet. I turned off the light and floated out the door on adrenaline. Exhausted was a stage I passed an hour ago.

I walked to the Interpol car a block away, feeling my mind running on hyperdrive. I noticed every little detail of the street yet remembered none of it when I put the key in the ignition. Driving through a maze of twisting streets, I curved downhill to Boulevard de Clichy marking the boundary of Montmartre. A fleet of tourist buses are always parked there, below nude show marquees blazing rings of light bulbs. On a median strip in the wide boulevard, prostitutes and transvestites were selling themselves, wearing bizarre costumes and fluorescent neck boas.

Beyond the neon sex district, Paris was an empty city, a blacked-out stage filled with buildings and sidewalks that were just props waiting for tomorrow's performance. The time was well beyond midnight and even Paris traffic had disappeared. I could sail along boulevards, paying no attention to details like red traffic lights. Suddenly, I swept into a vast plaza lined by classical buildings with rows of Greek columns. I was driving in the spacious Place Vendome, home to shops that are the Rodeo Drive of Paris, with a glamour and snobbery that pulls the wealthy from around the world.

All around the square, window displays were brilliantly lit despite the ridiculously late hour. The jewels of Cartier glittered next to Charvet's extravagantly expensive silk shirts and neckties. The center of the Place Vendome was highlighted by spotlights glinting on a huge cylindrical monument, the Vendome Column. The pillar's spiraling bronze tiles were melted from cannons won by Napoleon in battle. This was the spectacle of Paris at its most decadent – history, greed, fame, dramatically lit at night. One side of the plaza was even more brilliantly lit by floodlights illuminating the luxurious Regis hotel, where Taylor Hansen claimed he was waiting for me.

# 13

# Mistakes

I made the long walk up the hotel's steps, covered in a waterfall of red carpet. A doorman in gold overcoat and peaked hat pulled a massive oak-framed door open for me, nodding respectfully despite the time. He was used to people keeping late hours. Only normal people like me live during daylight. The rich haunt the night. World-class wealth drawn to the Regis start their day at noon and drink their last brandy and champagne to celebrate dawn before toddling into elegant suites, pulling drapes tight to shut out that ugly thing called sunlight.

The lobby was dripping in chandeliers, spattering bright drops of light on the carpet. I stopped at the check-in desk, standing before the head night clerk. He was dressed in a gray tuxedo with a fresh pink carnation pinned on his lapel, where a name plate below the carnation said Charles. He gave me the full snob treatment, complete with arched eyebrow and scornful look, but it didn't bother me. I'd lived in Paris long enough to know everyone on the Right Bank of the Seine behaves this way.

Charles ran his eyes up and down me. "You have business in the hotel?"

"I'm here to see a guest, Taylor Hansen," I said, ignoring his attitude.

"You're visiting Monsieur Hansen at this hour?" Charles slowly pulled his wrist up and tapped his watch with an irritating crooked finger. He calmly waited for me to give up and disappear.

I wasn't giving up. "I just got off the phone with Hansen. He asked me to come here and said it was urgent." I hunted in my purse and dug out the Interpol ID, holding it up for the head night clerk.

Charles flicked a condescending look at my ID card. "I see." He shrugged, his face drooping. "Very well. I will call Monsieur Hansen. You assure me he is awake and expecting you. This is true, yes?"

"True," I said.

Charles picked up a cordless phone and held it stiffly, precisely tapping keys with a forefinger. The phone was pressed tightly against his ear, but a ringing sound leaked out and I could hear a muffled "Hello."

The head night clerk replied, "Monsieur Hansen? This is Charles at the front desk. I am very sorry to disturb you. You have a visitor." He nervously fingered the knot of his tie. "Do you wish to receive her in your room?" Charles stole a peek at me.

I overheard Hansen asking, "Is it Inspector Foster of Interpol?" I laid my ID on the desktop.

Charles picked up my identification and held it very precisely between his thumb and forefinger. "Interpol, yes. A Nicki Foster. You were expecting her?" Charles looked at me with an eyebrow crooked in a question mark. He nodded. "Yes, at once, certainly." The head night clerk hung the phone in its recharging cradle. He ignored me and picked up a tiny brass bell, ringing it.

The tinkling sound of a little bell was lost in the lobby's deep carpet and plush furniture. I was sure no one could possibly hear the chime, but a bellhop popped off a chair hidden by a sprawling fern. The young boy ran over, masking a yawn with a white gloved hand.

Charles glowered at the bellhop for showing a yawn to a visitor in the Regis. Irritated by the young boy's lapse, Charles commanded, "Take Inspector Foster to Monsieur Hansen, in suite 312. Come back right away. No goofing off."

I didn't need anyone to show me Hansen's room but I didn't waste time on an argument. I knew the bellhop was more than a courtesy.

His escorting me was also a matter of security. They wanted to make sure I really went to Hansen's room.

I got in the elevator and sagged against the side. The late hour was catching up with me despite being wired with tension and I studied the bellhop to keep awake. The bellhop was a relic from the last century when Grand Dukes arrived in horse drawn carriages, with steamer trunks plastered in stamps from travels around the world. Bellhops carried the steamer trunks inside the Regis, wearing the same costume I was looking at tonight, rich blue pants and matching tunic with gold trim. Columns of brass buttons paraded around the vee shaped chest flap of the bellhop's cavalry tunic. A brimless jug cap was clamped on his head by a patent leather chin strap. The bellhop's face had the freshly scrubbed rosiness of a little boy. I gathered he hadn't made it into a technical school and was apprenticing at the Regis instead. Not a bad fate, when you consider the tips. He just had to survive his first years working the graveyard shift.

The elevator doors flowed open and I followed the bellhop along a hallway of red carpet and silk wallpaper. Typical of the Regis, gold adornment was draped over every object in sight, making the place feel overbearing and suffocating. It was like expensive perfume splashed around so much it makes you gag. I walked along the hallway toward Taylor Hansen, trying to ignore the ostentatious luxury.

When I got to Hansen's suite, I thanked the bellhop, giving him what was left of my smile. The bellhop waved and walked away so briskly he was almost skipping. He was used to the late hour, but I wasn't. I was exhausted and tense. I stood there a moment, wondering what would happen when I tapped on Hansen's door.

I raised my hand to knock and was startled by Hansen swinging the door open. He stared right through me and turned around, leaving me with a fist in mid-air. I felt like I did on the telephone when he'd hung up and left the dialtone in my ear. Anger simmered in me and I stood there, waiting for Taylor to acknowledge me with a simple hello.

He said nothing and walked away like I didn't exist. He'd been running his hands through his hair in agitation and it was a tangled mess. Hansen wore the same black silk turtleneck I'd seen at dinner but now the fine material was dark with sweat under his armpits and perspiration left a wet streak along his spine. I watched Hansen pick his way to the fireplace mantle in short unsure steps, rocking slightly. Even from the door, I could smell Hansen reeked of alcohol. He was drunk as you can get and still walk.

Taylor leaned against the fireplace, holding a snifter of cognac. Hansen brought the snifter toward his lips in a sloppy drunk motion and froze, the bowl an inch from his mouth. He saw me standing in the doorway and slowly Taylor's alcohol fogged mind realized I was there. He gave me a twisted smile and took a healthy swallow from his goblet. Hansen turned his head toward me and talked in a slurred voice. "Want some?"

"Sure, but I drink cognac, not swim in it. Pour mine in a glass, not a goldfish bowl."

Hansen removed a stopper from a crystal decanter and splashed brandy in a cocktail glass for me. Taylor wobbled in my direction, bringing me a highball glass with an inch of cognac.

I was too angry at Hansen to go in the room and meet him halfway. I made him take all the unsure steps that led to me. He held the tall, narrow glass out and I took it, feeling a damp sticky coating on the smooth glass from his sweat. The room wasn't hot, so it had to be fear sweat. Something was very wrong. I put my glass on the stone top of the entry table with a little clink. "What's going on?"

Taylor stared blankly at me, then talked in a blurry voice. "Come in and shut the door." I didn't obey and he added, "Please." He talked in a humble, almost pleading voice.

The pleading was so unlike Taylor Hansen that I felt ice drift along my spine, like I was a kid and someone jammed a snowball inside my parka. I edged inside the room and swung the door closed behind me, stopping before the latch clicked. I kept my hand on the doorknob so I could get out in a hurry. I talked in a flat, non-threatening voice. "You got me over here for a reason and you're getting drunk for a reason. What's the reason, Taylor?"

He put a hand in his pants pocket and fiddled with his keys, making a little clicking sound. Hansen cocked his head, looking at cornice molding on the ceiling. He rocked on his heels and said softly, "I have a problem." Taylor spoke much too calmly.

I felt very edgy and rushed my words out. "OK, you've got a problem. What kind of problem? Big, small, what?" I tapped fingers nervously on the doorknob. I could feel sweat forming on my own palms now.

Hansen leaned heavily on the mantelpiece and looked at himself in a mirror. His eyes slid to my reflection in the glass. Taylor said hoarsely, "My problem's in the bedroom. See for yourself."

"Why not just tell me?" I waited for a reply, but Taylor buried his mouth in the glass bowl and drained more cognac. He swirled the cognac and took another long drink from the goblet.

I wasn't going to get an answer. Taylor was lost in his own world, getting drunk. I'd never understand why he'd called me to the Regis unless I walked in his damned bedroom. I hated being trapped like this. Part of me wanted to leave and part of me knew I'd never get another chance to crack Hansen. My eyes jumped around, checking the suite, quickly touching everything I could see for threats, glancing at a dozen roses on the entry table, doubled by their reflection in the huge mirror behind them. Then my focus skipped to the bathroom and a massive cast-iron tub with golden swans as faucets to run hot water through their mouths. It was a surreal environment but that was standard fare in the Regis.

When I decided to walk in the bedroom, the light seemed dimmer, the air colder. Crossing the sitting room felt surreal, like I was floating. I walked in short even steps, angling my path around a couch and stopped, hit by a peculiar smell that clenched my stomach into a tight ball. I took a quick breath and smelled the sickly sweet odor of human blood, a lot of it.

My eyes ran over the bedroom, sweeping across the furniture, trying to find the victim. A makeup mirror was ringed in naked light bulbs like a theater dressing room for an actor. Taylor's shaving kit lay open on the makeup counter. I saw every vivid detail of the leather shaving kit, freezing an image in my mind of Hansen's brown comb sticking out of the unzipped bag. My eyes bounced off Hansen's shaving kit and hit the bed.

Taylor's leather overcoat was tossed carelessly across the dark blue comforter. I ran my eyes over the plush goosedown comforter to where bedcovers were peeled back, showing a pie slice of gleaming white sheets. Housekeeping had come in the room and turned down the bed, a normal custom in fine hotels. Chocolate roses wrapped in gold foil sat on a pillow and a linen card showed the time for Hansen's wakeup call in the morning.

My eyes jumped across the bed to mirrored closet doors. One door was slid open, showing Hansen's clothes pushed together at the end of the closet, crushing custom-made shirts against thousands of dollars worth of hand-tailored suits. Packing elegant clothing that tight creased the fabric and Hansen wouldn't wrinkle his precious wardrobe. He was fanatical about his appearance, down to new socks that seemed ironed on his ankles. Something was wrong.

I traced a fan of dark spots on the mirrored closet doors and realized it was blood splattered on the shiny glass. The victim must be lying behind the king-size bed, out of sight. I did a slow walk around the bed, tracing a finger along the comforter, trying to prepare myself for what I'd see. I knew I'd find a body and still I felt a jolt at what I saw.

I stared at a housekeeping maid lying on her back in a pool of blood, a nasty puddle soaking the white mohair carpet. The maid's young, attractive face was drenched in blood and a thick red stream painted her neck. My eyes followed the red trail to a long knife driven in the brain through the maid's eye. The punctured eyeball was runny soup around the black handle of the knife, a dagger sunk into cloudy gelatin that used to be a white globe with a pretty blue iris. The cold steel blade killed her mind but left her heart pumping blood out of a thoughtless body. Her last violent reaction was grabbing the knife in a useless effort to pull its sharp blade out of her mind. The maid's hands were convulsed on the knife handle, clenched so tightly her knuckles bulged with white tips, like they were going to pop.

Hit by the shock of what I saw, I felt lightheaded. I took a deep breath, recovering my composure. When I saw myself in the mirror, my face was ashen, bleached of color. There was nothing I could do for the dead maid, so I walked carefully out of the bedroom, my fists clenched tight. I found Taylor Hansen sitting on the couch, hunched over and staring at the carpet. He was holding onto his knees like they were all he had in the world.

"Why did you kill her?" I demanded.

"I didn't kill her." Hansen dragged his face into his knees like he could hide from me and avoid my questions.

"Then who did?" I glared at him.

Taylor mumbled something that sounded like, "I dunno."

I sighed in disgust. This wasn't going anywhere, so I lifted the phone and the dialtone made a loud buzzing.

Startled by the noise, Hansen looked at me. "Who are you calling?"

"The police," I said in a flat voice.

"You are the police," Taylor protested. "I . . . I thought you'd help me. You've got to fix this for me."

"I wouldn't fix this for you if I could. And I can't," I said with icy fury. In nervous energy, I picked up the heavy phone cradle and spun, pulling the wall cord around my hip. I dialed 911.

Hansen rose off the couch and spread his arms wide. He protested, "I didn't kill her. I returned from dinner and found the dead maid. I swear, Nicki. You've got to help me."

"Tell your story to the Surete. They'll be here soon." I picked anxiously at the curled phone cord, trying to figure out what happened here. I couldn't. Questions spun in my brain like Autumn leaves twisting in a storm.

"You've got to help me, Nicki. The Paris police, they'll . . ." Hansen waved his arms in tight circles, looking very scared.

"The Surete has to be called, Taylor. I'm Interpol, the International Police. The Paris cops have jurisdiction on this murder. Even you know that."

Hansen twisted on the couch and cursed, "Damn." Taylor mumbled. "This wrecks all my plans." He squeezed his knees and rocked his body, like he could make it all go away if he rocked hard enough.

Hansen's swinging motion played on my nerves like rats scratching in the attic above my bed at night. I couldn't stand to look at him and stared vacantly at the suite, waiting to talk with the Paris cops. When the Surete came on the line, I said numbly, "Hello. This is Nicki Foster of Interpol. There's been a murder in the Regis." I heard my own voice distantly, like someone else was talking in another room.

"Yes, a murder," I repeated. "I'm not joking. There's a dead body in the Regis hotel. No, not in my room. I can't stay at the Regis on an Interpol salary. The suite belongs to an American citizen, Taylor Hansen. Yes, Taylor's here with me in the room. I need you to send a coroner's team. Of course I'll wait for them to arrive." I hung up the phone.

I sagged against the wall and closed my eyes, trying to find some calm center in the midst of all this craziness. As soon as my eyes shut, my mind flashed on the knife stuck in the maid's eye and my body convulsed, then my eyelids snapped open. I heard Taylor Hansen mumbling something and fought to understand him through the gauze of my exhaustion.

"Nicki," Hansen pleaded. His rummy, drunken eyes looked in my general direction, seeming to barely recognize me.

"Yes?" I answered vaguely, feeling like I was lost inside a big cloud. The cloud was shock from seeing a dead maid staring at me with one eye, her other eyeball just runny soup floating the handle of a large dagger.

Taylor dragged anxious hands back and forth along his pants legs. He talked in a hollow voice. "I wish you wouldn't have called the Surete."

"Why?" Suddenly, I felt very alert. I watched Hansen intently and slowly repeated, "Why shouldn't I call the cops and get them over here, Taylor?"

"Because the Paris cops report to City Commissioner Alain Vernier, don't they?"

"Yes, the Surete reports to City Commissioner Vernier," I answered him. Suddenly I felt sick with fear. Hansen was holding something back, something very important that I needed to know as soon as possible. I had precious few minutes to pry the details out of him before the Surete arrived at the Regis. I snapped the huge tumbler of cognac from Taylor's hand.

When Taylor grasped for his drink, I swung the goblet away and he tried to stand. He didn't make it, falling on the couch with a little grunt. Hansen mumbled, "The maid was a mistake. It was supposed to be me dead in the bedroom. The housekeeper got knifed instead."

Shocked, I asked in a tense voice, "You think someone was trying to kill you and stabbed the maid by accident?"

He whimpered so quietly I was lip reading to hear it. "Yes." Hansen blubbered, "Vernier'll kill me." He ran anxious hands through his hair.

I put my face in front of Taylor to make eye contact and ugly, foul smells came out his drooling mouth. "Did you turn against Vernier, go out on your own? Is that why he wants to kill you?"

Hansen squeezed out a soft yes.

"How'd Vernier discover you turned on him, Taylor?"

Hansen whined like a frightened child. "Diane St. Remy told Vernier. She hates me now."

"Diane?" I was startled. "Diane has a crush on you, Taylor. She doesn't hate you."

"No," he insisted. "Diane killed the maid. She hid in the closet, thought I was in the bedroom, but I wasn't. A housekeeping maid was turning down the bed and Diane killed her by mistake."

A wave of pity and sadness hit me after I realized Hansen was telling the truth, that Diane St. Remy was a murderer. Her crush on Taylor Hansen must have turned into a jealous rage. Perhaps Diane caught Taylor having a liaison with another woman. But I knew there had to be more behind this killing than just sexual betrayal. A greedy conspiracy behind the arsons figured into this somehow because Hansen had driven Diane out of her logical mind and logic was 99% of

Diane St. Remy. Taylor must have taken something precious from Diane, something that promised to fulfill a lifetime of thwarted ambitions.

I felt very sad for Diane as I remembered sitting next to her in the Paris Archives, watching her wrap a bony, pale hand over the delicate handle of her expensive tea pot. It was hard to believe the same hand closed on a hunting knife and drove the long blade through a maid's eye, but it was true. I pieced together how the maid died and realized why Hansen's suits were crushed together at one side of his closet. Diane St. Remy pushed the suits over to make room for herself so she could hide in the bedroom closet.

Later, she heard someone walk into the bedroom and Diane slapped the closet door open. She lunged with a knife, thinking she was driving the blade into Taylor Hansen, but he wasn't in the room. Instead, a maid was turning down the bedcovers and leaving those stupid chocolates on the pillow. Diane's vicious blow knocked the maid on her back and spattered blood on the mirrored closet doors. In shock from her mistake, Diane left the knife stuck in the dying maid and fled the Regis. I'd walked around the bed and seen the mess left by Diane St. Remy. There was no doubt in my mind that Hansen's story fit the facts.

Taylor put his face in his hands and grunted, "I didn't think this would happen."

I was amazed at Hansen's attitude. "What'd you expect would happen? You tried to cut Diane out of the deal. She wasn't going to kiss you for double-crossing her."

Hansen pleaded, "You've got to fix this for me, Nicki."

I laughed sarcastically. "I can't fix this. Nobody can. Even you can guess what happens next, Taylor. Diane St. Remy is tracking down Vernier to plead with him for help. The Paris cops report to Vernier and we'll never make a precinct station. Vernier will get his hands on us and kill us both. We have to get out of the Regis."

I grabbed Taylor Hansen and tried to pull him to his feet, but it was useless. Pulling Hansen was like hauling the loose blubber of a dead whale, a ton of uncooperative flesh. I let go of Hansen and wiped his sweat off my hands. I gave Hansen a last look and started for the door, but I never made it.

There was a harsh rapping on the wooden door and a voice demanded, "Open at once. This is the Surete." Gendarmes pounded on the door with their clubs, demanding I open or they'd break the door down.

My eyes fled around the room, hoping for another way out of the suite and there wasn't any. I was trapped.

# 14

# Out of Time

I had to let the Surete into the room. Reluctantly, I opened the door of Taylor Hansen's suite and saw a pair of motorcycle cops leaning against the door frame like bookends. They had the surly attitude that seems to be standard police issue for motorcycle cops, part of their gear like a badge and a gun. Each cop wore a dark blue coat with a brown leather belt slanting across his chest in a military look. White gloves flared over their forearms, glistening like the white helmets they were carrying.

A cop with a dark skinned face, shadowed in coarse stubble, edged in the room. The thin brass nameplate on his chest read Sergeant Andre Laval. He gave the hotel suite a quick survey, then focused on me. The Sergeant grunted, "You called to report a murder. You're Foster?"

"Yeah, I'm Nicki Foster," I admitted.

Sergeant Laval snapped, "Mademoiselle, you will follow me and leave your friend in the suite."

"Where are we going?" I asked suspiciously.

"I will take you to another room. You'll wait there for the inspector. My partner stays with Hansen, in this suite."

"Why can't I wait here?" I protested.

Laval stepped aggressively toward me, wearing an ugly look. "You are ordered to leave."

"On whose authority?" I asked, hoping the answer wasn't City Commissioner Vernier.

Laval put an insistent hand on my shoulder, shoving me toward the doorway. "You and Hansen will be separated for questioning. The Surete Inspector gave orders."

"OK, OK, I'm going." I didn't like getting harassed by Laval, jabbed in the back every time I slowed down and yelled at like a three year old.

Sergeant Laval pressured me along the hallway, pushing me toward a service elevator, not the one normally used by guests. My pulse rate was high enough without being shoved in a small elevator smelling of ammonia from housekeeping carts. The elevator sagged to a stop on the ground floor and we walked along a battered service corridor that was in stark contrast to the opulent public areas of the Regis.

We stopped at a private office and Laval flattened a white gloved hand on the office door, pushing it open. He ordered, "Go in the room."

I didn't have any choice so I stepped in the office and the door immediately closed behind me. The lock clicked and I knew I was trapped until they let me out.

I looked around the room and found it instantly depressing, like being in a jail cell. The small office was furnished in rejects, scarred items and damaged furniture unsuitable for service elsewhere. Someone tried to fix upholstery on an antique chair and failed, leaving behind an ugly seam. The tarnished reflection of an old gilt framed mirror hung over the fireplace. A faded Persian rug sat in front of the hearth, its tapestry black with scars from embers popping off fires. The brass fireplace screen was dim with age and seemed almost ashamed to be there as it timidly reflected a green glow from the banker's light on a small desk.

Instinctively, I moved behind the wooden desk and tried its drawers, tugging on antique handles, but the drawers were locked and wouldn't budge. I looked for a telephone on the vacant desktop and spotted the empty jack at the baseboard. They'd taken the phone out before bringing me to the office. How thorough of them, I thought with disgust.

Damp cold seeped from the floor into my tired feet and I rubbed my arms to break the chill. Charred wood in the fireplace suggested I could start a fire to warm the room, but I was out of luck. The brass log cradle held only a litter of bark chips, not even kindling. Being trapped in a cold, windowless room added to my fear and depression. I had no idea how I was going to escape Vernier. A clock on the mantelpiece ticked off the seconds left in my life. My mind was tumbling frightened thoughts when the office door opened with a light squeal of its hinges. I blinked hazy eyes to clear them and saw a chunky man in his late forties outlined in the glare of the open door.

A Surete Inspector stood there, hands in the pockets of his baggy cardigan sweater, looking more like a professor than a cop. The elbows of his aging sweater were mended in coarse stitches that nursed another year from the tired garment. The light brown of his sweater matched thin strands of hair combed over a bald spot where a mole sprouted coarse black stubble. Blood was dried on his chin from nicking himself while shaving, no doubt after waking from a dead sleep and realizing he had to appear at the Regis hotel. He'd thrown on a thin, black tie for the Regis and the tie was stained with food. Worse, the stains were spread by inept use of cleaning fluid. None of his clothes matched any fashion in the last ten years, including green, heavy wool trousers. The trousers ended in wide cuffs that rumpled across dull, unpolished cop shoes.

The Inspector shuffled inside and stood there like a cold marble statue with only his eyes moving, surveying the office. His stare lingered on every object in the room as though he were taking an inventory of the furniture. Finally, he shut the door and announced, "I am Inspector Gilbert Villanueves." The Inspector pronounced his name "Jill—bear Villa—new—wave," dragging out the syllables with a nasal drone. "I am here to question you about the murder of a housekeeping maid."

Feeling uneasy, I asked him, "You've already interviewed Taylor Hansen?"

"I will speak to Monsieur Hansen after he sobers up. There is no rush, is there?"

I faked an indifferent shrug, pretending not to care how long our meeting lasted. This was Gilbert's moment of power and the harder I pushed to leave, the more he'd drag out the interview. I needed to look like I had all the time in the world and it wasn't easy. I felt more anxiety each wasted second I spent in that room, yet all I could do was sit there and stare at the Inspector.

Gilbert said coldly, "You are Nicki Foster, the person who called?"

"Yes, I'm Nicki. I made the phone call." I leaned my arms on the desk, waiting for Gilbert to ask more questions but he didn't. He surprised me by moving to the desk in quick steps, then flipping his palm up several times, motioning for me to stand.

He told me, "Come, mademoiselle. I am the inspector here. I sit behind the desk and take notes, not you."

"Sure," I muttered and got up awkwardly, my limbs stiff from the cold.

Gilbert exchanged places with me in tight, precise movements, sitting behind the desk. He looked harshly at me and said with icy conviction, "You came here tonight for a liaison and things did not go quite how you expected. The maid, she was very pretty and perhaps she forgot her role as housekeeper, hmm? You found her with Monsieur Hansen in a compromising position on the bed and you were not pleased. Hansen is your lover, yes?"

"Hansen's not my boyfriend," I said angrily. I sat in the wooden swivel chair facing the desk and it felt hard and sharp against my tired body.

Gilbert announced, "I expect you to deny your rendezvous with a lover, mademoiselle. Under these circumstances, you have no credibility." The Inspector smirked. "We could have a doctor examine you. He'll know if you've had sex with Hansen."

"Examine away, Gilbert. We didn't screw." I draped an arm over the chair and crossed my legs, forcing myself to look casual. I looked at Gilbert unblinkingly until he broke the stare. I won that round, at least.

I watched Gilbert pinch the thick flesh of his upper lip just below the nose. Abruptly, he stopped playing with his lip and asked, "Why did you go in the bedroom if it wasn't to screw, huh?"

I was startled that Gilbert knew I'd gone in the bedroom and looked at the body. Then I realized a lab tech from the coroner's office must've found my footprints on the carpet and told Gilbert.

I recovered from my surprise and explained, "After I got to the Regis, Taylor said he had a problem. I asked what kind of problem and he told me to see for myself. I didn't know there was a corpse in the bedroom. Hansen was too stressed and confused to explain anything. So I walked in the bedroom and found a dead maid. That's all there is, Inspector."

"Perhaps," Gilbert responded cynically. He was lost in thought, trying to match my story against the facts and then look at the million possibilities for what really happened. Understandably, his eyes glazed over as he examined the endless prospects for why the maid was killed. Gilbert took a tobacco pouch and a pipe from his sweater pocket, then began an elaborate ceremony of cleaning his pipe, scraping the pipe bowl out with a little metal stick. He lifted his eyes to look at me. "So, mademoiselle, how did you meet this Taylor Hansen?"

"Hansen works in the Paris Archives," I answered simply. I didn't volunteer any more information, fearing it would drag out the interview.

Gilbert laid down his pipe scraping tool. "Why did you go to the Archives?"

I hesitated to tell him about the arson cases since it would complicate everything. I said evasively, "The Paris Archives keep a lot of important documents and I needed some data."

"Go on." He jammed the pipe in his mouth and remembered the pipe wasn't filled. Reaching for his tobacco pouch, he looked at me expectantly. "Yes, I am waiting," he said, dragging out the "wait—ing."

I sighed. Dodging his questions was making me look guilty, so I had to tell him about the arsons, whether I liked it or not. I reluctantly said, "I went to the Paris Archives on a case. There's been some arsons recently and I was assigned to investigate them."

"Uh huh," Gilbert grunted. He absentmindedly used his thumb to pack tobacco in the pipe, then loosened the pack with a scraping tool. Eventually he lit the pipe, sucking the lighter flame into the bowl.

Puffs of blue smoke leaked from the corner of his mouth and smelled like a tobacconist shop on the corner of my block. Pipe tobacco was pleasant compared to cigarettes, but the smoke still irritated my lungs and nose. I didn't ask Gilbert to stop. I didn't want to waste time bickering about the Inspector's smoking habit. I had to escape the Regis before Vernier swung into action.

"How did you meet Monsieur Hansen?" Gilbert asked.

I answered Gilbert's question simply, hoping to save time. "Taylor Hansen's installing a computer system in the Archives. I needed data from the computer and I met Hansen."

Gilbert leaned back and sucked on his pipe. "Of course. You found Monsieur Hansen attractive, yes? He is a handsome man."

I gave Gilbert an ugly look. "No, Inspector, I don't have a crush on Hansen. I only wanted Taylor's help. I needed to find the owner of the arsoned warehouse."

"Why did you not ask a clerk to help you?" He waved the pipe at me.

"You can't just ask a clerk. Think about it this way, Inspector. If you want to own a home, you have to clear up title to the property before you buy the house and its land. Did you ever buy a house?"

He looked away and seemed almost to blush. Owning a home was not something a member of his social class did in Europe. "No," he muttered. "We rent a flat in Aubervilles." He snapped, "Just what are you driving at, mademoiselle?"

"Property titles are a mess in Europe," I explained. "Too many wars, too little recordkeeping. You need an expert to find a property owner."

Gilbert clamped the pipe in his teeth, freeing his hand for writing so he could take notes. He drew a huge plastic pen out of his shirt pocket. I saw blue ink on the pocket where the pen leaked, blossoming a dark stain on his gray dress shirt. He caught my glance and pulled his sweater over the stains. Gilbert fumbled the cap off his pen and wrote in a spiral bound notebook, making little shorthand notations. He asked, "Hansen's computer knows who owns things, these property titles you mentioned?"

"Yes. Eventually all of Paris will be in his computer." I studied my fingernails, trying to look casual.

"You cannot use this computer yourself to find the warehouse owner?" Gilbert asked skeptically.

"The computer is Hansen's bag. He put the whole thing in. He's an expert on the system."

Gilbert thought over my reply, trying to find holes. He wanted to shoot down my reasons for knowing Hansen and get back to the love affair motive. Then he tried a different tactic. Gilbert leaned on the desk and pointed his pipe at me accusingly. "When you went in the bedroom, you did not touch anything? You did not tamper with the evidence so Monsieur Hansen was free to help with your arson case?"

"No, I touched nothing." I shrugged to emphasize my honesty, trying to look like an innocent schoolgirl. I wasn't lying to Gilbert about what I'd done in the bedroom. I was too shocked by the dead maid to think about touching anything. I just wanted to get out of the room.

"Perhaps," Gilbert grudgingly admitted. He started to put his jumbo pen away with the felt tip exposed, staining his shirt pocket again. The Inspector saw me pointing at his mistake, frowned and snapped the cap on his pen. After he finished, Gilbert wrote a superior expression on his face. "Where were you tonight?"

His look and his tone of voice really got under my skin. I snapped at Gilbert, "I was in my apartment."

"And before then?" he demanded.

I sighed. "I went to dinner with Taylor Hansen." I looked around the room, trying to seem bored. It wasn't easy to look bored when Gilbert was dragging out this interview and every second mattered.

Gilbert cocked an eyebrow and acted smug. "Hansen took you to dinner. Where?"

"Olivier's. It was just a business dinner," I said firmly.

"At Olivier's, one of the most expensive restaurants in Paris?" Gilbert sneered. "But you are not lovers?" He rolled his eyes, emphasizing his disbelief. The Inspector cracked his fingers, then asked in a lewd voice, "What business did you discuss with Monsieur Hansen at dinner, hmm? How you were going to do it?"

I could see Gilbert wasn't going to let the lovers idea alone. Resisting was dragging out the interview so I tried a different approach, hoping to speed things up. "OK," I said contritely. "Hansen made a pass at me in the restaurant. I admit it."

I looked Gilbert in the eyes and said emphatically, "I turned Hansen down, Inspector. Taylor went to his hotel alone and I walked home. You don't have to believe me. Talk to the restaurant doorman. Check the phone records. Hansen called my apartment from his suite in this hotel. They can verify his phone call at the front desk." I leaned back and folded my arms over my chest.

"All right, let's assume Hansen called you. What did he say on the phone?"

"Taylor said he had a problem. He asked me to come over and he wouldn't say any more. When I drove over here, I found the dead maid. Then I called the Surete. That's all there is to it." I stared at Gilbert, hoping he'd believe me.

Gilbert didn't budge. He stuck to his accomplice theory and announced, "Ah, I see. Monsieur Hansen killed the maid. He wanted you to fix it for him. That's why he bought you an expensive dinner and played the handsome lover for you."

"Oh, brother," I moaned. "Look, there was a murder and I called you guys. I didn't run away." I put my hands up in frustration. "Why don't you check the time of death? The maid was probably killed while we were at the restaurant." I had a glimmer of hope. Would Gilbert listen to reason, I wondered?

Gilbert didn't say a word. He swiveled in the chair and stuck his legs out so far I could see his shoes peeking around the bottom of the desk. The Inspector tapped his toes together as he thought, gently puffing on his pipe. He looked at me, then at his watch. I waited for what felt like eternity and finally Gilbert pulled a cellular phone from his pocket.

I sat up straight in my chair, anxiously wondering who Gilbert was calling.

He saw the eager curiosity on my face and for the first time that night, he had some consideration for me. Gilbert covered the phone with his hand and told me quietly, "I'm calling the deputy coroner. Hector is in Monsieur Hansen's suite, examining the maid's body." Gilbert pulled his hand off the phone and spoke quickly in French. "Yes, this is Inspector Villanueves. Put Hector on the phone, please."

All I could do was wait. I listened to a desk clock tick, counting long seconds and my back went stiffer with each tick, the tension growing in me.

While I waited, Gilbert sat in the chair and sucked on his pipe. Finally, the deputy coroner came on the line. Gilbert said, "I'm sorry to bother you, Hector. I need to know the approximate time of death. Uh huh, yes." The Inspector wrote in his little notebook and looked at his scrawl carefully. He took the pipe out of his clamped teeth and asked, "You're sure the maid died that early? She did not die after midnight? Yes, OK. I got that. Thank you."

I let out a long sigh of relief. The maid was killed before Hansen and I left the restaurant.

Gilbert hung up the telephone and leaned back, staring at the ceiling, a little smoke curling out of his mouth.

I waited anxiously to see what would happen next, sliding my moist hands on the chair. Finally, I broke the silence. "Am I still a suspect?"

Gilbert thought my question over for an eternal moment. He flexed his hands, cracking his knuckles and the sound of his joints popping made me wince. The Inspector said reluctantly, "No. It appears you could not have done the murder."

I held my breath and asked tightly, "Hansen?"

Gilbert seemed not to hear my question. Absentmindedly, he nodded his head, indicating Hansen was cleared also.

My body relaxed and I suddenly felt every hard edge of the chair. "We're free to go?" I asked. I knew it was too good to be true.

"You will be free to go after I conclude tonight's investigation. I'm certain I'll want to speak to you again and you'll make yourself available to me." He didn't just say the words. He made a royal pronouncement. Gilbert pushed himself away from the desk and stood, walking quickly to the doorway. "Come," he ordered me. "I must return to Hansen's suite. There's much to be done." He bounced out of the tiny office and marched along the corridor.

I forced my stiff, tired body to trot after him, surprised by how quickly Gilbert walked for a heavy set man. We rode the elevator in silence and I leaned against the brass railing. The Inspector rocked on his heels, dragging on his pipe, little puffs of blue smoke leaking from the corner of his mouth. When we left the elevator, Gilbert resumed his quick strides and I lagged behind a bit, not wanting to crowd him.

The motorcycle cops were leaning against the wall outside Taylor Hansen's suite. They saw us approaching and straightened up, saluting crisply. Gilbert returned the salute with a slight curl of his hand and plowed through the doorway without a word to the motorcycle cops.

I tried to follow Gilbert into the room and was blocked by Sergeant Laval. "One moment, please, mademoiselle." Laval turned his head toward the suite. "Inspector?" he called out.

Gilbert responded in clipped syllables. "Yes, yes, she can come in." The Inspector disappeared inside the bedroom without waiting to see me released.

I slipped in the suite and spotted a dejected but sober Taylor Hansen sitting on the couch, reluctantly drinking a cup of hot coffee. I wanted to grab Hansen and leave, but Gilbert would become suspicious and stop me. Precious minutes were sliding away and all I could do was wait, wondering how long the coroner's team would stay.

Lab techs were using brilliant movie lights in the bedroom for videotaping and the glare shot through the door, carving shadows on the ceiling and walls. A tech exited the bedroom with a video camera and panned around, his floodlight swinging like a lighthouse beacon. The floodlight turned in my direction, painting me with glare and I shut my eyes, feeling the heat of the light brush over me.

Near me, a lab technician was applying fingerprint dust with a makeup brush. His slowness was maddening when he bent stiffly at the waist like a street mime, making fussy movements with the brush. He spread graphite over the entire suite, smearing black grime on walls and furnishings. After minutes of tedious waiting, the intense movie lighting melted away and the fingerprinted room looked dingy in normal light.

I watched a half dozen crime lab techs come and go through doorways, then I heard clasps snapping on toolkits, followed by grunts at lifting the heavy kits. A minute later, four lab techs walked out of the suite, hands gripping long black cases. I pushed off the wall and went toward the bedroom doorway, praying it was over.

In the bedroom, I saw the dead maid being stuffed in a body bag and I felt a pang of sadness for her. Ambulance operators were shoving the poor woman's jutting limbs inside a shiny plastic bag with difficulty as rigor mortis stiffened the maid's legs and arms. I'll always remember my last glimpse of her pale arm and dove gray uniform before they sealed the bag, the rasping zipper grating on my raw nerves.

Gilbert handed the ambulance operator a clipboard with a multipart form and the man absentmindedly signed for the maid's body like he was accepting a package from UPS. I heard the attendants calmly discussing where to eat breakfast after unloading at the morgue, surprisingly untouched by death. The ambulance attendants levered their gurney to waist height and wheeled the maid out like she was just a heavy box being carried to a moving van.

I slid through the doorway and stood near Gilbert, his droopy face looking like a depressed basset hound. He nervously fingered the pouch of tobacco in his sweater pocket and said, "Maybe, the murderer came to steal something. That is what I think now. I get some sleep and ponder this crime. Tomorrow, perhaps, I see things more sharply."

I just shrugged, not wanting a long discussion with Gilbert. I needed to scoop up Hansen and get the hell out of there.

Gilbert was slouching against the wall and looking at me with a smirk. "You are staying here tonight with Monsieur Hansen, yes?" The Inspector still believed I was having an affair with Taylor Hansen.

"No, I'm not staying here," I said firmly. "I'm going to my apartment."

"Yes, of course," Gilbert replied, a taunting smile on his face.

"Oh, think what you like, Inspector. I give up," I said in resignation and followed Gilbert out of the bedroom.

He gathered up his rumpled overcoat and nodded a sleepy goodnight. Moving to the open door of the suite, he gave us an intense stare. "You are very important witnesses and I will want to see you again soon. No one leaves Paris without my permission."

I nodded. When I nudged Hansen, he muttered, "Sure."

At long last, Gilbert went out of the suite, gently closing the door with a soft click of the lock.

I sighed in relief and rubbed my exhausted eyes, wishing I could call room service for a double espresso. I glanced at Taylor Hansen, stiffly poised on a gilded Empire chair. He had a look on his face like he was waiting for a dentist to do a root canal.

"I can't believe this," Hansen muttered. He was only half sober, his hair a matted tangle. His wrinkled silk turtleneck smelled of body odor and alcohol.

"Let's go, Taylor. We've go to get out of here before Vernier finds us. I'll get you a hotel room somewhere else where you can sleep it off."

Taylor got up like a robot and looked at me with glazed eyes. He rubbed his chin hard and seemed surprised to find stubble on it. "I, uh, better pack a few things."

"Make it fast or you won't need clothes ever again," I warned him.

"Sure," he said dully and lumbered into the bedroom. I heard a suitcase dragged off the closet shelf and clicked open, then his feet shuffled across the bedroom carpet and I saw him appear in front of the makeup mirror. Hansen looked at his toiletries like he'd already forgotten what he was doing.

"You're packing," I reminded him disgustedly and he started throwing toiletries in his shaving kit. I crossed my arms and leaned back against the liquor cabinet. Vaguely I remembered Taylor pouring me a little cognac in a tall glass and it seemed like he'd poured the brandy several days ago.

I briefly closed my eyes and when I tried to open them again, my eyelids felt like heavy suitcases I had to drag up a flight of stairs. Hansen wanting to pack a few things wasn't all bad, I thought, since I was drained and could use a moment to recover.

I walked toward the balcony of Hansen's suite and cranked elaborately curled handles to open a pair of doors. Stepping outside, I put my hands on a balcony railing, pressing moist cold into my palms. Damp chill hit me in the face, cutting through my fatigue. I needed to close my eyes and inhale, shake off my exhaustion. It'd been such an ugly long night.

Somewhere in the vast plaza, I heard the drone of a streetsweeper pushing dirt into storm drains with a flush of water like a loud toilet. I opened my eyes, expecting to see the empty boulevards of a sleeping Paris. Instead I saw City Commissioner Vernier slide out of the darkness below me.

Vernier grabbed Inspector Gilbert Villanueves as he left the hotel. Gilbert went from the exhausted man who'd spent hours questioning me about the dead maid to a frightened bureaucrat. Vernier's threats painted fear on Gilbert's face, intimidating the simple policeman in a few shocking moments. The abuse faded and Vernier shifted to the old reliable bribe, jamming an envelope thick with cash in the Inspector's overcoat. Then City Commissioner Vernier faded into a limousine and squealed away.

I didn't need to overhear their conversation to know I was in serious trouble. I knew Gilbert was told to get Hansen and me. Gilbert twisted around, craning his neck to look at the soft glow from Hansen's suite. Taylor's bright windows were isolated on the dark facade of the Regis. He saw me standing on the balcony and glared at me in rage.

I recoiled backwards, catching my ankle on the sharp edge of a glass table. A jolt of pain shot through me as I spun to keep from falling. The throbbing bruise on my ankle pumped me higher and I was already hyper. My problems were just beginning.

I saw police hop from patrol cars and run to assist Gilbert in apprehending me. SWAT teams were arriving, carrying submachine guns and sniper rifles. Vernier wasn't taking any chances. He was having the police seal the area and soon escape would be impossible. I had to run.

# 15

# Run

I shot through the open balcony doors and Taylor Hansen grabbed me, yanking me to a stop. Taylor was a mess. Coarse bristle shadowed his face and his hair was a greasy tangle. Under swollen eyelids, Hansen's bloodshot eyes were bright with panic, staring at me. He demanded, "Why're you running out on me?"

"Vernier," I answered, flipping my head toward the balcony. I pulled my wrist loose from his grip and tore the suite door open.

Taylor followed me and ran for the fire stairs, his lumbering footsteps echoing along the empty hallway. I said in a whisper, "I wouldn't use the stairs." My whisper was better than a scream and Taylor froze. His open mouth implied, "Why not take the stairs?"

I explained, "Gilbert isn't stupid. He has a dozen cops with him. He'll only send a few in the elevator. The rest will come up the stairs." I was right. We could both hear cops charging up the stairwell, their footsteps thundering on the metal stairs.

Hansen talked in a voice slurred by panic. "What're we going to do?"

I didn't have time to answer him. Soft chimes rang in the hallway, announcing the elevator was stopping on this floor. I was convinced Gilbert would step from the elevator and handcuff me. I waited, caught in the hallway with nowhere to run. Luckily, the elevator was empty, an open box with no one inside.

I ran into the elevator so hard I collided with the back wall and little stinging needles of pain shot along my ribcage. Taylor followed, grabbing a hand rail to slow himself. Hansen reached for the lobby button and I warned him, "Not the lobby." I caught a quick breath and said, "Cops are all over the lobby. Go for the basement."

"Oh, yeah," Taylor said dully. His finger was shaking from panic. He tried to poke the correct button and missed.

"Use your thumb, palm, anything," I suggested. "We have to get this elevator moving. You heard cops running up the fire stairs. They'll be on this level in a moment."

Hansen jabbed his hand against "Basement" and the plastic button lit up. He pulled his hand away in a jerky motion and stood there, looking shocked.

I waited for the elevator doors to gently squeeze shut, hiding me. It seemed to take hours for the door panels to slide together. Finally, the elevator doors kissed in front of me and I sagged against the wall in relief. Through the closed doors, I heard Gilbert arrive in the hallway, shouting orders at other cops.

The elevator jerked slightly, then sank toward the lobby. Gilbert's voice faded away but my shoulders tensed with every groan and clunk of the elevator on its long journey to the basement. I knew my chances for escape weren't good. "I'm not sure this will work."

"Why?" Hansen was confused.

"By now, Gilbert may have sent cops to the service basement."

Taylor glowered at me. "Why didn't you take us to the parking garage? We could get away in my rental car."

"You couldn't drive anywhere in your car. SWAT teams are blocking the hotel exits and searching the parking garage. Your car would have been priority number one when Gilbert didn't find us in the room."

The elevator dropped to the lobby level and I hoped the doors wouldn't open, revealing us inside the box. "Lobby" blinked out in the panel and we sank downward, one of a dozen miracles I'd need to escape. A long, hot minute passed before the elevator bobbed to a halt at the basement and the doors false started, then opened. I looked around, trying to find a path out of the Regis. There were no signs directing me to an exit and the basement was a maze of dingy tunnels.

I left the elevator and started along a narrow corridor, unable to move very fast. The runway ahead of me was blocked by big canvas carts heaped with dirty towels and uniforms. Bundles of pipes and wires were strapped to the ceiling, lowering head clearance, forcing me to bend over as I walked. The tunnel was dimly lit and I could barely see the obstacles in my path. I shuffled down the slick concrete hallway, stumbling against all kinds of litter in the dull lighting.

I tripped over an extension cord, yanking it out of a socket with hissing sparks. An electrician glowered at me as he shoved the plug back in the wall. I muttered an apology and went on, my eyes stinging. Pungent chlorine bleach burned the air from laundering bed linen. Steam leaked from pipes, making the ugly smelling air all the more suffocating. The service basement was a dirty stinking factory, an underground sweatshop making a pampered Regis possible.

The hotel was gearing up for another day and its service labyrinth was jammed with staff going about their business. Maids poked their heads out of storage bins, giving me curious stares. The farther I went, the more people I saw staring at me. Regis staffers were startled to see frightened guests racing through the service area. I imagined cops asking workers if anyone had seen me and I knew a dozen fingers would point at my back.

It looked hopeless, but I kept going, ducking under soggy insulation hanging from pipes. My feet ached from running in high heels on slick concrete floors. All the muscles in my legs were cramped and I had to quit for a moment. I leaned against a cold, gray wall but there was no way to rest in the middle of a factory. Machinery droned everywhere, drumming on walls, the floor and my aching head. I heard water dripping in a sink nearby and the leak was like an irritating, nagging conscience. The dripping water counted off the seconds left for me in annoying "plunks," feeding my anxiety instead of giving me a moment of rest.

I looked at Taylor and saw the alcohol hangover was killing him. Hansen bent over and vomited, spilling yellow mess on the floor. The air was filled with the rotten egg smell of his stomach bile, adding to my punishment.

Over Hansen's gagging, I heard cops slapping into the basement, flinging doors open. A whole squad of policemen were questioning Regis staffers, asking about Hansen and me, which direction had we gone, when had they last seen us. I didn't know which way to run with the cop's voices echoing around the hallways. In moments, they would turn a corner and spot me in this corridor, trap me in a chase I couldn't win.

I thought about diving in a laundry cart, hiding under a stack of dirty bed sheets, but then I saw something better. There was an unlocked door marked "Exit" only a few feet away. Nobody would see me go if I left now. I just had to be quiet. Any noise would give me away to the police, so I put my butt on the exit door and pushed slowly to muffle the sound. There was a hushed click and I felt a draft of cold air leak against me as the steel fire door opened. I slid outside and let the door close softly behind me, holding the sharp metal edge with my fingertips to the last possible moment.

I found myself at the bottom of a cement pit, damp with morning dew. In front of me, slick metal stairs led from the pit to a dark alley. I cautiously moved up the open metal steps, taking it very slowly. Finally, my eyes poked over the edge of the pit and I could look along the alley.

Kitchen workers were unloading crates of vegetables from a delivery truck crammed with produce for a day of meals at the Regis. Boxes were dragged from the back of the delivery van and slapped on top of each other, making a loud clattering that rang along the alley.

Unloading the delivery truck went on for several minutes. A chain of kitchen staffers wound through the narrow crowded area, stacking batches of crates. Wooden produce boxes were piled high until the stacks teetered, threatening to fall over.

At last I watched a Regis employee sign for the delivery, indicating today's unloading of fruits and vegetables was complete. I was delighted when the truck driver tore the top sheet off a clipboard, handing the receipt to an assistant chef. I thought they were done but to my annoyance, the Regis chef and the truck driver stood there trading dirty jokes.

The chef turned around and walked toward a steel prep cart right in front of my hiding place. There was nowhere to run and all I could do was crouch in the pit, listening. I heard footsteps crunch toward me. Finally, the chef pushed the prep cart away and a squeaking wheel on the cart slowly faded until I couldn't hear it anymore. I exhaled in relief.

The truck driver slammed his rear door and I peeked over the concrete pit, anxious to see if I could escape. The beefy driver shuffled in a sideways motion to the front of his vehicle. He got inside and the truck engine roared, billowing exhaust fumes along the alley. Maybe I could hop on the truck's rear bumper, hitch a ride for a few blocks to get away from the Regis. But I never got the chance to make a run for the truck.

The steel fire door at the bottom of the pit flew open and crashed loudly against the wall, scaring me. I twisted around, expecting to see the hard eyes and drawn gun of a cop. Instead I saw Taylor Hansen, his jaw speckled with vomit. I heard the delivery van rolling away behind me and knew I'd never catch the produce truck before it left the alley. I stared at Taylor in disgust. "Close the door. Give us a chance, why don't you?"

"Yeah, sure." Hansen let the door slam and the clank echoed along the inside hallway, making it obvious to the police where to look for us.

I said sarcastically, "Why didn't you just hang a sign on the door, Taylor? You could write 'They Left Here' on the sign, make it real easy for the cops."

"Sorry," Hansen mumbled, trying to look humble and failing. Hansen could act a lot of parts, but humble wasn't in him.

Taylor made a serious mistake letting the door slam, giving our position away, forcing me to move into the open where police could see me. I slid cautiously into the alley, hiding in shadows, letting the building's rough wall drag against my clothes. Cold stone pressed my back as I slinked along the alley one shadow at a time, always hiding. At the end of the narrow passageway, streetlights fanned blue glow on buildings and it would be easy to see me if I went any farther. I ran out of shadows and stopped. I peeked around the corner and saw my escape route went nowhere. The alley emptied in a wide square jammed with police.

A pair of German Shepherds leapt from a police car, looking keen and alert. They dragged their handlers behind on taut leashes like a boat towing a water skier. The excited dogs sensed a hunt and were wired to track someone down. With a keen sense of smell, finding my hiding place would be easy for them. One trip to Hansen's suite and the German Shepherds would have my scent. Then the dogs would quickly find me, following my path through the basement labyrinth and into the alley where I stood. How incredibly thorough of Vernier, I thought. I felt sick.

I heard Hansen saying something but I couldn't focus with my brain fuzzed by anxiety and tension. "What'd you say?"

Hansen got my full attention by grabbing my dress and tugging on me. He whispered in a frightened voice. "There's a car coming."

I was startled to see a van headed at me, pinning me against the wall. Headlights hit my face and a halo of light swelled around me. I instinctively put a hand up to shield my eyes against the harsh glare. When I pulled my hand away, I saw the little truck make a sharp turn, then brake to a stop. The van started backing into the alley like the produce truck had done, delivering crates of vegetables. The van came backwards so fast it couldn't go in a straight line but instead swerved in a corkscrew, making a loud grinding sound as its taillights came at me.

I hid from the approaching van by crouching in shadows behind a tall stack of boxes, using the produce crates to shield myself from discovery. Hansen quickly dragged himself under cover in the same place, jamming himself next to me. The vomit on his shirt made cabbage around me smell good even though I hated cabbage. Through a gap in the produce boxes, I watched the van settle to a stop, blocking the alley like a cork in a bottle. There was nowhere for me to run. I could only wait and see what happened next.

Time clocked off in routine events that are trivial under different circumstances but now they had all my focus. The idling van engine coughed to a halt and the glow of taillights melted away. For a moment all was quiet and then the van's door gronked open. Boots hit the pavement and the van's driver started along the alley toward me. I tucked even deeper behind the produce crates, listening to the shuffle of careful feet coming at my hiding place.

I heard the kitchen door surge open and a wedge of light fanned down the crowded alley. A Regis staffer was coming for more produce and his prep cart slapped noisily through the open door. The squeaky wheel of the cart rolled toward me, converging on my hiding place. I was trapped between the van driver and the kitchen staffer, squeezing me from both sides.

It looked like I was bound to be discovered but I got a break. The prep cart stopped before it reached me and the kitchen staffer started clanging boxes onto the metal cart. The prep cart got a last ringing slam from a produce box and began a slow journey back to the kitchen. I let out a cautious sigh of relief and turned in the van's direction.

The van seemed oddly familiar. I flashed on Paul Denis driving into an alley and meeting me to look at a phone company junction box. I heard his voice softly calling, "Nicki, where are you? It's Paul. Come out."

Paul was wearing an old charcoal sweater made of coarse seafaring wool flecked with white specks. It was the kind of sweater fishermen wear in the French port of Marseilles. Faded jeans tapered down his legs to white socks and scuffed work boots.

He called to me again, urging, "Nicki, come out. I know you're there. Hurry before we're trapped in this alley."

I stepped out of the shadows and asked in amazement, "How did you know I was at the Regis?"

Paul explained, "You left a message asking me to call your apartment but when I tried phoning, you didn't answer. My fire department credentials got your address from the phone company and I drove to your apartment. On the way to your place, I heard an 'All Units Call' for the Regis. As a fire captain, I have a police scanner in my van. The radio call mentioned Nicki Foster and Taylor Hansen, so I shot over here."

"How did you know I was in this alley?" I was still skeptical.

Paul shrugged. "This alley is a way of getting to a kitchen fire. The Regis is in my firefighting area. I've done practice walkthroughs for fighting a fire in the hotel. I was going to park my van in the alley and sneak in the Regis to find you. I got here and saw you hiding against the wall. It makes sense, yes?"

"Yeah, I guess so," I admitted. "Sorry, Paul. In the last few hours, I've gotten very paranoid."

"No problem. Just get in the van quickly, please." He waved his arm, urging me to get inside his truck. "There is little time." Regis staffers were standing in the kitchen doorway, gawking suspiciously at us. In moments, they'd notify the cops and police would swarm the alley.

"You get in first, Hansen," Paul ordered.

"Yeah, sure," Taylor Hansen said. The smell of his breath made me wince. Hansen went past me and clattered into the van.

I looked at the plaza. In the vast public square, police were clattering barricades in place and soon they would complete a circle, closing off the alley. I stared bleakly at the efficiency of the Paris police ringing the hotel with steel parade barriers normally used for crowd control. No one was driving away without being stopped and searched. We were locked inside police barricades, each exit manned by a four person squad with submachine guns. "How're you going to get past the cops?" I asked Paul.

"When I drive out of here, I'll tell them I'm moonlighting, delivering produce to the Regis. Lettuce, carrots, cabbage, that kind of stuff. For the hotel kitchen. They'll buy my story. I'll show them my firefighter's badge. Cops and firefighters, they're like brothers. It'll work," Paul assured me.

"Won't they look in the van?" I asked him.

"Yes. I have to hide you." He grabbed a wooden crate and shook it. "We'll use these boxes."

I didn't get in the van. I wasn't eager to bury myself under stinking produce cartons.

"There's no choice, Nicki. Lie down next to Hansen. I'll cover both of you with these crates." Paul shook water and damp leaves off a produce box and dumped it in his truck.

Taylor Hansen was lying on the ribbed flooring of the van, smirking at me like he enjoyed my discomfort. The idea of running a blockade pinned against a foul smelling Taylor Hansen was ugly, but I had no choice. It was my only hope for escaping. "Wonderful," I grumbled, sliding next to Taylor.

Paul Denis threw a tarp over our bodies and smoothed the canvas so it covered most of Hansen and me. Even though I couldn't see through the tarp, I felt Paul rapidly stacking boxes, building a wall around and over us. Crates of wet, leafy lettuce were dumped over my face, blotting out the light and smothering me in limp, smelly produce.

The back doors were slammed and locked. Then Paul got inside and I felt the van jiggle as he sat down. I heard the engine cough to life and the van began to roll, tires crunching on the pavement as we left the alley. The floor vibrated against my hip and shoulder from the van bouncing over cobblestones.

Laying there on the metal ribbing of the van's floor was a painful experience. Sharp floor screws jabbed my stomach and the corner of a wooden crate scraped my ankle like a rasping file, gouging me. We bumped over a pothole and my head slapped the cold metal ribbing hard enough to send little sparks flashing across my vision. I shifted my hand to cushion my skull from another bounce, but there was nothing I could do about the crate slicing into my ankle.

I heard the muffled sound of the engine die as we stopped at the police blockade, jerking to a halt. Paul rolled down his window and talked to the cops, trying to convince them everything was legitimate. When he finished explaining why he was at the Regis, Paul asked them to let his van go through the barriers and they wouldn't cooperate. The cops said they had to inspect the cargo before Paul could leave. They asked him to get out and unlock the back doors. I went from pain to fear, sure they'd find me hidden under the tarp and all those heavy produce crates.

The van's back doors clanged open and chilly night air swept under the canvas tarp, brushing cold air over me, leaving goosebumps on my naked arms. A cop jumped on the rear bumper and I dipped sharply, suppressing a groan from all the sharp objects jabbing me. The cop's bright flashlight probed the wooden crates, leaking glow through the tarp covering me and I wondered if he could see our hidden bodies. The white oval of his flashlight beam dragged slowly alongside me, poking through the leafy vegetables and revealing every crack in the camouflage hiding me. I watched in fascination and terror as the flashlight beam moved slowly toward my feet. I was convinced my shoes were sticking out, yet there was nothing I could do about it. I didn't dare move. I could only wait and see what happened. I held my breath, determined not to make the slightest motion, even from inhaling air.

Finally, the back doors slammed and the cop slapped the van's sheet metal side with his hand, making a loud ringing sound that hurt my ears. I heard the policeman order Paul to leave the area, then there was the scraping of barricades being moved aside. In the distance, I heard the excited howls of police dogs as they tracked my scent into the alley, barking and yelping.

I felt the van sag down and recover as Paul got inside, muttering, "That was much too close. The dogs almost got you, Nicki."

We started to move and his van went through the grinding of first and second gears, then the tires began singing on the pavement. Paul asked, "Where do you want to go?"

I thought it over for a moment and nothing made me feel comfortable or safe. Every place I went was a risk. The only way out was to solve the puzzle of these arsons. I debated several options and finally said, "Let's go to the Paris Archives. It's where this mess began."

# 16

# Hiding

**It** felt like a long trip to the Paris Archives and I was impatient to get out of my cramped position in the back of Paul's van. Finally, we thudded over a curb to park and the engine quit. I felt Paul Denis hop off the driver's seat. Door hinges squealed at the back of the van and Paul climbed on the rear bumper. I grunted in relief when he eased sharp boxes off me, then peeled a canvas tarp away. After lying under the dark tarp for more than half an hour, the dim streetlights of Paris felt painfully bright and I blinked my eyes, adjusting them.

Sliding out of the van, I looked around and the area was completely unfamiliar to me. Paul's van was parked between two buildings, jammed against short concrete posts lining the passageway. The only landmark was a tiny sandwich shop with stacks of white plastic chairs chained together. I said, "I've never seen this little street before. Where are we?"

Paul Denis answered, "We're in an alley behind the Archives." He swung the van's doors closed. "I can't park on the street. The Surete are looking for my van."

"Sure," I agreed, rubbing my ankle, wiping away dried blood. I heard a noise and turned to look at Taylor Hansen brushing vegetable leaves off his shirt.

His pants were stained with rust from the van's floor and vomit clung to his expensive silk turtleneck, yet none of that dimmed his conceit. He conveniently forgot he was running for his life and stood there arrogantly surveying the alley, acting like a Wall Street stock trader with a master of the universe attitude.

His behavior grated on me and I could barely restrain my sarcasm. "Taylor, if it's not too much trouble, maybe you can get us inside the Archives before Vernier finds us."

Hansen answered with his usual false warmth. "Sure. I'm in this with you."

"You're in this for yourself, Taylor. Let's get inside the Archives and talk." I put out my hand. "The key."

"Yeah, sure." Hansen sulked, irritated his charm didn't work. Taylor reached inside his pocket and dangled a key ring in front of me, giving me a fake smile. Hansen was trying his "see, we're all buddies" attitude, teasing me instead of putting the keys in my open hand.

I didn't want to depend on Hansen so I snatched the key ring from his hand, tucking it in my fist.

Taylor gave me an innocent, wounded look. "I was going to give it to you."

"Sure." I knew Taylor was lying and he'd never intended to hand me the keys.

Paul broke the tension. "We'd better go," he said. "It'll be dawn soon. Look at the sky."

I looked up and pink sunlight was edging rooftops, a soft glow fading into the dark sky. Checking my watch, I saw it was quarter to six in the morning. Soon Paris would come to life with commuters surging from doorways and crowding the sidewalks.

I hadn't gone more than a few steps when I heard a loud clanking sound. Startled, I turned toward the noise, concerned I was being followed. Faint sunlight slid past me and brightened a stairwell where a boy was skipping downstairs with his bicycle. The bike clattered down a flight of stairs, a woven basket bouncing on the handlebars.

The basket was jammed with textbooks and a spiral bound notebook, indicating he was attending a local polytechnic institute as preparation for entering the Sorbonne University.

I moved aside to let the student go past in the narrow confines of the alley. I was relieved he didn't pay me any special notice. He spun a bicycle pedal to level it, put a foot on the pedal and started off, chattering over cobblestones. I thought I was safe, but the bicyclist turned in my direction. He cocked his head in a puzzled look, like a curious bird sitting on a fence. I forced myself to smile and act friendly, but the bicyclist kept a hard expression on his face. Riding away, the young man's curious stare tracked me as though I were someone he couldn't quite place.

I was worried the young boy saw my picture on early morning television news and I wanted more than ever to get off the streets, vanish inside the Archives. I ran to join Paul and Taylor, catching them at a huge carriage door, the entrance to the Paris Archives. Unlocking the door seemed to take an hour, yet I knew it only took seconds. Paul helped me force the heavy door open and its rusty hinges moaned, sounding like a crying child. The mournful sound echoed along the quiet street, calling attention to us and I pressed quickly through the open doorway to get out of sight.

It was dark inside the lobby and I couldn't see anything, not even the floor. I patted the wall with my hands, trying to find a light switch. When I came up empty, I asked Hansen, "Are the lights on timers?"

Taylor answered in a snobby voice. "How should I know? I never get to work at this hour. Diane's the first one in the Archives and she's the last one to leave. Workaholic is Diane's hang-up, not mine."

"I'll go downstairs and look for a light switch," Paul Denis suggested. He pushed around me and grabbed the iron handrail twisting into the old mineshaft that served as entrance to the Paris Archives.

I put a hand on Paul's arm, restraining him from going down the spiral staircase. "Better let me go. I know the place. I've been here before." I nodded toward Taylor, indicating the real reason I wanted Paul to stay in the lobby. I was afraid Hansen might try to run off.

Paul caught on and said, "Sure Nicki, you go down the staircase. Just be careful."

"She'll be careful," Hansen said sarcastically, mimicking Paul's voice. Taylor leaned against the wall, disgusted that he didn't have a chance to escape.

I ignored Hansen and went down the spiral staircase, carefully picking my steps. Any light quickly vanished and I had to feel my way in darkness until I hit bottom. I clung to the damp stone wall of the cave, sliding my fingers along sticky limestone until I hit a light switch. I flipped it on and fluorescent lights blinked to life across the vast abandoned limestone quarry. The lights flickered at first and gained strength, brightening the cave so I could see the document storage area with its thousands of shelves.

I looked up the staircase and saw the lobby illuminated by an old river navigation lantern. Yellow ripples of light pushed through bubbles in the lantern's ancient glass and fell on the narrow, twisting steps. I urged Paul and Hansen, "Come on down. It's OK."

I listened to their footsteps clatter on the iron stairs until they got to my level. I led them into the storage cavern, walking through a maze of tall shelves, our footsteps echoing off the cavern's high ceiling. Besides our steps, the only sound was a soft trickling of water leaking down the walls of the abandoned limestone quarry, keeping the area damp and moldy. My nose was filled with the ugly smell of mildew and in that early morning hour, the smell was even more pungent. I was grateful to swing open the rusty iron door to the office area, warm and dry with the normal odors of stale coffee and toner cartridges from copiers.

I led Paul and Taylor along a narrow carpeted hallway going to Diane St. Remy's office. On one side, the corridor was painted white with framed pictures hung between office doors. Ancient sketches of the city showed Paris as just some crude huts at the river's edge, a trading post at the outskirts of the Roman Empire. The faded ink drawings depicted Paris as it was in 500 A.D. Next to them, aerial photographs showed the same neighborhood fifteen hundred years later, a bustling modern city.

The inner wall with its framed pictures looked like a normal office area, but the other side was quite different. The hallway's outer wall resembled the glass display windows of a New York City department store. The row of plate glass windows was coated in water droplets from garden sprinklers making a soft hissing sound as they misted a garden alcove. Outside the windows was a beautiful atrium filled with lush ferns and gray plants shaped like elephant ears. The plants bathed in an eerie glow from the hazy sun of early morning. I walked along the hallway in that unusual light until I came to Diane's office.

When I hit a switch, bright lights snapped on and the glare was painful to my dry, exhausted eyes. I stood there blinking until my eyes gradually adjusted and I could see Diane's room clearly. There was no mistaking that Diane was boss of the Paris Archives. Facing the door was her power desk, a large rosewood piece that matched her cabinets and conference table. The desk was sterile – no personal photographs, no toys. There was only a huge leather blotter and an antique dagger Diane used as a letter opener. I avoided the cold arrogance of Diane's desk and sat at a small conference table in the corner.

Paul Denis walked past me and sat in a conference chair, bending his legs under him. He rocked forward and leaned aggressively over the table. His only expression was a tight smile that worried me. I sensed a lot of rage simmering in him and it was all directed at Taylor Hansen. I could understand Paul's reaction. Taylor was easy to hate and making it easier by the moment.

Hansen didn't sit with us. Instead he slid behind Diane St. Remy's power desk, running his hands along the smooth, rich desktop like he was boss of the world.

Taylor's arrogance provoked me and I knew Hansen's attitude enraged Paul. I watched a cheek muscle tighten, relax, and tighten again on Paul's face. I sensed an ugly mood gathering in the room like static before a summer lightning storm. I hoped to break the angry mood by getting Hansen to talk about the arsons.

I said, "OK, Taylor, we came here to get answers. I know Vernier's looking for something and you know what he wants. It must be worth a fortune because Vernier's killed a lot of people."

"Oh, what Vernier wants is definitely worth killing people." Hansen whispered in a slow tease. "There's plenty of money for us to share, money and power for all."

"I see." Paul Denis said it quietly, running a fingertip along a ruled pad, leaving a deep crease from the pressure of his rigid finger. He folded the sheet very precisely in a simple, controlled gesture and the absolute perfection of it frightened me.

I put my hand on Paul's forearm, trying to soothe him but it didn't work. His arm stayed rigid, a measure of his tightly coiled anger. I gave up trying to calm Paul and continued questioning Taylor, hoping he'd volunteer some information. "You're after millions of dollars, hmm?"

"You're getting the idea," Hansen answered. "But there's more, much more." He shot me a nasty look. "Better than your Interpol salary, huh, Foster?"

"Yes, providing you're alive to spend the money. And you haven't been very good at staying alive, Taylor. It could easily have been you killed in the Regis. Diane missed with her knife but she'll have better aim next time. How about a little cooperation so I can help you?"

Hansen gave me a twisted smirk. "You got it backwards. You're gonna help me or I'll cut a deal with the fire captain and leave you out." Taylor jabbed a thumb in Paul's direction.

Paul said, "We'll split the money equally, Monsieur Hansen. If there is anything to split. In a little while, we can all be dead. So, quickly, eh?"

Hansen's voice was icy cold. "I don't have to rush. I have what you want. You have to play ball with me, do things my way."

"I do?" Paul asked idly. I saw Paul's hand slip under his bulky sweater and curl around a tire iron. The heavy steel bar came from Paul's van.

I didn't like where this was going. I tried to head off violence. "Look, Taylor, you need help. You can't do this all by yourself."

Instead of talking to me, Taylor leaned over and picked up the antique dagger lying on Diane's desk. Hansen aimed the pointed blade at me. "You think I can't take care of myself?"

"I believe you, Taylor. You can take care of yourself. But Vernier's murdered a lot of people. Paul and I can't stand around and let these arsons go on. More innocent people will die." Innocent people like me, I thought. I'm not a hero and I was worried about my own future, as well as the unfortunate victims of these crimes. I watched Hansen intently, hoping he'd be logical for a change.

Hansen's eyes narrowed. "I don't give a damn about innocent people getting killed. If they're in the way, they die. That's life."

Paul spoke in a tight voice. "And that's why you kill the firefighters. Dead firefighters can't put out a fire, so the burn cooks up and destroys all evidence. That's what you said, Taylor. Kill everyone and burn all the clues. Firefighters get in the way and they get killed also."

"Right," Hansen agreed. He toyed with the dagger, pointing it at me again. "So, I'm in charge."

"Sure," Paul agreed, his voice much too calm. I saw Paul Denis slip the tire iron under the table. Before I could stop him, Paul lunged. He brought his tire iron down, smashing Taylor's hand with a sickening crunch. The dagger shot from Hansen's broken hand and went flying down the hallway. I heard the knife skitter along the floor, slapping against a baseboard.

Paul had thrown the conference table in front of me, blocking me so I couldn't interfere. I shoved the table out of my way and moved toward Paul. "Hansen's got the message. You don't need to hit him again."

"I'm not going to hit him again – provided Hansen cooperates." Paul taunted Hansen. "You can really take care of yourself, can't you, smart boy? Little Taylor want his dagger back? I'm willing to go a second round, Taylor. Are you?"

"Paul," I demanded, "He's had enough."

Paul Denis exhaled loudly, the breath whistling through his tight mouth. "OK, I'll try it your way. But Hansen cooperates." Paul slapped the tire iron against the desk. "I don't want any more firefighters killed. What's the arsonist burning next?"

Hansen didn't answer. He stared at his twisted fingers in disbelief, seeming unable to grasp that his hand was mangled. Pain shot up the arm and bleached Taylor's face.

Paul grabbed Taylor's good hand and held it against the blotter. "I don't have time to play games, Hansen. I want answers now. Tell me what the arsonist burns next or I'll crush the other hand."

"No, Paul. Enough," I insisted. I was going to grab the weapon and stop him from breaking Taylor's other hand, but I didn't have to worry. Hansen cracked.

Tugging his pinned wrist, Hansen whimpered, "No, don't hit me. I'll tell you everything."

When Paul released Hansen's good hand, Taylor hid it in his armpit. Hansen tried to speak and couldn't. "Some water," he gasped, licking his lips. Shock from his mangled hand made Hansen desperately thirsty.

Paul groaned. "He doesn't need water. He needs to talk."

I reassured Paul, "Don't worry. You've made your point. Taylor's going to tell us everything." I grabbed one of Diane's carafes from a side table and splashed water in a cup.

Hansen greedily tore the mug off the desk, holding it in his shaking hand. Taylor's eyes sent me a grateful look as he drained the water. Hansen dropped the mug on the desk and pushed it toward me, nodding in a silent request for more.

I opened Diane's cabinet, hoping to find plastic water bottles, but there weren't any. I straightened up and dusted off my hands. I poured Hansen the last water in the carafe, shaking the jug to get a final drop out, then slid the cup toward Hansen. I saw Paul tense, resenting Hansen getting any comfort.

"Taylor didn't kill your friends, Paul. He's not the arsonist. Vernier and Diane are behind the crimes. Taylor just cut himself into the deal." I saw Paul relax but I knew it wouldn't last.

I quickly asked Hansen, "The computer system you put in the Archives ties into these crimes somehow. I'm guessing the computer tells the arsonist where to strike, right?"

"Yeah." Hansen nodded his head. "Diane used my system to build a secret file. I broke Diane's password and found a list of addresses."

I pressed Hansen. "How do you know this list is for the arsonist?" I didn't get an immediate answer and Paul Denis leaned menacingly over Taylor.

Hansen recoiled in his chair, looking like a shadow painted on the angled seat. "This has to be the arsonist's target list. The torched warehouse and apartment building are at the top of the list." Taylor's frightened eyes darted to me.

"OK, I'll buy that," I said. "I assume the arsonist searches these places looking for something hidden and later burns them down. What exactly is the arsonist hoping to find, Taylor?"

"Don't get mad," Hansen pleaded. "I'll tell you. Just don't hit me. OK?"

I assured him, "No one's going to hit you."

Paul went along. He let the tire iron drop to his side. "Go on," he urged Hansen.

"OK," Taylor muttered. He cleared his throat. "Well, you're not going to believe this."

"Try me." I was irritated at Taylor for dragging this out.

Hansen swallowed hard, afraid he was going to be hit again. "The arsonist is looking for old furniture. That's all he wants, some old furniture."

I stared at Hansen, convinced he was finally telling me the truth. His answer was too bizarre to be a lie. Taylor claimed the arsonist tore a warehouse apart to find the right pieces of antique furniture and afterwards burned the warehouse to the ground, destroying all evidence. At the apartment building, the arsonist followed the same pattern, going through each unit, then burning the building to hide his search. Fire crews were killed at both places to make sure everything burned, destroying all clues.

I should have felt relieved at seeing a pattern to these crimes, but I didn't. I had a sick feeling the more I knew about these arsons, the worse it would be. Despite how I felt, I couldn't stop asking questions now. City Commissioner Vernier was burning Paris down to find antiques and there had to be some very intriguing reason why he was willing to risk his career for a collection of old furniture.

# 17

# Evidence

I put a restraining hand on Paul's arm, making sure he didn't hit Taylor again. "You know, I think Hansen's right. The arsonist could be looking for old furniture."

"Nobody kills for old furniture," Paul Denis said angrily. "Hansen claims they're searching for a huge fortune. No antiques are worth that much." Paul leaned menacingly over the desk. "I don't buy it. You're lying, Hansen."

Hansen cringed. He shrank in his chair and looked to me for support. "Help me, Nicki. I'm telling the truth, I swear."

I tugged on Paul's arm, trying to move him away and all I got was a reluctant half step. Paul wasn't backing off, so I tried a different approach. I encouraged Hansen to open up and tell us more, hoping additional data would calm Paul Denis. I challenged Hansen, "We don't understand the crimes yet. For example, how does this lost treasure link to the apartment building in Menilmontant?"

Taylor didn't answer me and instead nervously cleared his throat. He looked at the desk like he was desperately searching for a distraction. When he couldn't find any objects on Diane's bald desktop, he began picking at his clothes.

I had to bring him back or he'd sit there all night, fiddling with a hole in his torn pants. "Go on," I prodded Hansen. "Tell us how the apartment building is tied to the search for a missing fortune."

"OK," Taylor sighed. "Diane said the arsonist wanted to examine two apartments. The old furniture, the key to this lost fortune, might be in those flats. I asked Diane why the arsonist went at night, when people are sure to be home. Diane just laughed and said I was stupid."

I acted sympathetic. "I believe you, Taylor. Diane likes making people feel stupid for asking a question because then she feels superior giving you the answer. Why did the arsonist go at night?"

"He wanted people home to question them. Maybe they sold a chair or table. Maybe they gave a desk to a relative. He wanted to track down all the pieces of furniture so he tortured people to make sure they were telling the truth. Once the arsonist finished his interrogation, he killed the people and burned the building, destroying any evidence."

"Maybe," Paul grumbled, rubbing his chin. "Hansen might be telling the truth." To my relief, Paul backed away from Taylor.

I stepped closer to Hansen. "So the search is over and there won't be any more fires. The arsonist found the furniture?"

Taylor shook his head. "No. I'm sure the arsonist didn't find what he wanted. None of the furniture was in the warehouse and there wasn't anything in the apartment building either."

"How do you know?" Paul demanded.

Hansen managed a thin smile despite his pain. "Diane was depressed after both arsons. Diane would be insufferable if she found the fortune."

"Yes," I sadly agreed. "A rich Diane St. Remy would be arrogant, not depressed. But I still don't quite understand. Why did the arsonist kill firefighters? A dead fire crew called a lot of attention to the warehouse arson."

Hansen shrugged. "How am I supposed to know? Diane didn't tell me everything."

I looked at Paul. Maybe he understood why firefighters were being ambushed when they arrived at an arson and began fighting a blaze consuming the building.

Paul explained, "The arsonist killed the fire crew to make sure his burn got hot enough to destroy any clues. Even using rocket fuel won't destroy all the evidence unless there's time for a longer burn."

"You can stop rocket fuel with water?" I asked skeptically.

"With enough water, yes. That's how launch pads and gantry cranes are protected, with a thick spray of water. The arsonist sets a trap for us at the fire scene to make sure we don't stop the blaze before all the clues are gone. He doesn't want anyone knowing he's searched the building."

"Great," I said in disgust. "Any fire can be an ambush."

"Yes," Paul agreed. "We need clues to stop the arsonist."

"Maybe there's a clue in the furniture itself." I asked Hansen, "Do you know anything about this furniture? Like why these antiques are so important."

Taylor was evasive. "How should I know? I don't have all the pieces to this puzzle." Taylor held his twisted fingers and whined, "I've got to get out of here. I need a doctor."

I knew the broken fingers hurt and needed treatment, but they were also an excuse for ducking my question about why the furniture was important. "The sooner you talk, the sooner you get medical attention for your fingers, Taylor." I pushed on him. "You know more about this furniture, don't you?"

"Yeah, kinda," Taylor hedged.

I crossed my arms and stared at Hansen. "You think those fingers hurt? You said the arsonist tortured people in the apartment building. Imagine the arsonist working on your body. Keep stalling and he'll find us. You'll know real pain."

Taylor sagged in his chair. He took a deep breath and let the air out slowly, his cheeks deflating like an old bicycle tire going flat. "All right," he said quietly. "It's like this. The furniture comes from an old hotel. It was once the most elegant hotel in Paris. The penthouse suite was huge, the whole top floor of the building. Vernier's looking for furniture from the penthouse suite."

Paul asked, "Why isn't the furniture in the hotel?"

Taylor had an answer. "The building was wrecked in World War II. The French Resistance blew up the hotel, killing a bunch of Nazis. It was a huge bomb. The front of the hotel looked like the blasted courthouse in Oklahoma City, a caved-in shell. The damaged building was torn down."

"Let me guess," I offered. "Furniture from the wrecked hotel was put in a warehouse. Many years later, the arsonist searched that same warehouse. He didn't find what he wanted and burned the place down. Right?"

Taylor eagerly agreed. "Yeah, right, it was the same warehouse." He told Paul Denis, "See, guy. I'm giving it to you straight."

Paul rolled his eyes in disgust. "You gave me a little piece of this puzzle, but it had to be pried from you with a tire iron." Paul slapped the heavy iron bar against his palm. "OK, prove you're giving it to me straight. What makes this furniture worth billions?"

Hansen didn't answer and nervously picked lint off his pants leg. He squirmed uneasily in his chair, pushing his chin down against his chest.

I prodded Taylor. "Come on, tell us. Time's running out. We have to leave the Archives soon. What makes this antique furniture valuable?"

Hansen muttered and it was hard to hear him. "The furniture itself isn't valuable." He talked in a pained voice, but it wasn't from the pain of his fingers. Hansen hated losing control over the treasure. Reluctantly, Taylor explained, "Important things are hidden in the furniture."

Paul Denis slapped the desk blotter with his tire iron. "What's hidden inside the furniture?"

Hansen sighed. "Jewels. Nice stuff, easily broken up and sold on the black market."

I said, "Jewels will get a few million at most, even crown jewels. You're holding out, Taylor. Something else is hidden in that furniture."

"There's more," Taylor said reluctantly.

"Keep going," I pressured him. "You're on a roll. Let's have it all."

"There's only one more thing," Hansen pleaded.

"I'm sure you've saved the best for last," Paul said sarcastically.

"I was going to tell you," Taylor whined.

I was cynical. "Yeah, you were going to tell us, all right. What else is hidden inside the furniture?"

"Just some property titles." Hansen said it meekly.

"Property titles?" Paul asked, puzzled.

I explained, "Property titles are like grant deeds for homes in America. Buy a house and you get a document saying you own the land and the building. That's a property title. The deeds hidden in this furniture must be worth a lot more than a house."

"Yeah," Taylor said. He radiated greed again. His eyes were so alert they felt hypnotic.

I ignored Hansen and looked at Paul. "Maybe that's why City Commissioner Vernier spent money on the Paris Archives. It's where property titles are kept and Diane is an expert on them."

Paul was curious. "You told me Hansen was putting property titles in his computer. But Vernier hasn't found the furniture. They don't have the property titles. It doesn't make sense."

"Not yet," I agreed. "We need to know a lot more. And we need some evidence."

Paul was upset. "We can't look around this place for evidence. We have to get out of here. Vernier is turning Paris inside out to find us and soon he'll look here, in the Archives."

I knew Paul was right. I couldn't hang around here and expect to live, but staying a few minutes longer was the only way to get more information from Taylor Hansen. I'd spent a frustrating, dangerous hour getting Hansen in a receptive mood and I had to get clues while he was willing to talk.

My mind was racing, considering all the options, but I tried to look calm on the outside. I idly fingered a water carafe, toying with the plastic handle while I suggested, "Let's leave after we get that target list Diane built for the arsonist on her computer. It'll help prove there's a conspiracy. The target list also warns the fire department."

Hansen didn't care about the fire department. He wanted pain killer and help for his broken fingers. "Staying here is dumb. I can sneak back in the Archives tonight. I'll print the target list later."

I was firm. "No. The Archives will be watched night and day. You'll never get in here again. Print the list now. It'll only take five minutes."

"Print the target list," Paul Denis insisted. "We're not leaving without that list. No more ambushes. My firefighters aren't getting killed again."

Hansen gave in to our pressure. He sighed, reached under the table and hit a switch. The computer gronked and beeped, then the screen powered up with a snap of static electricity. Hansen squinted at the computer screen and typed some commands.

Paul urged Hansen, "Hurry."

"I am hurrying," Hansen complained bitterly. Taylor gave the keyboard a final tap and announced, "There's nothing to do but wait."

I said, "There's one thing you can do."

"What?" Hansen snapped.

"Show me some evidence. How do I know this treasure hunt is for real? All I have is your word against Vernier's. Your testimony won't be enough in court, assuming you aren't lying."

"I'm not lying," Hansen grumbled. He talked very softly. "The money's real."

"How do you know?" I asked.

Hansen ignored my question and sat there, looking sullen. He studied his broken fingers, pain and anger clouding his face.

Paul leaned over the desk. "You threatened to cut Nicki out of the deal. Now, I'm playing that game on you, Hansen. I'm cutting a deal with Vernier, giving you to the City Commissioner."

"Vernier won't go for it. He wants all three of us," Hansen said defensively.

I played along. "I think Paul may be right. There's a way out for Paul and me. We sell you to Vernier."

"You're not going to do that," Hansen said, but his voice showed fear. His face turned pasty and grew moist, looking damp and white in the harsh office lighting.

I let Hansen squirm for a moment and then said, "Maybe I won't cut a deal with Vernier. But I have to believe the treasure is real." I pressed Taylor. "Go on. Convince me."

Taylor looked at his broken fingers, stalling. Finally, he said, "Diane and Vernier are looking for a lost treasure that's never been found. There weren't any clues until now."

"And you're going to tell us about it," Paul said firmly.

Hansen reluctantly agreed. "Yeah," he sighed. "I'll tell you what happened. It's based on a true unsolved mystery. Billions of dollars disappeared in Paris and were never found. The treasure is right here, waiting for someone to discover it. Somebody has it and doesn't know. They put their socks in a drawer loaded with a fortune. They're sleeping on the treasure every night in their bed, ignorant that they're rich."

"You're serious?" I found Taylor's story hard to believe.

"Yes," Hansen quickly answered. "The facts are in the history books. You can check. Billions of dollars are missing. There's no reason we can't be the first people to find the treasure."

# 18

# An Unsolved Mystery

I pressed Hansen, "Go on. Tell us why the treasure's for real. You said it's based on a true crime, an unsolved mystery."

Taylor shifted uneasily in his chair. "We don't have to discuss this now. I need help. My fingers are killing me." He held out his hand. The thumb was bent at an unnatural angle and the forefinger had a bone pressing so hard against the flesh that the bone almost stuck out. Swollen and discolored, the hand was an ugly, frightening sight.

I knew Hansen was in a lot of pain, yet I had to balance his discomfort against stopping the arsonist from killing more firefighters and innocent victims. I was firm with Hansen. "You'll get help for your fingers after you tell us about the treasure. The faster you talk, the sooner you get help."

Paul Denis grabbed a corner of Taylor's chair and talked in a menacing voice, reminding Hansen of the story. "You told us about furniture in the penthouse suite of a hotel. Jewels and deeds to valuable property were hidden in the furniture. How did all this happen?"

Even in great pain, Hansen was reluctant to tell everything. He sighed. "It started a long time ago, in June 1940, at the very beginning of World War II. Adolf Hitler's tanks rolled into Paris and the Germans helped themselves to the finest of everything. The top Nazi claimed the penthouse of the best hotel for his private suite." Taylor shrugged and looked at me as though this little scrap of information explained everything.

I deliberately prodded Hansen to get more details. "Are you making this story up, Taylor?"

"Check it for yourself," Hansen snapped. "The man staying in the penthouse suite was Rudolf Hess. Hess is a real person, not a fictional character. Rudolf Hess was Hitler's closest friend, an ally from the beginning when they shared a prison cell after the Munich beer hall riots. Hess is in the encyclopedias, the history books, everything. Hess plundered France for Hitler."

"I've read about Hess," Paul Denis said. "Rudolf Hess was Hitler's trusted henchman, the number two guy. Hess was second in command at the start of World War II."

"Did Hess go to France?" I asked Paul.

"Yes," he confirmed. "Rudolf Hess looted Paris like Hansen said. Hess was terrible. He tortured whole families to get their money. His reputation spread and people signed away everything to escape Hess. They gave him fine art, jewels, homes. Hess stripped Paris of its treasures."

"Amazing. It's beginning to make sense." I turned to Hansen and asked him, "What did Rudolf Hess do with the treasure he got?"

Taylor answered, "Hess was supposed to send the loot to Adolf Hitler, but things didn't go the way Hitler planned."

"Let me guess," I said cynically. "Rudolf Hess sent enough stolen art and jewels to keep Hitler asleep. But Hess skimmed the best for himself, kept the finest stuff in his penthouse."

"Sure." Hansen shrugged. "Wouldn't you? I'd keep the best."

I ignored Taylor's comment. "Let's get back to the furniture in that penthouse suite. The pieces were probably massive antiques and it was easy to hide jewels or property deeds in hidden compartments. Is that why the hotel furniture is so important?"

Hansen nodded. "Yes. Hess had carpenters hollow out bedposts and make hidden compartments in dressers and nightstands. Hess probably killed the carpenters to keep his fortune secret. Afterwards he stuffed the furniture with all the loot it would hold."

"Nice guy." Paul Denis was being sarcastic.

"Smart guy," Hansen contradicted Paul. Taylor, of course, sided with Rudolf Hess and his greed. "Hess had a good scheme. He could move out of the hotel penthouse and take the furniture without raising suspicion. He'd say he was using the furniture to decorate his country estate."

I teased Hansen. "You said Hess is so smart, Taylor. Yet all this treasure is floating around lost. Why didn't Hess keep his fortune?"

Hansen talked wistfully, like Hess was some champion athlete who never got to play in the Olympics, not a cruel Nazi. "Something happened and Hess never got his chance to escape with his treasure. Maybe Hitler discovered Rudolf Hess was skimming, keeping the best for himself. The history books say Hess fled Paris one night, chased by Hitler's personal guard. Hess got to Austria, stole a plane and took off in a panic. Bailing out over Scotland, he was arrested and interrogated. Hess claimed he was on a secret peace mission, but nobody believed the story. After the war, Hess was tried at Nuremberg with other Nazis and served a life sentence in Spandau prison."

Paul Denis was deliberately skeptical, hoping to get more information out of Hansen. "That's all you have? It isn't much."

"No, uh, there's more," Hansen said defensively.

"What is it?" I prodded.

"I did some checking. I tracked down the prison guards that handled Rudolf Hess and two of them were still alive. The guards said Hess tried to bribe them with stories about a fortune hidden in Paris. Hess wanted to escape and said he'd take them to the loot." Taylor's eyes looked pleadingly at me. "You believe me, don't you?" He shifted uneasily.

I said, "Maybe there's some truth in what you're saying. According to you, Rudolf Hess ran out of Paris and left his treasure stuffed in hotel furniture."

"Yes," Taylor confirmed. "After Hess flew to Scotland, an explosion blew up the hotel. The hotel was too damaged to rebuild. The building was torn down and the rooms were gutted. The nicest antiques, like furniture in the penthouse suite, were auctioned to raise money for the hotel's owners. Now that furniture is scattered all over Paris and has to be hunted down."

"Our only way of tracking down the furniture is the arsonist's target list," I reminded Hansen.

"OK, I'm printing the list," Hansen said angrily. "Chill out." Hansen pecked at the keyboard with his good hand and said, "The document's printing. I'll go get it." He got up and started around the desk.

Paul put a hand on Taylor's chest, pushing Hansen backwards. "You're not going anywhere, Hansen. Where's the printer?"

Taylor babbled. "Uh, it's a long way from here, in the conference room. I better go. You'd get lost."

I volunteered, "I know where the conference room is. I'll go." I was suspicious why Hansen printed the list so far away. "Diane has a personal desk printer. Why didn't you do the list here?"

Hansen responded nervously, "I needed a faster printer. It's a long list and I knew we had to get out of here. It would take too long on Diane's machine." Taylor used all his false sincerity to convince me. "I need you guys. I'm not going to run out on you."

Paul looked at Taylor with contempt and asked me, "You know how to find this conference room?"

"Yeah, I was in the conference room a few days ago. I'll run over there and be right back. Then we'll get out of here. You got any idea where to go next? We need a place to hide."

Paul shrugged. "I have some ideas. I'll think about it."

"OK." I turned to go and hesitated, worried about leaving Hansen with Paul. I didn't want more violence. I knew how stupidly provocative Hansen could be and I asked Paul for a promise. "You won't do anything to Hansen, right? Taylor's my witness against Vernier."

"Sure," Paul answered in a mocking way. "I won't do anything that keeps Hansen from talking. The rest is up to him."

I hoped Paul was only posturing to keep Hansen in line. I warned Taylor, "Please behave while I'm gone."

Hansen slouched in his chair, giving me a surly look with his body language and glaring at me in resentment. His stare made me feel uncomfortable and I stopped in the doorway of the office, turning around to study Taylor. His attitude was strange. I had an intuition Hansen wanted to get the arsonist's target list by himself because something valuable was hidden in the conference room. I decided to make a quick search of the conference room and grab anything I found. Hansen probably wanted some computer files. I might find a backup cartridge in a drawer.

I walked along the office hallway and into the cavernous document storage area. The old cave was huge with a ceiling high enough to cover a three story building. Light from the few bulbs tacked on that tall ceiling barely lit the area. I felt unprotected and vulnerable walking between rows of gray industrial shelving towering over me, forming a disorienting maze. I doubted Paul could hear me if I needed help and he certainly couldn't get to me in time, trying to follow my voice as it echoed around the old limestone quarry. It wasn't a reassuring thought for me as I followed old hand-lettered signs toward the sunken grotto where Hansen had worked.

I cautiously stepped into the little cave Diane used for a conference room and hit the light switch. A garage fixture on the ceiling sputtered to life. Long fluorescent tubes flickered and finally pushed soft glow on the cave's stone walls. The lights got brighter as the tubes warmed up. In one corner icicle-shaped stalactites hung in twisting spires from the ceiling. Five of the crystallized limestone formations were like a giant's fingers pinching a round boulder between their tips.

The far wall was made of discarded blocks resembling hand-made loaves of bread, stacked to the ceiling with no mortar between them, leaking a soft draft of icy air. A sign was hung on the wall warning occupants not to eat any of the death cap mushrooms that always sprouted between the wall blocks despite repeated attempts to eradicate the poisonous fungi. Every wall was irregular, none of them at right angles to each other and the ceiling buckled in sweeping arches. I was careful to watch my steps because the floor sloped and was etched in chisel marks where the room had been quarried out.

The exotic setting contrasted sharply with the cheap conference furniture that was a motley collection of military surplus discards and deep discount store purchases. The table was a slab of pressboard on folding legs, surrounded with metal chairs like the kind used in schools. I'd punished my back on cold metal chairs like that for hours in the high school multi-purpose room, then janitors stacked them in a closet to clear the gym for basketball games.

I picked my way around the folding chairs, exploring the conference room. The area was filled with the distinctive smell that comes from laser printers and in one corner, a laser printer was slipping pages in a tray, spinning out the arsonist's target list. The long inventory of potential targets was still printing, so I used the time to search the area.

I looked around to find anything hidden in the room by Hansen. I ran out the drawer from a table and looked inside. Nothing was worth taking. I slid reams of white paper around to look behind and found only a dusty stone wall.

Then my eyes caught a small door that I assumed was a closet since the door had a flip latch, not a doorknob. I pulled the thin plywood door open and was hit by dank mildew smell from a basement. Alongside the door frame, an old fashioned ceramic switch was nailed to a wooden beam. When I flipped the switch, a naked bulb glowed on the basement ceiling, giving enough light to see dusty wooden stairs leading downward. I couldn't make out anything beyond the stairs.

I felt pulled to go in the basement and stepped downward, sliding my feet from one creaking stair to the next. The dusty wooden staircase led me to the dirt floor of a small room lined by stone walls. Against the walls, empty shelves were layered in fine orange dust. There was only a single cardboard box on the shelves.

In the dark cellar, I moved slowly toward a battered cardboard box with torn sides and a crushed top. I flattened my hands on the soft, damp cardboard, brushing aside a thick layer of dust. My hands dragged over coarse waxy strings and I felt a knot hidden under the dust. I pulled, the waxy strings fell to the side and the box's top flaps sagged limply open.

Dim glow from the single lightbulb crept inside the box, flowing over a jumble of useless items. The carton held the remnants of a man's lifetime. I pulled out relics from the past, a windup alarm clock, shoe polish and a brush for shaving cream. Finally, I saw a small book, bound in dark blue calfskin.

I lifted the book from the battered cardboard box and opened the manuscript. I flipped pages again and again, trying to understand what I'd found. It appeared to be a diary written a long time ago. Every page in the book looked the same, filled with handwritten entries on blue ruled paper. The handwriting was perfect script, drawn in rich green ink from an expensive fountain pen. The handwritten script was almost calligraphy, the elaborate lettering used on wedding invitations. I turned to the front of the little blue leather book and discovered this was the private diary of the Nazi Rudolf Hess.

The diary was written in German and I knew enough of the language to realize this was an obsolete dialect called High German. A scholar of old languages was needed to translate the writing, a person with a real mind for details. Fortunately such a person had read the diary, Diane St. Remy. Her careful French translation was printed between the lines of German script. I'd seen that same printing on notes she sent me and the neat, precise lettering was undeniably Diane's. This translation was her talented mind at work.

I assumed Taylor Hansen stole the Hess diary from Diane St. Remy after she completed her translation. I wondered how Hansen knew about the diary. Taylor must have grown suspicious of Diane and Vernier, wondering what they were really doing with the computer system. When Taylor put the pieces together, he began following Diane through the Archives and caught her reading the old leather diary. Hansen watched Diane finish with the book, then hide it inside a battered cardboard box. After she left, Taylor stole the box for his own use. Hansen was worried hidden security cameras might spot him taking the box out of the Archives so he hid it in the conference room and this little basement closet was a perfect spot.

Taylor looked inside the box and realized he had the lost diary of the Nazi Rudolf Hess. The diary precisely listed a huge fortune stuffed in old hotel furniture. An Impressionist masterpiece was rolled up and slid inside a bedpost. A twelve row diamond tiara in platinum setting was carefully wrapped in velvet and hidden in the false bottom of a dresser drawer. The list of valuables included secret codes to Swiss accounts with gold bullion and property titles for exclusive areas of Paris. The property titles were clearly the most valuable, worth many billions. It was like owning blocks of Manhattan that included Rockefeller Center and the 77-story Chrysler Building.

The treasure was staggering and greed put Hansen on overdrive. There was no reason to split the fortune with anyone. Taylor knew the computer system and he hacked Diane's password, copying her private files. A little searching and he found the arsonist's target list. Now Hansen could look for the treasure on his own, without Diane and Vernier. In his own mind, Taylor already had the fortune and started worrying about how to cash out the stolen valuables.

Hansen knew he needed help fencing jewels and artwork hidden in the antique furniture. Taylor didn't know how to contact international fences who deal in rare, precious items, but Interpol agents track stolen goods and know all the great fences by heart. He decided to bribe an Interpol agent he'd met and that agent was me. Hansen pulled my business card from his pocket and gave me a call, leaving me voicemail to have dinner with him in a fine restaurant. He invited me to dinner at Olivier's, one of the most expensive restaurants in Paris. Taylor played cat and mouse with me over dinner, teasing me with how rich I'd be after helping him. Naturally, he didn't want to say I'd be fencing stolen jewels. I might arrest him, not help him.

Hansen was at dinner with me and Diane took a stroll through the Archives. She went to check on the diary and was shocked to find the battered cardboard box missing. It didn't take her brilliant mind long to crosscheck the facts since correlating facts is what she did for a living. Diane concluded Taylor Hansen must have stolen the diary. For the first time in her life, Diane St. Remy went crazy and lost it. She went to the Regis intending to butcher Taylor Hansen with a knife and killed an hotel maid by mistake.

By now, Diane was back to her normal self, a calculating machine logical as a chess computer. Diane asked herself what Taylor Hansen did with the cardboard box and realized Hansen put it in the conference room where he worked. He'd hide the box in the little basement storage area and I was standing there now, an easy target.

How long ago had Diane figured it all out? Too long ago was the answer. Somewhere in the distance, I heard faint scratching noises. I waited and heard the sound again, closer this time. I knew Diane was already in the Archives, armed for revenge. It wasn't hard to know. The lightbulb dangling above my head went out and I was standing in darkness.

Blind in the dark, I listened to my ragged, tense breathing. Then I listened to a more sinister sound, the muffled scraping of Diane quietly working her way through the underground quarry. She was stalking me, slowly and deliberately hunting me down. I had no doubt she intended to kill me. We'd all like to believe killing someone is unthinkable, but the margin between sane and a killer is whisper thin, the slice left in paper after you drag a razor blade across.

When Diane drove a knife in the eye of an hotel maid, she crossed the imaginary line between normal and deadly. Now Diane St. Remy made a perfect killer, emotionless and logical. She wouldn't hesitate to murder anyone who got in her way and I was definitely in the way. I knew enough to ruin her plans and I held the evidence in my hands, the arsonist's target list.

# 19

# Stalked

I couldn't just wait there to die, standing in the dark, surrounded by the smell of rot and damp cold air. I had to get out of that basement, escape the Archives. But Diane cut power to the lights and in the dark I couldn't even see my own body. The wooden stairs leading to a thin plywood door were a vague memory. I slowly turned and groped in the dark, moving like an insect patting with its feelers, having only the dullest idea of the world around me.

My fingertips hit the jagged edge of a metal shelf and I felt rust crumble under my fingers, flaking in gritty layers. I'd gone the wrong way and hit empty shelves lining a basement wall. I patted my way down the metal shelving and got on my hands and knees, crawling to find the low staircase. Dirt from the basement floor caked on my hands like flour as I fumbled in the blackness, trying to locate the stairs.

I was startled when my ankle jabbed the corner of a board. I realized I'd bumped into the low steps leading out of the basement, but I didn't dare stand up. I might lose my orientation and waste precious time trying to find the stairs again. I crawled up the rough wood steps on hands and knees, pressing slivers into my palms. The emotional and physical strain exaggerated my need for each new breath. I stopped, out of breath and fought to see where I was. I could tell I was at the top of the stairs because there were no more steps in front of me.

I tried moving my eyes around the conference room and saw nothing. Like the basement, the conference room was a black hole and trying to sense an exit in the utter darkness all around me was futile. Still I had to try going somewhere and began crawling, sliding along the cold stone floor. In my anxiety, I crept forward too fast, running my forehead into a table with a soft thud. Flashes of pain raced through my head and false echoes of light jabbed across my vision, disorienting me. I recoiled backwards and sat there, fighting to calm down.

I couldn't crawl on my hands and knees forever. I'd never get out of the Archives. When I tried to stand, my legs were numb and I groped for something to lean on. I felt the warmth of the laser printer and used its table to help myself get up. Wobbling to my feet, I teetered, jabbing a hand on the printer to stop from falling. I felt a warm, soft crush of paper. It was the arsonist's target list and instinctively I swept up the wad of pages. My other hand clung to the diary like it was part of me. I wasn't leaving without the Hess diary, my only way of proving there was a conspiracy behind the arsons.

I saw a thin slice in the distance, a wedge less dark than the rest of the blackness and hoped it was an exit. Cautiously, I made my way forward, trying not to make a sound. Diane hearing me in the conference room would be fatal, giving her all the advantage she needed to kill me.

I was wound tight by the time I brushed against stairs leading to the document storage cavern. Hoping a tread wouldn't squeak and give my position away, I gently went up the stairs. When I got to the top, I waited, searching for Diane. My eyes were getting used to the darkness and I was startled to see an eerie green glow twinkling across the underground cavern of the Paris Archives.

The abandoned limestone cavern lived in muted twilight from fungus growing on damp walls. The fungus glowed the way sea organisms fluoresce in the wake of an ocean liner. At night, cruise ships leave a trail of softly glowing water and the same thing was happening in the Archives. Glowing fungus ran along rotted cartons, drawing a green twinkling spider web where tall rows of bookcases formed glistening canyons.

I started walking on a quilt of twinkling lines and became disoriented by the flickering. It was very hard to keep my bearings with the eerie glow moving back and forth like weak strobe lights pulsing. I was afraid of bumping a shelf and knocking something off since the clatter would show Diane exactly where I was. My cautious, stealthy walk along an aisle took forever. Finally, I stopped at the center corridor leading out of the Archives and listened for Diane. I hoped to hear a telltale sound, like her shoe scraping in a missed step.

I didn't hear the whispered glide of Diane's shoes. Instead, my heart jumped as I heard a loud scream echo across the cavern. Taylor Hansen begged for mercy. Hansen stuttered in half words, pleading for his life. I could make out Hansen saying, "No, Diane. No, you don't have to. Don't hurt. I'll give you the diary. Please, Diane."

Then I heard soft popping, like a lightbulb breaking and Hansen screamed in agony. There was another pop and Taylor couldn't scream. He moaned a low wail, like a dog hit by a car. Diane was torturing Hansen, firing silenced bullets into his knees, crushing his joints. It was exactly what Diane would do to me.

I planted a foot to run, not caring where I was going, as long as I was running away from Diane. I scrambled along the center aisle and bumped into tall shelving. A box slid off, falling on the floor in a clatter of books. Startled by the noise, I ran faster, panting to catch my breath. In front of me, there was nothing but green twinkling spider webs hung on velvet blackness, a disorienting landscape with no landmarks to help me find my way out of the maze of shelves. I kept running anyway and my footsteps echoed in the cavern. My feet slapped the rock floor as I ran, getting more tired with each step.

Finally I was out of breath and I bent over, trying to get some wind in my lungs. I realized I was an easy target standing there in the dark. The noise I made would lead Diane straight to me. I started to move again, but didn't make it. When I bent forward, a hand clamped tightly on my face, pulling me back. I struggled against the grip, my heart racing as I punched and kicked in an attempt to get free.

Paul Denis whispered, "Nicki, calm down. It's all right." His hand was on my mouth to keep me quiet and he kept it there until I calmed down.

I asked in a low, hushed voice, "Where have you been?"

"Working my way to you. I thought Hansen was right behind me. He must have stayed in Diane's office, the damned fool."

"How'd Diane find Hansen in the dark?"

"Diane's wearing night vision goggles." Paul waved his hands at the dull glow twinkling on walls and bookshelves. "For her, this place looks like daylight and it's no accident. I'm sure Vernier got the equipment for her."

I sighed in disgust. "She has everything money can buy and we don't even have a gun."

Paul suggested, "Let's get out of here before Diane finishes torturing Hansen. I have a good sense of direction. I think I can find that spiral staircase going to the lobby. We can leave that way." He turned to go.

I stopped him. "I don't think we can use that stairway anymore."

"Why not?"

"I heard Diane doing something to the staircase. I'm afraid she set some sort of trap. Diane knows you and I are here, not just Hansen. I think she's baiting us with Hansen screaming. Diane knows we'll try to escape and run into her booby trap."

"Damn. There has to be some other way out of this cavern, another exit from the Archives."

I shrugged. "I don't know how to find the other exits, but it doesn't matter. They won't do us any good."

"What do you mean they won't do us any good?" he asked. Paul jerked his head around to follow a noise in the distance.

"Diane once told me there are several exits from the Archives, old tunnels leading out of the limestone quarry. These old tunnels dump you in catacombs that undermine Paris, miles of sewers and aqueducts linking to underground reservoirs and ancient cellars. Many tunnels are dead ends from caved-in excavations. Most of this underground world was dug six hundred years ago so there's no map or blueprint. Every year, people get lost in the catacombs and die before they're found." I sadly admitted, "We're trapped."

"Not quite," Paul argued. "There's still a way out. Diane certainly won't expect us to go that way."

I realized what he intended to do and it scared the hell out of me. "You're suggesting we try climbing Diane's garden cliff? We'd have to go in the office corridor and break the glass wall."

"Yes. It's our only chance."

"Breaking glass makes a loud noise. Diane's not going to stand around. She'll come and get us. How're you going to avoid her?" I stared at Paul's shape, a dark outline on the fuzzy green glow behind him.

"We can shield ourselves from Diane," Paul suggested. "We wait behind that thick iron door to the office corridor. Eventually, Diane will come out to look for us. We sneak around her and slam the iron door, shutting her out of the office corridor. Her bullets can't shoot through a thick metal door. Am I right?"

"Assuming everything goes according to plan. If not, we're dead."

"Do you have another idea?" Paul asked.

"No," I admitted. It was impossible to think with Hansen moaning in the distance. There was another horrible popping sound and Taylor pleaded, "I told you, Nicki's in the conference room."

"Great," I muttered. Diane knew where I was.

Paul urged, "We've got to go."

"All right. How do we get to the iron door? I'm all turned around in the dark, Paul."

"I have to find my way in buildings with no light. It's my job as a firefighter. I just came through that door and I'll lead you back there. Come on." He started walking away.

I had to follow him or be alone in the darkness. I tracked Paul along rows of shelving, following his body as a shadow on the green glow. It felt like an hour before I saw the iron door's dim shape. I could faintly make out details and saw that rust bubbled everywhere on the metal surface. The leprosy of rust was eating corners off steel plates, chewing holes in panels.

The metal door was a relic, its iron forged before the Statue of Liberty floated into New York Harbor, a gift from France. This antique was supposed to stop Diane St. Remy from shooting me, but it looked like a mouse could poke holes in the rusty metal. However, I had no better plan, so I moved behind the tall steel panel and crouched near Paul.

All I could do was wait and the tension made me aware of each change, however slight. I hung on every sound, listening to a slight rasping in Paul's tight breaths and the soft rippling of water trickling down a far wall in the cavern. Little dribbles and plops of water gave way to a long, tense silence. I rolled forward, trying to be poised and ready.

Then I heard the dull thud of Diane's boot kicking Hansen and Taylor moaned. Diane unloaded on him, emptying bullets into Hansen's limp body. In the quiet, even her distant firing sounded like thunder and I winced with each shot. After a brief silence, I heard the snick of fresh bullets jammed in Diane's gun. My mouth and throat stuck to themselves, gummy as a New York sidewalk in August. I knew Diane was coming for me, her gun fully loaded with a new clip of bullets.

# 20

# Next

I ran through our escape plan, making sure I remembered the steps, rehearsing the moves in my mind. Diane walks past us and we twist our bodies around the door. We pull the iron door shut and clamp it tight. The thick metal stops her bullets and we have time to escape. The trick was getting around Diane before she shot me. It was all timing and luck. I tried to ignore sweat trickling down my armpits and pretend I was confident. Listening for Diane, I struggled to predict her next move, hoping I'd be ready for the moment she came through the door.

I turned and watched Paul nervously rub a sweaty hand on his pants. His other hand clenched our only weapon, a rusty tire iron from his van. Muscles tensed in Paul's face each time Diane slammed a boot down, marching along the hallway. Paul was rocking slightly on the toes of his work boots, poised for the moment Diane would come through the metal door.

For a second, it was quiet and no one moved, no one breathed. We waited behind the old iron door while Diane tapped a pensive finger against her gun. Perhaps Diane was trying to psych us out and get a mental advantage by stalling. The waiting went on for an eternal moment and it seemed nothing was going to happen. A bead of sweat fell from my forehead and I watched the droplet fall to the floor in slow motion. My eyes had just come up level again when Diane sprang through the door. She quickly turned and pointed her gun straight at me.

Diane didn't shoot me right away. Instead she smiled, enjoying her moment of power, feeling unbeatable dressed in protective gear. Diane was wearing a dull gray riot helmet, like the crash helmet motorcyclists wear. Night vision goggles bugged from her eye sockets, letting her see in the dark, a great advantage over us. She was wearing a black nylon uniform, her chest covered by a thick bullet proof vest. The vest rode over a web belt carrying extra bullet clips for her gun.

Diane held an Israeli-made machine pistol, basically a small Uzi designed for carrying in a shoulder holster and favored by Secret

Service details all over the world. Vernier had given Diane the best weapon money could buy, a small gun she could handle yet it could stand up against larger assault rifles. Each high-velocity bullet in a 35 round clip was capable of tearing a lethal hole through body armor and I didn't want to think about what a tumbling bullet would do to my flesh or Paul's. We didn't stand much chance against Diane, but we had to try anyway.

Paul took his best shot and threw the tire iron at Diane, whipping the bar at her head. The steel rod viciously twisted past Diane, barely missing her as she ducked. Diane's gun barrel came up, pointing straight at my stomach and her finger snugged around the trigger. I had no weapon but the heavy iron door and I swung it at Diane with all my strength. The door hit her in the chest and she was knocked backwards, nearly falling. The night vision goggles twisted on Diane's face and she couldn't see properly.

I had a moment of freedom and I used it to get past Diane. I jumped around her and into the office hallway. Paul ran behind me, dragging the door shut and we both slammed home locks securing the door. Drained from tension and exertion, I sank back and tried to catch some breath. I didn't get the first breath before Diane fired bullets into the door. Each shot made the iron bulge like a dented fender, chipping off pieces of steel that scattered around me like hot popcorn, burning me where they touched.

The iron was rusted from more than a hundred years of corrosion, weakening every rivet and plate. Each blast from her gun tore out another chunk. There was very little time before Diane shot her way through. I shouted over bullets ringing against the door, "Paul, break the glass wall so we can get out."

"I can't break the glass," he replied sadly. "I threw my tire iron at Diane. I've got nothing to smash the window."

"Let's break it with a chair. We can get one from Diane's office." I got to my feet and rolled down the hallway, my side aching from lack of breath. The sound of Diane's bullets ringing on the iron door pushed me down the hallway despite my exhaustion.

A bullet went cleanly through the door and ricocheted along the office corridor. The bullet pinged around and hit a framed aerial photograph of Paris. The picture tilted wildly and crashed to the floor, sending jagged shards of glass along the hallway. I jumped to avoid being cut by flying glass.

Losing my balance, I stumbled through Diane's office door, unable to stop. Knowing what was going to happen revolted me, yet there was nothing I could do. I stepped in the remains of Taylor Hansen's mangled body, the mess left after Diane tortured him.

My foot pressed on Taylor's wounded kneecap and the knee joint popped like a water balloon. Cartilage, bone and fluid squirted on the floor. My ankle twisted on the liquidy mess and I fell forward. I threw my foot out to stop my fall and kicked Hansen's leg, swinging the leg to a very unnatural angle. The leg was detached at the hip and the hip joint was smashed to pulp. Diane had run her gun along Taylor's limbs, shooting bullets into every joint and every bone. Arms and legs were mashed flat. Hansen's bloody shirt sleeves looked like deflated balloons.

I winced and jammed a hand against Diane's cabinet to steady myself, my head poised over Taylor's face. His handsome features were contorted in agony. The top of Taylor's head was gone and his brain was spilled on the carpet like a dumped bowl of Jell-O, a gray jiggly mass. It was quite a shock to see Hansen's mind lying on the carpet in a pool of fluid and blood. I realized this was how I would look if Diane caught me. I had to get out of the Archives. I forced myself to turn away from Hansen's corpse.

My eyes hit Paul Denis coming in the room. I saw Paul recoil from looking at Taylor Hansen. I said, "Get a chair. Break the glass. We've got to get away from Diane."

"Sure," Paul Denis replied in a sick voice. His eyes stayed on Hansen's shattered body, running over the bloody mess, too shocked to turn away. Paul's gaze stayed riveted on Taylor's shredded remains as his hands reached for a chair. Paul tumbled into the office corridor, dragging a heavy conference chair with him. He was going to throw the chair through the plate glass in the hallway, letting us escape. It was a race against Diane cutting her way through the antique metal door with a submachine gun.

I heard Diane heave against the iron door and it groaned loudly but didn't give. She backed away and fired bursts from her gun. Her bullets chipped off hunks of plating and the broken plating slammed on the hallway floor with a ringing sound. I knew there wasn't much door left to hold Diane back.

I had to get out of there and I couldn't worry about how I treated Hansen's corpse. I wobbled and slid through the mess, my shoes coated in a thick goo of flesh and bone chips. I was horrified by goo slipping through the open toes of my high heeled shoes and sticking between my toes. Sliding out of Diane's office, I tried to ignore the hideous mess on my feet. Taylor's bone gristle and his soft, bloody flesh were caught between my toes, squishing inside my shoes as I walked.

I left a trail of bloody footprints behind me until I stopped near Paul Denis. He picked up the heavy conference chair and smashed it against the glass wall. With a surprisingly quiet pop, the glass sheet exploded in a spray of chips. The entire sheet of thick, tempered glass disappeared and cold morning air shocked my face. One moment I was in an overheated hallway and the next second I felt all the cold of early morning rushing at me. I recovered from my surprise and stepped through the open window frame, ignoring how cold I felt in the chilly garden.

When I tried walking on the garden paving stones, there was absolutely no traction. The tempered glass shattered into little balls that skated freely under my shoes. It was like walking on a treadmill and I couldn't get anywhere despite all my efforts. Paul's work boots had a better grip and he pulled me across the paving stones like I was water skiing.

In a few steps, we hit the garden's steep outer wall and came to an abrupt stop. The garden ended in a sheer cliff, thirty feet straight up. It was made of moss-covered stones that were dripping water. The wet rocks looked slick as ice. I watched Paul make repeated attempts to climb, but he couldn't get anywhere. All he got for his efforts were ripped Levi's and skin torn from his knees. Slippery and wet, the vertical cliff was impossible to climb.

He slapped at the wall in frustration. "There must be a way out," Paul insisted. "Where's the fire escape? There has to be a folding ladder. It's required by the building codes."

I couldn't see any fire escape ladder, building codes or not. I gave up looking for a ladder and kicked off my shoes. They were useless anyhow. I asked Paul, "Can you give me a lift up? Maybe I can find a handhold on the wall."

"Go," he said, bending over and cupping his hands. I stepped in his hands like a stirrup for mounting a horse and he pushed my feet upward, almost to his chest.

I grabbed the wall for balance, pulling on a stag fern and the plant came out of the rocks in a shower of dirt and moss. Sputtering dirt from my mouth, I tried again. I snagged my fingers in a small cleft, grunted and pulled myself upward. The rock crumbled and I fell, tumbling backward on the paving stones. Paul broke my fall and pulled me to my feet.

"Try standing on my shoulders," he suggested. "You can reach higher. It's worth a try."

"Sure," I said. I flunked gymnastics in high school and this move really scared me. I put a foot in his hands and stepped up. After I got high enough, I stuck both feet on his shoulders. I teetered badly, about to fall and Paul grabbed my legs, steadying me. I desperately pulled at anything and everything on the cliff and all I did was knock junk down on Paul. My ankles were painfully tired from the wobbly foothold on his shoulders. "I've got to get down or fall. I can't grab anything up here."

"OK," he grunted.

I tumbled off, thumping hard on my butt. Looking at the old iron door, I was shocked to see Diane's gun poking through. All she had to do was pull the trigger and bullets would fly right at us. I hurried to my feet and dragged Paul with me, racing inside a niche of the garden wall.

We barely got out of the way before Diane sent bullets flying in our direction. Bullets hit the cliff wall and rock sprayed violently across the paving stones. Diane fired again and sharp pieces of rock hit my feet and legs, cutting me. I cursed and hugged the side wall even tighter. Finally, Diane's gun clicked blankly on an empty clip. She was temporarily out of bullets.

"We have to get out of here. Quickly, before Diane reloads," Paul urged. "Is there any other exit?"

"Diane's office is a dead end. There's no exit in there. We've got to go up that cliff."

I didn't stand much chance of climbing the wall but maybe Paul had a better grip. I suggested, "I'll boost you up. You try the wall." I couldn't begin to hold his weight on my shoulders. I knelt down and let Paul step on my back.

His work boots dug into my exhausted muscles. Then he got on his toes and stretched to go higher, concentrating all his weight on the sharp toes of his boots, pinching my flesh. I heard Paul frantically claw at the rock face, scraping with his fingers to get a grip. Ferns, leaves and dirt rained on me, running down my neck and under my dress, sticking to my damp skin. My knees and hands burned from the pressure of having Paul on my back. Sharp glass chips were scattered on the paving stones, the chips cutting into my bare hands.

For all the discomfort, I was upset when Paul quit trying and jumped off my back. I exhaled a grunt and slowly stood up, scraping rock chips and bits of broken glass from my knees. I panted from exertion, my breath fogging in the icy morning air.

"Only thirty lousy feet from safety," Paul said. He was disgusted.

"It's thirty feet straight up. There's no handholds and the moldy rock is like slimy grease. We can't get any traction." My torn, bleeding hands were covered in a black slime that wouldn't wipe away and my feet were covered in the same black muck. I searched the cliff for a section that wasn't coated in greasy slime and found none despite the brighter light of early day.

The blue shadows of morning had faded and sunlight filtered along the cliff, leaking down to us. Daylight was shining in the alley behind the Archives and I heard faint sounds of a normal day above. A bicycle bell tinkled along the alley and vanished, leaving a moment of silence. I didn't think yelling would do any good, but I had to try.

"Help," I screamed. "We're trapped down here. We need help right away. Please, somebody, help us."

Paul shouted with me in loud bellows. After a moment, we quit yelling and listened, desperately hoping for some response but it was painfully quiet. Then there was some ragged noise in the alley that sounded like the stack of plastic cafe tables were unchained and dragged inside the sandwich shop. It was infuriating to be so close to safety, listening to the sounds of a normal life. In contrast, I stood in an area littered with dented bullets, mute witnesses to the fear I felt. I wasn't alone in my anxiety. I looked at Paul Denis standing nearby.

Paul was clenching his fingers, showing his own tension and fear. His denim shirt was torn, shredded by attempts to climb the rock wall. His hair was littered with torn plant leaves and beard stubble glistening on his dirty cheeks. Every muscle in his face was tight, giving him an angry expression. There was a loud noise and Paul's eyes jumped to the bullet riddled iron door that kept us safe.

Diane's gun rattled like a jackhammer against the rusted door, sawing away metal plates. She peeled off hunks of iron throwing them down with ringing clangs. Then Diane threw her weight against the steel door and it groaned. There was a snap and the dented metal plates swung open.

I saw her leg move cautiously through the open doorway. Her dark shape squeezed along the hallway, clinging to shadows, sliding like a ghost. I could smell Diane's cologne overriding musky garden scents and the pungent ash smell of fired bullets. In seconds she would be close enough to shoot me. I searched for a weapon, a rock, anything. Paul used a chair to break the glass wall of the garden but it was too far away. Diane would kill me long before I touched the chair. I looked around and there was nowhere to run, no weapon and no protection.

# 21

# Complications

Diane St. Remy stepped over the empty window frame and into the garden, her boots crunching on broken glass scattered across the stone floor. She moved slowly toward me, feeding on the scene, enjoying her moment of power. She gloated, a lewd smile forming on her lips. Diane took off her night vision goggles, letting them dangle around her throat like some weird tribal necklace. Her eyes were wide and glowing on her pale narrow face. Diane stopped a few feet from me, close enough to invite a foolish rush at her. She held the submachine gun almost carelessly at her waist with the thick, silenced barrel pointed at my belly.

I bent down cautiously, picking up the diary and the arsonist's target list from a small stone bench in the garden. "Is this what you came for?" I asked her. I bought some time, stalling by holding out the diary and the computer listing.

Diane didn't answer my question. Instead, she laughed. Giddy on her power trip, Diane's laughing sounded like a bird chirping in hollow, high-pitched notes. "Very thoughtful of you. Now I don't have to search the conference room for the diary. I see you also printed the arsonist's target list for me. Or did you think the list was yours, Nicki?"

I ignored Diane's sarcastic attitude, knowing I couldn't win by tying into her arrogance. Instead, I tossed the diary softly toward her so it landed flat. I followed by throwing the printout toward Diane and the sheets fluttered to the ground, spreading around the blue leather diary. "You've got what you want. We'll leave, get out of your way." I didn't risk a step toward her, knowing she was looking for the slightest reason to shoot me. I just shrugged toward the hallway, indicating I wanted to go.

Diane's reply was sliding the bolt on her submachine gun, arming it. "You're not going anywhere, Nicki. You're going to die with your boyfriend here, the firefighter. Or was Hansen your lover? Sometimes I get confused." She said it coyly, toying with me. Diane was never confused about anything.

I ignored her provocations, knowing Diane was looking for an excuse to shoot me. Reasoning with her wouldn't work, but it might keep me alive for a few more seconds. "You've got the evidence and all you need to search for the treasure. There's no reason to kill us. It just complicates things."

"Complicates things?" Diane smirked. "No, killing you simplifies everything."

I offered, "No one can prove you stabbed a maid in the Regis and I'll say you shot Hansen in self-defense. Paul and I can be on your side, witnesses to your innocence."

"No," was Diane's simple reply.

I kept stalling. "We don't have to be enemies, Diane. I appreciate how much you want the treasure."

"Do you?" Diane sneered. "I doubt it. I've spent fifteen years working underground in these Archives. You don't know what it's like working for nothing in a pit. People send old paper to rot in the Archives like they send old relatives into the hospital to die. Everyone in Paris depends on my Archives and none of you gives a damn about me."

"Let me try," I offered. "Tell me where I'm wrong." I left a silence for Diane to talk, hoping to drag everything out, delay the inevitable.

She didn't say a word. Instead, her face hardened and her gray eyes clouded into a mask.

I quickly said, "Diane, I understand your hatred of Taylor Hansen. He used women like you and me, then dumped them. Taylor was cutting you out of the deal, trying to get the treasure on his own. It wasn't fair. You found the diary and translated it, Diane." I wanted to soothe her and buy us more time. I was trying to show I understood her point of view. "You put the deal together, a search for the lost fortune. You did the research to find the old furniture. You did all the work and you deserve the payoff."

"You're right about that." Diane was cold and haughty. "There's no one else in the world that can do my job."

"Sure," Paul confirmed. "You're unique. But you can't do it alone. You need help." He shifted his weight in a subtle way, putting a foot slightly behind him.

I could see Paul was getting ready for a try at Diane when we ran out of talk and I didn't think rushing Diane would work. We'd both die. I wanted to keep the conversation going but I needed a new topic. I asked Diane, "I assume you're the arsonist. How'd you learn to make fires so hot?"

"I didn't," Diane answered in a tight, controlled voice. "I don't have time to run around Paris and set fires. Someone else does those errands. They burn a warehouse for me, check out an apartment building and get rid of the evidence."

"You're not the arsonist," Paul said in astonishment.

I was skeptical. Diane was callous enough to be the arsonist, torturing people to find what happened to the old furniture. I saw how Diane inflicted pain on Taylor Hansen, forcing the last bit of information from Hansen before she killed him. I studied Diane intently, wondering if she was telling me the truth.

"Curious even when you're going to die, hmm? You want all the details," Diane taunted me. Behind her, a timer clicked and drip irrigation plinked little droplets on garden plants. There was a gentle hissing of a sprinkler misting a fern, but she didn't react to the sounds, keeping herself focused on Paul and me.

"You've got nothing to lose by telling us more," I said, hoping for a longer conversation. I certainly had nothing to lose by listening to her story. I knew what happened after we stopped talking. I'd look like Taylor Hansen and know his pain. The idea of being tortured made me so alert I saw every color in the garden like it was wet artist's paint, freshly squeezed from a tube. Every faint sound came to me like a whispered scream.

I was surprised to hear a car slide into the alley behind me, sounding like someone parking. The engine died and a door clicked open.

Maybe I'd get lucky and the driver would look down the cliff, see us in the garden, and wonder why we were being held at gunpoint. I stalled again, hoping something would break. I tried flattering Diane. "So you only do the hard stuff, like research?"

"Research," Diane laughed. "I did the whole plan. I laid it out like chess and Hansen wrecked things by dragging you into this game. Now I'm cleaning up." She pointed the gun at my legs. My kneecaps were going to be jellied mush like Taylor Hansen.

"I know you're going to kill me, Diane." I talked calmly, but I was scared. "Don't you want the satisfaction of telling me how you did the crimes? You'll never be able to share your plan with anyone else. The only person you can tell is me. I'm going to die. I won't be able to testify against you." I stopped. I'd run out of ideas and my mouth was too dry from fear to talk anymore.

Paul Denis picked up where I left off. "Diane, how'd you ever find that old diary?" He said it with amazing calm, but I saw his hand run nervously along the seam of his pants. His tongue licked dry lips after he finished speaking.

"Fate sent the diary to me." Diane was smug.

"Which fate?" I pressed her. It was nice to know some of my old, spunky self was left, even staring at death. I listened to soft footsteps in the alley behind me. I didn't think Diane heard the sound because her thick riot helmet blocked soft noises. I stalled, asking her, "Go on. What's the story behind the diary?"

Diane talked and her eyes held a cold fixation. "A French Resistance fighter swept through the ruins of a Paris hotel bombed at the end of World War II. He had only minutes before German troops arrived to guard the hotel. He searched dead Nazis and office desks, looking for valuable papers. Most of what he found was thrown in a box and forgotten, never looked at again because a few days later, the Germans fled Paris. They left to escape capture by American soldiers sweeping across France, winning the war. The war was basically over and Nazi papers didn't matter anymore. The cardboard box holding the diary sat in a closet for decades. Finally, the French Resistance fighter died and his concierge sent the box to me, thinking it might hold some valuable papers." Diane laughed. "Well, the concierge was right. The Resistance fighter died penniless in a rooming house. But he had a diary worth billions."

I flattered Diane to keep her going. "That's an amazing story. You're very clever to figure it all out." I heard a slight noise above me and felt dirt spray on my neck. Someone was walking on the cliff behind me and when they kicked dirt over the edge, I felt fine grit dribble down my back.

I talked in a louder voice, hoping to attract attention. "The concierge sent the box to the Archives. You looked inside and found the diary. Then, you went to City Commissioner Vernier. You wanted Vernier's help, his connections for financing a search, right?"

Diane didn't answer. She was becoming suspicious and her eyes swept cautiously around the area. The alcove had been a little jewel, a model of a Japanese bonsai garden with miniature trees, polished black stones, swirls of exactly raked gravel flowing through clusters of rare plants. Before tonight the garden was immaculate, every leaf groomed, every fallen petal swept away. Now the place was wrecked, the floor covered in glass shards and rock chips mixed with crushed plants. Ferns torn out of the cliff were layered in messy clumps, withering in the warm morning sun.

The wrecked garden was another reminder how my presence warped Diane's precise world. Everything I did bent her perfect plans and Diane was furious at being thwarted. She pointed the gun at me with an even greater desire to kill me and her finger snugged over the trigger. There wasn't going to be any more conversation. But suddenly Diane lost interest in me.

Something hit the guard railing atop the cliff and there was a metallic clink. Diane's eyes flew upward and she winced, blinded by glaring sun. Diane moved to get a better look and instantly her gun pointed away from me. The submachine gun pivoted toward the cliff, but the gun never finished swinging up.

I heard a shot. The loud gunshot was very brief, nothing like gunshots in movies, just the snap of a firecracker. The crack of the gun was followed with a hollow plop, a kind of thud and everything seemed to happen in slow motion. A chunk of riot helmet was blown off Diane's head. Flesh and hair were matted into a bloody golf ball that skipped crazily across paving stones in the garden, driven by the force of the bullet. My eyes went back to Diane and I stared at a large hole in her forehead.

Diane fell like a cut tree, in a stiff arc, her body completely rigid. She clattered to the ground, slapping against a flat paving stone and lay there motionless. I thought the shooting was over but I was wrong. The gun banged again and Diane's head bounced, a second hole appearing on her temple. Blood gushed from her temple in spurts, a bizarre red fountain. After a moment, blood quit spurting, ran limply down her face and finally stopped.

I should have felt relief at Diane's death but I didn't. The second precise shot was the signature of a professional killer, a paid assassin. The man above me was sent by Vernier to eliminate Diane and now he was pointing his gun at me. I glanced at Paul and saw a depressed look on his face. He'd come to the same conclusion I had, that we weren't being rescued.

I craned my neck and looked up the garden's mossy cliff. There was a large caliber pistol pointed at me and even from a distance the gun looked like a cannon. The pistol was cradled in a pair of familiar hands. I was staring into a gun held by my Interpol partner, Pierre Corday. My partner had been hired by the City Commissioner to kill Diane St. Remy.

Once again, there were unforeseen complications in Vernier's plans. I was sure the City Commissioner told Corday to wait until after we were dead to kill Diane St. Remy. The story was then very simple. Pierre Corday got there too late to save us. In self defense, he shot Diane. At the press conference, Corday killed Diane St. Remy in the line of duty, case closed, wrapped up tight. But Vernier wasn't in charge now. It was Corday who was planning the moves. First Hansen changed the game by going after the fortune on his own and now Corday was acting as a wildcard, shooting Diane but leaving me alive.

He'd overheard my conversation with Diane about a lost fortune and now Corday was after the treasure himself. I knew Pierre was always calculating what was in a situation for him. Greed was tugging violently on that side of his personality and I had no choice but to follow his directions. Corday's voice was colder than the body of

Diane St. Remy when he said, "Climb up here. Bring the diary and those papers."

He kicked a chain link ladder under the metal railing and I realized this was the missing fire escape ladder. Diane pulled the chain ladder up before she went inside the Archives. She didn't want anyone using that fire ladder to escape. The collapsible chain ladder slapped against the stone wall, unfolding downward with a loud clattering.

I looked up at him and saw that Corday was a mess. He hadn't shaved in days and his normally oily skin had a greasy sheen. His much laundered dress shirt was missing a button, stained with food and wrinkled like he'd slept in it. Bloodshot eyes confirmed he'd been drinking cheap tap beer at his neighborhood bar and I knew from experience that left him in a terrible mood, with a fragility where everything was perceived as an insult, an excuse for violence.

I reluctantly put a foot on the wobbly ladder and pushed my tired body upward, wrapping my arms around the chains. Climbing was an ugly, painful job. It was painful as the bitter truth about my situation. I wasn't Corday's partner, his buddy. I was his prisoner.

# 22

# The Arsonist's List

**My** prospects for a long healthy life didn't improve after I climbed a wobbly chain ladder out of the Paris Archives and sat in the passenger seat of Pierre Corday's car. There was no reason for Pierre to keep me alive once we found the lost fortune. At that point, I was just a liability, someone who knew too much and could make a lot of trouble, even if I wanted no share of the valuables.

"Where's this treasure?" Corday demanded. He was in a foul mood.

"Give me a moment. I haven't found page one yet." I was trying to put the arsonist's target list in order, shuffling pages in my hands and it didn't help to have Pierre's gun jabbed in my ribs. I had difficulty getting my fingers to act normally with the barrel of his gun poking my spine.

I found the first page of the arsonist's target list from the stack of papers in my hands. My eyes skipped over the initial entries on the list, the torched warehouse and the destroyed apartment building. I glanced at the next entry and relaxed a bit. I'd finally gotten a break for the first time in a long horrible night. I pointed at the third line and said, "We should try this place."

Paul Denis nodded. "Yes, surely. That one is best." He appreciated my choice since the address was a long drive out of Paris, buying us time to live. A quick smile flitted across Paul's face.

Paul Denis still had life twinkling in his tired face despite little pouches saddling his exhausted eyes. His sun baked forehead was lined with creases, as though he'd aged ten years in a night. Exhausted, Paul was seated behind the wheel of Pierre's Citroen sedan, sagging against the worn upholstery of the bucket seat. Like me, Paul was Corday's prisoner.

Corday grabbed the sheets of paper from my hand and scanned the list. He looked at me suspiciously. "Why'd you pick that address, huh? There are more than a hundred sites on this list."

"The first two places were searched already so I picked the third entry. This is the next target Diane intended to hit. She thought this place was most likely to have the treasure and Diane knew a lot more than we do." I sighed, trying to summon my vanishing patience.

Corday snapped at me. "It's such a good spot, huh. So why didn't Diane go there already?"

I jabbed back at him sarcastically. It was the only way to keep Pierre in line. "Diane couldn't go there. You killed her, remember? She isn't going anywhere with two bullets in her brain."

"I can put bullets in your head also," Pierre warned me. I didn't need another reminder. I had his gun jabbing my kidney.

"This place is a logical choice." Paul Denis tried to calm Pierre.

Corday snorted and rolled his eyes in disgust. "Logical choice or not, it doesn't matter. We aren't going there. We can't drive out of Paris. Vernier sealed the city. He's got riot police covering every highway. On my way to the Archives, I saw police watching every major boulevard."

"I can get us out." Paul Denis talked in a soothing voice. "I'm a fire captain, yes?"

Corday responded angrily. "It doesn't matter you're a fire captain. I have the gun. You aren't so damned smart. Are you, my big dick fire captain?"

"It's true you have the gun." Paul agreed patiently and then returned to the real issue, how to get out of Paris. "Vernier sealed major boulevards and highways. He won't know about the other ways to exit

Paris. I can find a way around the road blocks. I've memorized every little street. A fire captain must get around the worst of Paris traffic, even at rush hour. I know alleys that wind through ancient parts of the city and lead to the outskirts of Paris. Trust me."

"It's your life," Corday warned. "Don't screw up." Pierre let the cold metal of his gun barrel rest against Paul's neck.

"I know," Paul said calmly. Then he waited and I held my breath. Corday finally pulled the gun off Paul's neck.

Paul Denis put the car in gear and the old Citroen sedan bumped off a curb, rumbling slowly along the alley's paving stones. Relieved, I took a deep breath and regretted it. The smells in Pierre's car were so gross I wanted to gag. Fast food wrappers littered the back seat, their secret sauce rotted from hot sun. Pierre's car was a mess with little bent straws stuck in every slit. His kids left the straws after draining a carton of fruit juice. Two empty glass bottles of Orangina were rolling under my feet and metal lids for the bottles were scattered on the gummy floor mat.

Even trapped in that messy car, I was glad to leave the Paris Archives behind, but my relief was temporary. Corday's patience lasted only to the corner and he started nagging me again.

Pierre snapped, "I don't buy it. This place you're taking me is near the Swiss border. Switzerland is too far away. That Nazi Hess stored his treasure in a Paris hotel. Your idea doesn't make sense." Pierre Corday was getting on my nerves like he always did. Starting an argument with me was his morning cup of coffee, his way of waking himself up.

I twisted in my seat to look Pierre in the eye. My dress clung to the sticky seat, pulling on me. I held the target list in front of Corday and ran a finger along the entries. "See," I said firmly, "the first three addresses are the best targets. The rest of the list is in alphabetical order. The arsonist hit #1 and #2 on the list and didn't find anything. We're going to #3. Doesn't that make sense? Besides, Hess originally planned on escaping with his treasure to Switzerland. Maybe most of the fortune was moved to this house on Lake Geneva, near the Swiss border. It could have been done before Hess had to flee Paris."

Corday's face tightened at being confronted, yet he couldn't deny my logic. Pierre sagged against the rear seat, looking sullen. His eyes were rummy with the same exhaustion we all felt, but Corday's eyes held a vicious edge. He wiped greasy hair back and muttered sarcastically. "Fine choice. You're a genius."

"Diane's the genius," I corrected him. "She was a ranked master at chess, Pierre."

"OK, you're both geniuses," Corday snorted. Greed brought out a side of Pierre I'd never seen before, a mean streak that made him dangerous. He sat coiled in the back seat, wound tight and radiating hostility.

"I'm no genius," I said, hoping to lessen Corday's antagonism. "I'm only reading Diane's notes. She did the work. And paid for it." I flashed on the hole in Diane's head and a chunk of her skull slapping the ground after Corday shot her.

"She had it coming," Corday said coldly.

"Sure," Paul Denis agreed, trying to soothe Corday. "No one cried over Diane St. Remy. This Diane helped kill my buddies. I don't care about her. Nicki wasn't complaining, were you?"

"No," I said quietly, "I wasn't complaining about your shooting Diane." I couldn't look at Corday anymore, so I turned around to sit normally in my seat, facing forward. I was too drained to think. Nothing seemed real to me as I sat there and looked out the windshield.

Paul cranked the steering wheel and the hydraulic suspension of the Citroen glided silkily around a hairpin turn. He slid the full-size car in a tiny alley and it was a very tight fit for the sedan. On Paul's side, the car brushed past metal garbage cans. The scraping of cans against the car grated on my tired nerves.

I looked out my window and tires on my side were thumping over a stone step outside a back door. The ancient stone was worn smooth from five hundred years of footsteps. Rainwater had trickled off the roof for centuries, carving a ditch in the stone. The stone had all those years but I had only hours left. I was certain Corday would shoot me when we found the treasure. With a sharp pang, I felt how much I wanted to do before I died. I tried not to think about the pain and focused on the alley.

The next turn brought harsh glare flashing on the windshield. Sunlight danced on the glass, bruising my exhausted eyes. The sunlight flew away and my vision recovered. I saw brightly colored laundry hung on lines across the alley, shirts and underwear snapping like flags in the wind.

In the next alley, we stumbled on a group of kids playing street hockey and I envied their freedom. They raced along on Rollerblades, yelling and elbowing each other. Their heavily bandaged hockey sticks were slapping at a pink foam ball instead of a hockey puck. Discarded cardboard boxes served as goal nets and the score was written in chalk on a brick wall. The kids saw the car and scampered in doorways to let the Citroen pass.

Beyond the street hockey game, an arch bridged across the alley. The connecting arch was actually a room in someone's townhouse. The arch was ancient half-timbered construction with exposed hand-cut beams. A pair of diamond pane windows let sunlight into the center of the arch. The windows were ornamented by flower boxes with a jumble of red carnations. Delicate lace window curtains were open, revealing an antique headboard of golden brass and white porcelain. Blue pillows were propped on the headboard, an invitation to lie down and relax. The room was a wonderful place to curl up with hot cocoa and read. I looked at the cozy room and felt pain that my life was stolen.

I'd dreamed of exploring this area yet never had time. Now I was seeing the neighborhood under the worst of circumstances. I couldn't reconcile idyllic scenes with stepping in Hansen's mutilated corpse and watching Diane's head explode. I fought to detach myself from those ugly experiences and I grew numb, exhausted.

My eyes squeezed closed and my neck fell against the head rest. The car bounced sharply and my eyes snapped open, then slowly drew closed again. I worried I'd embarrass myself by snoring and laughed at the idea. Snoring was the least of my problems. I'd only close my eyes for a few seconds, get a little rest. The nap would help me face a bleak future.

I heard Paul Denis talking with Pierre Corday and fought to wake up. I realized I'd been asleep for several hours. My eyelids were like a heavy shop curtain I had to crank upward and my neck was lumpy with sore muscles. I put a hand on my neck, massaging a library of kinks. It was close to noon and the car was hot, baked in sunlight, making Corday's messy car smell even worse. I pushed my stiff body upright and looked out the windshield.

Road was peeling under the car like a gray ribbon. The tires sprayed pebbles against the fenders in a loud rattling sound. We were rumbling along a gravel side road, kicking up a tail of dust. White powder coated the side windows, making the outside world look gray. I turned away and looked at Paul Denis. Soft fuzz shadowed his cheeks like a peach with bald spots. Paul could never grow a beard. "Where are we?" I asked him.

"About thirty miles outside Paris. I've been using service roads to avoid police road blocks. Driving back roads takes longer than highways, so we're still many hours from Lake Geneva. How're you feeling?" Paul asked.

"Lousy," was my candid reply.

Paul smiled and offered me a bottle of water. "We stopped for gas and got something to eat off racks in the station. You didn't even wake up."

I took a long sip from the water bottle. "Thanks," I said. "You got any food?"

"Some." Paul tossed a sealed packet of granola on my lap.

I stared at the health food in amazement. "Um, Paul, you get anything else at the station? Like a candy bar, maybe."

"Bag of nuts," he answered. "But they're gone. I ate them all. Nuts give you a lot of energy. It's how I keep driving. Try that granola. It's got seeds in it."

"Yeah, sure," I replied, hiding my true feelings about nuts and their cousins, yogurt and tofu. I stared at the granola, balancing my growling stomach against eating dry, unsweetened cereal. Starvation won over my basic dislike of health foods. Grabbing the plastic granola pouch, I tried to rip it open. I thought my hands would tear before the plastic did. I finally worked a small hole in the pouch and dumped granola in my palm.

Cramming dry cereal in my mouth, I pretended I was eating a candy bar without chocolate and caramel. My pretense didn't work. The wad of nuts and grain was so dry I couldn't swallow. I washed the lump down with water and put the granola away. I'd had enough health for a while.

I stared out the windshield at scenery rolling by the sloping hood of the Citroen. Fields of mustard plants spread across low hills. A light wind rippled the yellow mustard flowers, brushing waves over a sea of lush green bushes. Overhead, clouds bumped against each other, surfing an intense blue sky you never see through the haze of a big city like Paris or New York.

I envied the cotton puff clouds, going wherever the wind took them. I was only going straight toward the end of my luck. Each mile of road disappearing under the car brought more anxiety. I tried to be calm and pretend I had a chance. I wanted to look at all the possibilities, be prepared for anything. It was silly. Nothing could prepare me for what really happened at Lake Geneva.

# 23

# Diane's Notes

We were driving the shoreline of Lake Geneva and out on the water a large excursion boat glided lazily on the calm lake. The slow yacht was surrounded by zigzagging sailboats, looking like white moths chasing colorful party lights strung along the excursion boat's decks. A setting sun glinted on the lake's blue waters, but the tranquility and natural beauty of the lake were lost on me. My eyes flitted off the water and I picked anxiously at loose threads on my torn and sweaty dress. I felt miserable and I had a killer neck ache from the car seat. I needed aspirin and a hot bath, but I wasn't going to get them while Pierre Corday was poking his gun in my back.

The only thing keeping me alive was Corday's greed, his desperation for the lost treasure allegedly worth billions of dollars. It was supposed to be in an old villa on Lake Geneva, according to Diane St. Remy's notes. Her list gave a street address but no description of the place. We were having a hard time finding it despite slowly cruising the lake's shoreline.

Corday stared at every mansion's private gate, trying to read the street number off small, almost hidden signs. Twice we drove past the address somehow, turned around and tried again, perplexed at how we'd missed the place. Then we came to a neglected driveway, a stub of road clogged by overgrown hedges. This little orphaned road only remotely looked like the entrance to an estate, yet it was sandwiched between street numbers bracketing the villa's address.

Pierre wagged his gun, pointing at the gravel lane branching off the highway. Corday demanded, "Pull over there."

Paul Denis was driving Corday's old Citroen sedan. Paul rotated the steering wheel and the car tires gave up their low singing on smooth highway pavement. The Citroen rumbled over gravel, kicking up a cloud of fine dust. We came to a stop and waited while the cloud billowed over the hood of the car, leaving a coat of gray powder on the windshield.

"Run the wipers," Corday ordered Paul Denis.

Paul flicked a switch and water squirted on the windshield. The rubber wipers snapped free and squeaked across the glass, smearing wet dust.

It was difficult to see through the windshield and Corday tugged on my headrest, levering himself up for a better look. Pierre's tug yanked my stiff neck backwards and it really hurt.

"Ow," I complained, rubbing my neck.

"Be quiet," Corday snapped. He was in a lovely mood and we hadn't found any treasure yet. Pierre barked, "Don't just sit there. Look for a street address."

I strained forward, squinting for a mailbox to confirm the street number. It was useless. Any signs were swallowed by the thick brush curled around a derelict fence leaning into the driveway. I gave Paul a questioning glance, hoping he didn't see anything.

Paul Denis gave me a sympathetic look and the pit of my stomach tightened. Paul shrugged his eyebrows, flicking his gaze upward and looking at a vine arching over the country lane. A twisted web of green leaves on thick runners formed a canopy over the driveway.

I realized the vine wove through an iron arch. There was a name scripted on the arch, formed by metal rods bent in the shape of handwritten letters. The vine meshed through the letters, making it difficult to read the name. A few seconds passed before I made out "Villa Toth." This was the place mentioned in Diane St. Remy's notes and I whispered a quiet damn. I was out of time.

"This is it," Corday hissed excitedly. "Drive," he ordered.

"Are you sure?" Paul Denis stalled. "I mean, this doesn't look right."

Corday jabbed the gun barrel against the back of Paul's head. "Drive," Corday snarled. He cocked the pistol menacingly.

"OK, I'm driving," Paul replied. He put the Citroen in gear and eased the car forward. The gravel lane vanished and we were on a narrow track of wet earth, rutted in a lumpy mess. Even the Citroen's smooth hydraulic suspension was challenged by deep holes in the driveway pavement. I bobbed like a toy in a bathtub, floating up and down with every dip in the asphalt.

No one had tended this access road in years and the bushes were growing wild, meshing with each other, nearly closing the road. Bramble grew in the trees, coiling overhead like intertwined fingers. The thick nest of branches formed a roof, blotting out the sky, making riding under the bramble like being in a tunnel. It was dark enough that Paul turned on the car's headlights, but even high beams didn't do much good. The headlights lit only a short piece of road choked with brush before dense bushes swallowed the light, leaving the car in a black tunnel. Out of the dark, a clutching tree limb shot at me and I gasped, startled. The limb snapped against my window and screeched along the car's body.

Paul turned to follow a sharp bend in the road and the car's headlights slid across the rough wooden planks of an antique bridge. We rolled over the arching bridge, car tires rumbling on loose boards. A heavy Spring runoff rushed loudly under us and even through closed windows, I was almost deafened by the creek's loud roar. No one could hear a gunshot over that noise, a cascade of sound like the drumming of a waterfall. This would certainly be a great place for Corday to put a bullet in me. That thought brought me wide awake despite hours trapped in a car seat and I watched the road intently.

We drove for a few minutes, tires crunching over dead branches and loose rocks in the road before the dense vegetation finally thinned. For a moment, I glimpsed lake water shining in late afternoon sunlight. The car rolled into a large pasture covered in waist high grass. Pungent odors from the soggy grass rushed through the car's vents and the ugly smell of rotting vegetation added to the depressing feel of the neglected meadow.

Paul slowly ran the Citroen through the field of grass to an impassable washout in the road. He stopped the car alongside a crumbling barn. Most of the window glass was broken out and it was easy to look through the open holes. Only black shadows and bird nests lived inside the barn's dusty stalls. The shed leaned heavily to one side and its door sagged, almost off the hinges. Red stain on the barn's sides was bleached to gray from years of rain and neglect. The shingle roof was torn off by many winter storms, exposing a skeleton of weathered beams. The wooden beams were covered with patches of vivid green lichen, alive from Spring rains. Knowing how slowly lichen grows, I guessed the thick, furry lichen was very old. It looked like the last repairs were done more than fifty years ago. Long neglect also showed in the dense high grass clogging the meadow.

I looked around the pasture but couldn't immediately spot Villa Toth. I bargained with myself that we were in the wrong place and we hadn't found the home listed in Diane's notes. We were going to turn around and go back, keep searching. Then my eyes tracked a weed infested driveway as it swept to the shore of Lake Geneva and spread before a large mansion. There was no doubt we were at our destination and my heart sank into my stomach. This had to be the place Diane referenced in her notes.

The setting sun ran long shadows across the villa, cutting the estate into dark and light patches. I couldn't see much detail in that light, but the building was huge, like a manor home on Long Island. Once elegant, the mansion was now in shabby condition. It looked like someone left suddenly half a century ago and never returned. I had the feeling my life was going the opposite way. I arrived here but would never leave. Once I got out of the car, I knew I'd be shot and we were about to get out of the car.

The door behind me snicked open and Pierre talked in a voice that was sickeningly casual. "We've been in the car a long time. Let's get out and stretch our legs, eh? Toss me the car keys, Paul. Gently."

"Sure," Paul replied calmly. He yanked the keychain out and flung it backwards in a gentle arc. I knew Paul's heart was thumping like mine, despite the calm tone of his voice. We were both wondering what Corday would do next.

Corday talked with the charm of a cocktail party host. "Let's go for a walk, get a little exercise before I call Vernier and negotiate." He smiled engagingly and it turned me cold. He intended to walk us into the dense woods, making sure no one would find our bodies. Corday only had to fire two muffled shots and it would be over. Paul and I were dead.

I cranked the door handle and rolled my body out of the car, hoping to run away. I stood for the first time in many hours and my legs were barely able to prop me up. Looking across the car, I saw Corday was pointing the gun straight at me and I knew I couldn't escape.

Pierre wagged the gun at thick brush surrounding the meadow. "Walk," he ordered and his face turned to stone.

Paul Denis was rubbing his legs, his body numb like mine. He stalled, "You need to keep us alive. You want to trade us to Vernier, don't you?"

"No," Pierre said coldly.

"Why?" I asked, not expecting an answer. But I got one.

"The treasure's in that villa. Once I get it, I have to move fast. You'll slow me down," Pierre replied.

"Keep the damned treasure, all of it. Let us go," Paul argued. "We'll walk to the shoreline highway and hitchhike. It'll be hours before Vernier finds us. You'll be long gone."

"I can't take that chance." Corday pointed the gun toward the woods and snarled, "Walk and you'll live longer. I can shoot you here and drag the bodies." Pierre cocked the gun.

I was desperate and I had to try something. I argued, "This villa is abandoned. Nobody lived here for decades, more than fifty years. You can tell from the condition of the buildings. The treasure isn't here."

"Yes it is," Corday smirked. "You thought you were smart, eh, Nicki? You dragged me to Lake Geneva as a stall, a wild goose chase. You picked this place for a long drive, thinking you were putting one over on me. But you were taking me where I wanted to go."

"I was taking you to the treasure. Is that what you mean?"

"Yes," Corday answered smugly. "You thought I was stupid, didn't you, Nicki? But I'm a lot smarter than you think. You were sleeping and I was busy reading the printout, going over Diane's notes. I saw things you missed."

"Like what?" I prodded Corday, stalling to buy a few more seconds of life.

Pierre said, "I discovered an auctioneer bought all the old hotel furniture. The same guy owned the burned warehouse where the first arson happened. I think he stored the furniture in that warehouse after he bought all those massive hotel pieces, many of them from the penthouse suite where Hess stayed. I think this auctioneer inspected the furniture and found the lost fortune. This villa was built with part of the treasure."

It looked like Corday might be right, but I had one last reason for Pierre to keep us alive. "There's still missing pieces to your story. Suppose the auctioneer spent the whole fortune and there's no treasure in the villa. You need Paul and me alive, as bait for Vernier. Kill us and you have nothing to trade Vernier for your life."

"She has a point," Paul Denis argued. "There's no way of knowing what really happened. We have to go inside the house and find out."

"That's right, Pierre. It'll only take a few minutes to explore the mansion. You've got nothing to lose by keeping us alive and possibly a lot to gain."

I saw Pierre hesitate, trying to decide what to do. He was wavering, licking the corner of his mouth. His eyes darted to the villa, then back to me and I could feel the anger clouding his face, narrowing his eyes. He hated doing anything I recommended, even when I made perfect sense. He could go either way, shoot me or walk inside the house, but it didn't look good.

The longer I waited, the worse Corday acted. I couldn't stall anymore so I started toward the old villa, hoping I didn't get shot in the back. I stepped in the washout beside the car, waddling through ankle deep mud. I didn't turn around to look at Corday, afraid that would break the spell. I was pulling on him to follow me, hoping it would work. Maybe I'd get a bullet in my back, but I had nothing to lose.

I sucked my feet out of the mud, taking each step in a wobbly struggle. Nearly falling, I put my hand down for balance and the hand sank into muck up to my wrist. I slid to the bottom of the washout and fought my way up the other side, panting from exertion. The effort to climb only a few feet was exhausting, plopping one foot into sticky goo and dragging the other out.

Finally, I reached level ground and went toward the ruined house, knowing that in a few more steps Corday would have to shoot me. My heart tightened with anxiety. Then there was a snick and Corday uncocked the gun, letting the hammer down. I heard Pierre's footsteps sloshing behind me and sighed in relief. We were going inside the villa.

I kept walking, rocking in the mud with each footstep, wading in muck toward the derelict mansion looming in front of me. My bare legs were coated with icy mud and my body was painfully frozen under a thin dress that was a joke against the cold wind rushing off Lake Geneva. I had a hard time seeing where to walk because it was almost dark. When Paul came alongside, I sensed his eyes on me and I tried to look calm, like I had all the answers. But nothing was farther from the truth. I had no idea what was in that old, abandoned house. Only Villa Toth knew the secrets of the last sixty years.

# 24

# Inside Villa Toth

The setting sun painted a deceptively warm glow on Villa Toth. The mansion had a full second story with large windows along the front giving the occupants sweeping views of Lake Geneva. The building was a huge wood framed structure with turrets on both ends. A balcony ran around each turret like the deck around a lighthouse, shielding windows underneath from strong afternoon sunlight. The estate had a country elegance, like a diplomat's retreat, ready for escaping job stress or formally entertaining VIPs and rich socialites.

In the middle was a grand entry with a flat roof extending from the house and supported on wooden columns, a porte cochere. This entrance was a sort of carport, shielding guests from rain after they slid out of limousines. Their ball gowns and tuxedos would stay dry during their walk to the house, keeping their clothes perfect when they were announced by the butler. It was like movie stars arriving at the Academy Awards and I could easily imagine a fleet of limos gliding up the long driveway, stopping under the porte cochere.

I was surprised to see an antique limousine parked under the overhang, the long hood of the old Packard badly weathered, its black paint faded to chalky gray. A bird's nest messed the chauffeur's open seating area and the tires were flat from all the air slowly leaking out over the years. A wheel had been taken off its axle and propped against a running board. That side of the limo was supported by a rusted jack holding the front axle up, so the car sat on three tires and one metal crutch.

Paul Denis walked past me and lifted a cross shaped tire wrench off the ground. He ran a thumb along the heavy iron tool, chipping flakes of rust from it, then tossed the metal wrench on the driveway with a loud clang. "It looks like the chauffeur was changing a tire and never finished the job." Paul brushed rust off his hands and looked the house over carefully. He frowned. "Something bad happened here. They went away in a hurry and left the limousine behind."

"Maybe they tried to run away and didn't make it," I suggested.

He nodded. "It's possible they didn't escape. I hope something inside tells more of their story."

"Sure you want to know?" I asked.

"Yes," Paul answered. "I feel like I've walked in the middle of a dream and I want to know the rest."

"I don't have any time for dreams," Pierre Corday complained. He ran a hand over stubble darkening his cheeks, then nervously pushed strands of greasy hair off his forehead. His eyes darted to the villa and back to me. "Hurry up. The sun is setting. It's getting dark." He waved a hand, urging us forward.

"OK," I said irritably, "I'm going."

I cautiously put my foot on the entry stairs and a tread bent, squeaking loudly. I tried the end of the plank where there was more support. When the tread held, I dared the remaining steps and they sagged deeply, each board springing like a trampoline. I got on the porch and the front door was still elegant despite neglect. Elaborately carved, the door held an oval window of frosted glass and a richly detailed brass saucer was the mounting plate for a massive doorknob.

I put a hand on the large ball of the doorknob and twisted against years of rust and dirt. The door lock gave a harsh click, unlocking with great reluctance. I pushed and the door barely moved despite my leaning heavily against the dark mahogany wood. When I shoved harder, the door swung back on screeching hinges, yielded to half open and stuck, refusing to move any more.

I craned my neck to look around the door into an entry hall, a brief corridor that opened on a living room cluttered with massive furniture. The furnishings were covered in dust that turned them into gray shadows, making the antiques appear as the ghosts of a sofa bracketed by armchairs. An open book was turned face-down on the chair seat and its leather binding was a fuzzy lump on the cushion. Next to the chair, a tall standing lamp seemed to be growing out of the dirt on the carpet like a thin tree. Its top branched into three naked bulbs shrouded in the tatters of a skirted lampshade. The fireplace brass was so badly tarnished it looked like a black spider web. Charred logs were jumbled in the fireplace, coated in soot knocked from the chimney by wind.

The front windows were nearly opaque with grime but a broken window pane let a beam of sunlight through and it looked like a theater spotlight painting a halo on the floor of a dark stage. Under the thick carpet of dust on the floor, I could see a tree limb blown through the window years ago by a storm.

Paul Denis pointed to little pieces of broken glass dimly visible under the dust. "That tree limb fell through the window decades ago and no one fixed the broken glass. I think we're the only people to enter the house in more than sixty years."

Corday was impatient. "Go on," Pierre urged.

Reluctantly, I stepped across the threshold and entered the mansion. An overpowering stench hit me, a combination of rot and dust. My ears itched from mold growing everywhere. The building was saturated by rains pouring through the leaky roof for years and it actually felt colder inside the house than outside.

I walked over to a grandfather clock with its brass weights run down and softly held a drooping chain in my fingers, letting the cold brass links slide across my palm. Grandfather clocks were one of my favorite things and I was sad to see this beautiful antique timepiece abandoned and forgotten. The clock sat on a long Persian rug whose bright colors were muted shadows under the cake of dirt on the floor. The rug ran along the entry hall to a flight of stairs and I asked Corday, "Do you want to explore the second story?"

"I don't know." Pierre hesitated, showing his first sign of fear. He fidgeted in the doorway and glanced nervously around the house. Corday talked in an unusually soft voice. "I want to see this level before I go upstairs."

"OK, we stay on the ground floor." I didn't really care. I didn't expect to find anything unusual on this level, but I was wrong. I turned to face the dining room and was surprised to see a long table loaded in a full place setting, decorated in fine linen mats, elegant silverware and domed serving dishes. Gold filigree in the china managed a dim glint, smiling at me despite ages of neglect, inviting me to join what had been an every night family ritual dinner.

On the dining table, several plates held old slices of roast beef. The meat had decayed to a repulsive slime, an ugly combination of grease and bacteria. Sweet potatoes were dried and collapsed, looking like worn out ballet slippers. Blackened lumps on the plates may have once been cauliflower. On a side board, a dessert cake was covered by a glass dome. The cake was petrified in a leathery, shrunken head version of its real self. I picked up a linen napkin, brushing off a mat of cobwebs and looked at the monogram, then respectfully put the napkin back.

"The chairs are all pushed away from the table and one chair is toppled over," Paul commented. "The family was eating here and left in a hurry, abandoning the house for some reason."

"Yes." I was struck by a feeling of tragedy that clung to the room. I tried to understand what happened here. Clearly a wealthy family was eating dinner and I imagined a butler pouring dessert wine at the head of the table. I saw the butler with a white bow tie gleaming over the rigid collar of his shirt, his black tuxedo running down long arms to white cotton gloves. Maids in starched white aprons and black skirts cleared dishes, getting the table ready for dessert service.

Children of various ages, from kindergarten to high school, sat in the righteously stiff dining room chairs. They were laughing and giggling to each other. The house was alive again, warm and inviting and it felt more real than just my imagination. Car headlights streaked across the dining room window and it shuddered like a gust of wind hit the glass. I heard car doors thrown open and boots hitting dry, hard ground. People were talking outside in loud voices, shouting at each other. I was so convinced someone was outside that I ran to the window and looked, only to see an empty darkness settling on the soggy earth. I turned around to look at the family eating dinner but suddenly the memories that weren't mine vanished, brushed away by an icy wind.

"Let's go upstairs," Pierre croaked from a nervous, dry throat. He looked skittishly at me, catching my eyes indirectly. He was staring at my reflection in the window glass.

I asked Pierre, "Did you see the family?"

"No," Corday said. It was easy to tell Pierre was lying. He cleared his throat. "Come on, let's get this over with."

I looked at Paul Denis, wondering what he'd seen. Was it just my imagination, or had the family really been there in the dining room for a moment?

"The house is trying to tell us something," Paul explained. "Don't worry. I think it's on your side."

"I hope so. I could use some help."

"Knock it off," Pierre ordered us. "I want both of you to go upstairs. You walk ahead of me."

"Right." I shrugged and moved to the staircase, but I didn't go very far. I put one foot on the stairs and stopped, frozen in mid-step by the image in front of me. I was staring at something so obvious I couldn't believe I overlooked the clue on entering the house.

"What's holding you up?" Corday was impatient.

"Oh, nothing much," I replied sarcastically. "You wouldn't want to know."

"What the hell's she talking about?" Corday asked Paul.

Paul Denis hesitated a moment. "We aren't the only people to visit the house." He gestured at footprints in thick dust on the floor.

I added, "Someone came inside Villa Toth before we entered the old mansion. Their tracks lead right up the stairs." In the dark shadows of the old house, an outline of footsteps made sharp cutouts in thick gray dust on the floor. The heel and toe of shoe prints indicated two people came here recently, a man and a woman. Small women's pumps wove up the dusty carpet on the stairway and the woman's footprints were trailed by men's dress shoes.

# 25

# Previous Visitors

Behind me, warped floorboards squeaked as Pierre Corday moved to get a better look at the footprints. Corday pointed his gun at an outline of footsteps leading up the staircase and sputtered, "There weren't any tire marks on the road from another car. How did anyone get inside this house without us seeing a trace of them?"

I shrugged. "I don't know. Let's backtrack and see where they entered the house." Paul Denis was standing behind me and I squeezed past him to look down the hall. Beyond the grandfather clock, hazy light let me track the footsteps until the hallway bent toward servants quarters. At that point, a sagging doorway was framed in moldy plaster, buckled from rain water leaking down the back wall of the mansion and peeling off ornate wallpaper, leaving bubbles of green slime on the raw plaster. The warped door was recently opened, sweeping a clean arc on the dusty floor. I said, "They came in the rear door."

Paul brushed past me and pointed at the long trail of footprints. "That's why we didn't see any sign of them in front. But why come in the back door?"

"I have an idea why, but I don't think we're going to like the reason." Without waiting for Corday's permission, I walked toward a small window at the rear of the house, a diamond-shaped pane of glass clouded with grime. I pressed my face against the window and peered out, trying to distinguish objects in the fading light.

"What do you see?" Corday demanded.

"There's a huge circle pressed in the meadow where downblast from a helicopter mashed the grass flat. The helicopter's landing skids tore a pair of gashes in the center of the circle. Traveling by helicopter is Vernier's style."

"Maybe it wasn't Vernier," Pierre said lamely. "Somebody else came by helicopter, a rich buyer and their agent."

I disagreed. "No one's cared about this place for more than sixty years. Only Diane knew Villa Toth exists. I'm sure the visitors were Diane

St. Remy and City Commissioner Vernier. The woman's footprints indicate Diane was here."

"Can you be sure it was Diane and Vernier?" Paul asked. He squatted to get a better look. His fingertip carefully traced the outline of a footprint as though Paul were trying for a psychic link to the owner of the shoe.

I suggested, "The shoe marks fit Diane and Vernier. Diane was tiny and City Commissioner Vernier's a small man. You remember how short Vernier is, right Pierre?"

"Damn," Pierre cursed.

I said, "They came here before Diane went to the Archives and killed Taylor Hansen. I think Vernier may have the treasure."

Corday's face dropped and he looked sick. "I don't believe it." Pierre was just being stubborn. He didn't want to believe the huge fortune was gone and there was nothing left for him. Corday wanted the money for himself and believed it was all right to steal treasure from Vernier since he was part of the conspiracy behind the arsons.

In Pierre's mind, stealing from Vernier was like skimming cash off a million dollar drug bust. Some narcs felt skimming was legitimate pay for risks they took, like a waiter getting a nice tip for doing a good job. Pierre had the same belief, taking money away from criminals was fine. Corday had been fixated on stealing Vernier's treasure, dreaming of an easy life. Without the treasure, though, Pierre was like the rest of us, a little person trapped in a crazy world, trying to survive. Pierre seemed lost and disoriented. He just stood there, looking melancholy and didn't say anything.

Perhaps I should've felt rage at Corday for the ordeal he put me through, threatening to kill me, but I couldn't bring myself to hate him. So far he hadn't done anything really criminal. Shooting Diane could be viewed as saving my life and Paul's. Maybe I could get Pierre to put his gun away. I said, "Pierre, you haven't done anything illegal so far. Even shooting Diane can be explained."

"I shot Diane in the line of duty," Corday hedged. "I had to shoot her." Then he muttered softly, "Vernier threatened to kill my family if I didn't get rid of Diane."

"Of course," I agreed. "When Vernier didn't need Diane anymore, she became just a liability. Diane was a witness tying Vernier to the arsons and the City Commissioner wanted to get rid of her."

"Nicki's right," Paul Denis agreed. "Diane would've testified against Vernier to get a shorter prison sentence."

I went on, "So City Commissioner Vernier got in touch with you, Pierre. He threatened your kids, forcing you to shoot Diane." I added,

"It was lucky for me you showed up at the Archives. You saved my life."

Pierre couldn't look at me and he seemed shy, almost bashful. Corday stared at his pistol like the gun was a strange growth sprouted on his hand, a huge wart. He shifted the gun nervously, then slid the pistol in his shoulder holster. Corday snapped the flap over the gun, securing it.

Pierre talked quietly. "If that bastard Vernier found the treasure, it's hopeless. I'm dead. I'm the last witness and Vernier will kill me."

I said, "He'll kill all three of us. We all know too much. Maybe something upstairs will help." I started walking up the stairway.

"What do you think you're doing?" Corday asked. His voice was worried, not hostile.

I said quietly, "I'm going upstairs. Diane went there with Vernier. I want to see what they found." I pointed toward the second floor of the house.

"Be careful," Pierre warned me.

Paul said, "Diane may have left a booby trap. I should go first."

Corday elbowed past, his body wound tight with anxiety as he brushed against me. He mumbled, "I have to know if they found the treasure."

"Hey," I shouted, "go slower. You said to be careful, remember?"

"Yeah," Corday muttered bitterly. He stopped when he got to the top of the stairs and rubbed sweaty hands on his hips. Pierre twisted his head, peering along the second floor hallway, squinting at the darkness. The upstairs hallway melted into dust, becoming nothing more than vague shapes and gray shadows. There was so little light I couldn't tell dusky walls from gray haze leaking downward.

In that dim interior, I could only see Corday's legs clearly, not even his torso. Above, his head vanished in a misty gloom like he was standing in a damaged photograph, partly erased. We waited there on the stairway, listening. I kept expecting the grandfather clock in the hall to tick but the clock was silent as the house.

Then I heard the stairway squeak and Paul Denis wedged past me. He stopped alongside Pierre at the top of the stairs. They were both wary, hesitant to move any farther.

Paul asked Corday, "You smell it?"

"Yes," Corday answered. "I smell gasoline and sawdust. Diane ran a chainsaw."

"Diane was probably cutting up furniture."

"I think you're right Nicki," Paul agreed. "Diane was looking for treasure in hidden compartments and she sliced the furniture open with the chainsaw."

I moved closer to them, hoping to get a look at the furniture but their bodies blocked any view. Standing at the top of the stairs, the pair were like a cork in the neck of a wine bottle. I raised myself on tiptoe and craned my neck, peering at the gloom along the hallway toward a faint glow marking the door of the master bedroom suite.

Paul sensed I was behind him and he waved me back. "You stay there as backup. One of us will go along the hallway to check it out."

"OK," I replied sullenly. I didn't like staying behind, but part of me was grateful not to be walking along the dark corridor.

I could see fear working on Corday. He licked dry lips and leaned against the wall for a better look. "I'll go," Pierre said and he slid along the second floor hallway before Paul could stop him.

"Look out," Paul Denis shouted and he grabbed Pierre's ankle, tugging the leg backward. Corday fell, thudding on the floor just before an explosion banged along the hallway. The boom of the explosion was followed by a terrible shredding noise, a hundred holes punched in the walls from metal fragments tearing through the plaster. A few of the iron splinters hit Corday and he moaned in pain, writhing on the hallway floor.

Acrid fumes and a cloud of plaster dust fell on me. I rushed upstairs and found Paul Denis tearing Corday's pant leg. Pierre's wounds were an ugly sight. Steel fragments had ripped through Corday's leg and jagged metal slivers were sticking out of his torn muscles, dripping blood at an alarming rate. Pierre's leg was discoloring and swelling rapidly, terribly bruised by the force of the explosion.

"Grenade?" I asked.

Paul nodded. "Not very high tech. Only a trip wire and a grenade, but the booby trap almost worked. Another step and Pierre would be dead." Paul assured Corday, "The leg only looks bad. It'll heal up fine." Paul improvised a tourniquet from torn cloth and tied it below the knee, stopping the flow of blood.

Pierre grunted a "Thanks."

"Sure," Paul responded automatically. He fingered a length of coarse piano wire, the trip wire for the grenade. "I hope Diane didn't leave any other gifts behind."

"Probably not," I guessed. "Didn't have time. That's why this old fashioned hand grenade was used. The trip wire would be easy to spot in daylight, but she didn't have time to be subtle."

Dust from the explosion had settled out and I looked along the hallway. The setting sun moved across the master bedroom windows, making it easier to see along the corridor and spot booby traps. I'm not very brave and without the light, I wouldn't have done what I did next.

I started down the hallway, hoping to explore the bedroom before it got dark.

"Hey, Nicki," Paul shouted after me.

"I'll be careful," I assured him but I almost wasn't careful enough. The next trip wire dragged against my ankle and I barely felt its feather touch. I froze and stood there, feeling the tight strand of piano wire cut into my skin. I'd almost set off another booby trap, an explosion sending a hundred sharp metal fragments into my body.

I slowly looked down, lifted my foot slightly and let the wire's tension push my ankle back. My eyes tracked the strand of wire to a grenade where the safety pin was pulled half out. I carefully bent down and pushed the pin back in the grenade, then unwrapped the tough strand of piano wire from the explosive device. The wire snapped out of my fingers and curled against the wall with a vicious twang.

I let Paul know what happened. "I found a second booby trap and defused it."

"Damn," Paul muttered. "Hang on. Don't move again."

"OK," I agreed. I watched Paul Denis inch his way past me and slide cautiously toward the bedroom door. His steps were paced like slow drip from a leaky faucet. He slid his feet forward, his work boots scraping the floorboards like sandpaper, feeling for the trip wire of an explosive device. Sweat beaded on Paul's forehead and dripped on the floor, each drop of sweat boring a dark hole in a thick cake of dust covering the floorboards. His foot moved forward and stopped abruptly, poised an inch off the ground, then slid ever so gently backwards. I saw Paul's face tense and he said quietly, "Another booby trap."

Paul slowly knelt down. "I need a pin to make the grenade safe. You see a loose nail around?"

"I don't think so," I answered, patting the dark walls. "There's no safety pin in the handle?"

"No," Paul grunted, looking around for something to use. "Diane must have taken the safety pin with her. She wanted this third booby trap to have a hair trigger. Any sudden movement against the trip wire sets off the explosion."

"Lovely," I said sarcastically. Even dead, Diane was easy to hate. I suggested, "Maybe a paper clip could be used as a pin in the grenade. Pierre might have one in his pockets. I'll check."

Corday was sitting on the hallway floor and in the dim light all I could see of Pierre were his shoes sticking out of a dull gloom. Corday shifted his weight to check in his pockets. He grunted in pain and said, "Here. I got a paper clip."

I walked the few steps to Corday and was shocked at the change in him after only a couple of minutes. Even in that faint light, Pierre's face was white from blood loss. His hair was a sponge clogged with plaster dust from the explosion and blood was drying on his forehead.

My eyes flashed to Corday's hand trembling in front of me, holding a paper clip. I took it and said, "Thanks. Don't forget to loosen the tourniquet every few minutes. OK?"

"Yeah," Corday grunted. Pierre leaned his head back in exhaustion and his head hit the wall with a thump.

"We're getting out of here soon, taking you to a doctor," I reassured Corday. He didn't answer. His blood loss was serious despite the tourniquet and Pierre was fading in and out of consciousness. I gently touched his arm.

Corday's eyelids fluttered open. He murmured, "I'm all right. Go help Paul."

"Sure. Get some rest." I turned away and went back to Paul, handing him the paper clip.

He bent the metal clip and forced the straightened wire in the grenade's lever mechanism. There was a light snick. "There, it's safe," he said quietly. Paul stood up and brushed off his hands.

"You should take a look at Corday," I suggested. "He's lost a lot of blood."

"Sure, I'll check on him. Then we better get out of here. In five minutes, it'll be completely black inside the house and we won't be able to see where we're going."

"OK. While you check Pierre, I'll look inside the master bedroom. I think it holds the answers to a lot of our questions."

Paul shook his head. "Nicki, that's not a good idea. Diane may have another booby trap in there. You can get killed. Get us killed as well."

"I have to go in the bedroom. It's the last chance to put this puzzle together. Tomorrow, Vernier will have the arsonist torch this house. The whole villa will be gone."

Paul sighed, but he didn't argue with me. "All right," he reluctantly agreed. "Watch out."

"Yeah, I'll be cautious." I knew it wasn't safe to go in the bedroom but I wanted to know what happened to the lost fortune.

# 26

# The Ledger

Standing in the doorway, I had a sweeping view of Lake Geneva through a long run of windows, taking up most of the outside walls. The open feel of the glass transformed the master suite from bedroom to sunroom, an effect that naturally led to a large balcony. It was as though I were in the lobby of a resort hotel with a grand terrace rolling to the lakeshore. The suite was enormous, with a sitting area and two private bathrooms. I guessed this area took most of the mansion's upper floor, deliberately built large to hold the furniture from a hotel penthouse suite. It was the penthouse Rudolf Hess occupied when he hoarded a fortune in stolen treasure.

The master bedroom suite of Villa Toth wasn't decorated for a Nazi, though. The room had been lovingly furnished by a wife to share with her husband. The bedroom's feminine elegance was undeniable. The woman who decorated this suite was the Laura Ashley of her day, using sunny pastels and floral patterns to give the room a soft brightness and an uplifting mood. Blue window curtains were a counterpoint to earth tones in the wallpaper, but time faded all the pretty colors to muted shadows. For more than sixty years, rain leaked through the roof, ruining the décor. The finely detailed wallpaper hung limply on rotted plaster walls. Over the years, velvet window curtains faded, bleached by the sun until the heavy curtains rotted and fell off their rods. Now they added a heap of yellowed cloth to the mess Diane St. Remy made in the room with her chainsaw.

An old four poster bed was cut into thick chunks and its canopy was shredded fabric peppered with sawdust. The canopied bed was made of thick hardwood planks and must have weighed nearly a ton. I could no longer tell what picture had been carved into the thick headboard, but the scene looked like an outdoor, woodsy setting with birds and deer. The headboard was now scarred with fresh woodcuts slicing through the pale grain, ripping away the deep red stain and rich varnish. After destroying the bed, Diane used her chainsaw to rip apart all the bedroom furniture.

Shards of broken glass jutted from the splintered doors of an armoire. The mirrored glass glistened in the last rays of sunset, posturing like an old actor vainly attempting to regain his glory days at center stage. I could reconstruct the armoire and its twin brothers into three giant closets with sculpted crests along their top. Butted together, the sculpted tops of the armoires would have formed another forest scene complementing the headboard's woodland motif. After Diane, the closets were just broken remnants, part of a junk pile strewn across the floor like a garbage dump.

In the rubble, I could see hollowed out bedposts and drawers with false bottoms, hidden compartments large enough for jewels, rolled up paintings, cash and title deeds. But did they still hold this treasure when Diane walked in the room? The only way to answer that question was to risk a step inside the suite, yet there was hardly any light in the room.

The sun's orange ball was only a slim crescent sinking into Lake Geneva. The setting sun forced its way through grimy window panes, painting the bedroom in reddish shadows, coloring the scene like an early photograph, a tintype done in sepia tones. Dust choked the air, making it even harder to spot a trap. When I walked on a pile of rubble, anything could be hidden underneath. I got a few steps inside and stopped.

One bedpost was near me, a carved wooden piece thick as my leg, with elaborate crosscut patterns like a pineapple. I squatted and reached for the heavy post, teasing it toward me using my fingertips, rolling the post over the smooth hardwood floor. Finally, I was able to lift the chunk and was surprised at how light the hardwood felt. The bedpost was hollow, weighing a fraction of what I expected. The empty center was easily large enough to hold title deeds to whole blocks of central Paris, worth a billion dollars each. This was indeed the furniture an arsonist murdered people to find, antiques that once held a Nazi fortune. But there was nothing inside the furniture's hidden compartments now. I tossed the bedpost on the floor and it hit with a thunk, rolling to a stop against a warped floorboard.

The corners of the bedroom disappeared in dark shadows that inched toward me with every passing second. There wasn't time to look through everything to see if part of the treasure remained. I had to hope a quick scan of the area would lead to some answers. I felt pulled toward the remains of a "secretary," a small desk used for composing letters. Thomas Jefferson would have written to friends at such a desk. The "secretary" was sitting in the corner where the piece had stood for decades, waiting for its owner to return and pull out a sheet of linen stationary, ink a fountain pen inlaid with mother of pearl and compose a note. This was the kind of desk where you lift the lid and put your papers inside. I bent over the shattered desk and pulled up its lid, now sliced in two pieces.

There was nothing inside the "secretary" but wood shavings and a dead cockroach. I was puzzled why I'd felt drawn to an empty desk. I was about to leave when I saw a black ledger nearby, thrown against the wall. I assumed the accounting ledger was once kept inside the writing desk for daily use by its owner. Jammed in a corner, the thin black ledger was covered in plaster dust and wood chips. It looked like the book had been taken from the desk and hidden under a pile of debris. Later, the explosion that injured Pierre Corday tore a hole in the wall and threw the ledger into the corner.

I picked up the book and despite the years, the ledger was in remarkably good shape from being sheltered inside the little writing desk. Opening the book, I turned its green and red ruled pages, smoothing bent sheets of paper. I heard Paul's careful footsteps approaching me.

"You found something?" He was eager to know what happened.

"Oh, yes." I thumbed a few more pages. "I think Vernier and Diane walked in the bedroom and she began sawing open the furniture. City Commissioner Vernier did a little exploring on his own, lifting the lid on the writing desk. He found this ledger."

"What's it say?" Paul leaned over my shoulder to read the book.

"The ledger details every piece of the treasure."

Paul said, "The City Commissioner must have been happy. He finally discovered what he killed people to have."

"No. On the contrary, when Vernier read this accounting ledger he saw there wasn't any fortune left. It had all been spent. But he didn't tell Diane anything. Vernier was cunning and hid the ledger under some rubble. He wanted Diane to think they were still hunting for the lost fortune. But in fact the treasure was gone and City Commissioner Vernier didn't need Diane anymore. He decided to kill her. She was a witness who could testify against him, tying him to the arsons."

"It makes sense," Paul agreed, frowning. "Diane wasn't expecting to be shot in the Paris Archives. She was taken by surprise because she thought Vernier was still backing her search. The City Commissioner is a very cunning man and we still have to deal with him. But what happened to the Nazi treasure?"

I explained, "The ledger says a Mr. Abraham Toth bought the bedroom furniture from the bombed out hotel. Toth was an auctioneer by trade. He examined the furniture in detail to catalogue it for an auction and found the treasure. There's a real irony in Mr. Toth finding the loot."

"Irony?" Paul asked, craning his neck for a better look at the ledger.

I held the book so Paul could see. "Yes, it's very ironic Toth found the treasure. Mr. Toth wrote a passage from the *Torah* in Hebrew script at the beginning of the ledger. Abraham Toth and his family were

Jewish. The irony is that they saved people from Nazi concentration camps using a fortune stolen by a Nazi."

"It was a wonderful accident Toth found the money," Paul commented. "Or was it fate? We'll never know, but I like to think it was destined to happen. Either way, Villa Toth was probably built on the shores of Lake Geneva because it was an escape route to Switzerland. People could cross the lake in boats and avoid Nazi patrols."

I glanced out the window at what little I could see of the lake. The water was a black mirror where an orange streak of sunlight pointed like an arrow toward city lights twinkling on the far shore. This edge of the lake was France, but the lights I saw twinkling on the other side were in Switzerland.

I guessed, "Toth had this house built in the early 1940s, after Nazis occupied France. When the villa was complete, Toth left Paris and lived here with his family. He went to Paris often, making a note of his visits in the ledger. Each trip, he returned with people who'd been hiding from the Nazis. Toth kept them hidden on the grounds of the villa until they could flee to Switzerland."

Paul mused, "I wonder where these rescued people lived? I think it was in that old barn that was so run down."

"Really. Why there? I didn't see any living quarters inside that shed."

Paul said, "I think they lived in a cellar under the barn. Then one night, after arrangements were made, the escapees slipped through a tunnel to the edge of the lake and went by boat to Switzerland."

"Your story makes sense, but I wonder why they lived in the barn's cellar. Why not have them live in the mansion? The house is certainly large enough for several families."

"Too risky, Nicki. A neighbor comes by and sees people he doesn't know. Country folk have nothing to keep them occupied but gossip. Soon the gossip spreads to authorities and the Nazis visit without warning. You see?"

"Yes. Your tunnel theory comes from that shallow ditch near the barn," I guessed.

Paul nodded. "I'm certain the ditch is actually a collapsed tunnel. At first, I thought it was a trench dug to bring lake water to barn animals. But the ditch stops many yards short of the lake and water can't flow into the ditch. I think the tunnel was supported by wooden planks and the planks rotted over the years. The roof fell in and now we see a shallow trench."

Paul shrugged. "That much, I understand. What I don't get is why it took so much money for each person to get into Switzerland." He pointed to entries in the accounting ledger.

I read aloud. "A diamond studded tiara, a crown jewel of the Hapsburgs, is debited. Credited is a family of eight." I was astonished by the next line. The crew of a downed American bomber had been hiding on the outskirts of Paris and they were sent to Switzerland, their safety traded for the deed to the last remaining vineyard in Paris, in Montmartre. "It's the same vineyard I look at every night through the window of my studio apartment."

"Quite a coincidence," he agreed. "Why were such expensive items needed as bribes? Switzerland was neutral during World War II and refugees would be safe there."

"In theory, yes," I explained. "But the Swiss were under a lot of pressure from the Nazis. Swiss officials often handed refugees to the Germans rather than risk an invasion by Hitler's army. It took heavy bribes to keep an escaping family safe in Switzerland. Most bribes went to Nazi officials acting as negotiating agents between the Swiss and Hitler. The agents were really spies. It took a lot of money to keep them quiet about Jewish refugees."

"So the entire fortune was spent saving lives. There isn't any left." Paul whistled in astonishment.

"Not a penny of the original treasure remains," I confirmed. I pointed to the end of the neat rows in the accounting ledger. A line was drawn and beneath it, Abraham Toth wrote that all the money was gone, even cash hidden in Swiss bank accounts.

"Wow," Paul said. "So, Diane flew to this villa expecting to be queen and found nothing inside the hollowed-out furniture. It put her into a rage. After she helicoptered back to Paris, Diane went to the Archives and took out her anger on poor Taylor Hansen. Then she tried to kill us. We were lucky to escape, Nicki."

"Yes. I hope the Toth family also escaped. They saved a lot of lives. I think that meal downstairs was the Toth family's final dinner here, a celebration of the lives they saved. My guess is that Abraham Toth was using his own money to get his family and servants out. They were leaving the very next morning, the last group escaping to Switzerland."

My eyes moved to the windows overlooking the water. Paul was standing before the panoramic view, gazing out the windows with a blank stare. I put the ledger on the floor next to the diary and walked toward Paul, sad and happy at the same time. When I tried to join him, Paul pushed me away. "Don't look."

"I have to know," I said firmly. I turned into the last embers of the sun. Even in that nearly extinct light, I knew instantly what happened to the Toth family and their servants.

Abandoned on the shoreline were three very weathered boats. Their wooden planking was shattered with bullet holes. Dark blood stains were still visible on the wooden seats after all these years. It seemed the Toths died on their last night in the mansion, surprised by Hitler's ghouls. I wanted to believe there'd been a fourth boat and it got away, that somewhere, Toth's grandchildren were raising children of their own right now.

I knew it was just my imagination but I could hear the roar of the engine and see white froth from the boat surging across the water. I left the story as I wanted to see it, with a fourth boat speeding into the night. The image gradually faded and I melted into reality, standing in a room that was nearly dark. There was no more time for sentiment, even with all the pain I felt for the Toth family. I sighed, then picked the diary and ledger off the bedroom floor, grasping the beginning and end of a tragic story in my hands. I walked slowly toward Paul Denis and together, we helped Pierre Corday to the car.

It was a long walk to Pierre's Citroen. The walk was even longer in the absolute darkness that only happens in the countryside, never in a city where streetlights leak glow into the dingiest alleys. It was a relief to hear the car start and see its headlights pick out a fuzzy horizon. Paul gently rolled the car over bumps, going slow to ease Corday's pain, carefully navigating the Citroen over the deeply rutted driveway.

For a moment, I had the illusion I was going home to the life I'd known before the phone rang and I was asked to look at a warehouse arson. I'd stop for cheese at Madame Delbey's Fromagerie, get some fresh strawberries and a Sunday *New York Times*. I'd take a week off and soap this case out of me in some very long, hot showers.

Then the truth hit me and I knew my life would never be the same. I couldn't convict Vernier of a conspiracy because I had no witnesses. Taylor Hansen and Diane St. Remy were dead, so all I had were theories. Publishing my theories would ruin Vernier with a scandal. In return, he would kill me. So I couldn't touch Vernier. The City Commissioner and I were going to co-exist in a kind of Cold War tension, always wary and afraid. It was an ugly way to live.

I thought about leaving Paris, quitting Interpol, but it wouldn't buy me anything. Vernier could reach me anywhere in the world. I was better off staying in plain sight where the City Commissioner could watch me and realize I just wanted to be left alone.

I was completely drained. I'd gone beyond exhaustion hours ago and only the courage of the Toth family gave me strength. I wouldn't like the deal I worked out with Vernier any more than I liked what happened to Abraham Toth and his children. But like them, I'd learn to live with it.

# 27

# Paris Again

I was back at my desk in the Interpol bullpen and happy to be leading a somewhat normal life again. Many things weren't the same, including my hands and feet, which were wrapped in gauze bandages like an Egyptian mummy. A very tired emergency room intern spent two hours cleaning and treating cuts I'd gotten in the Paris Archives. My aching muscles dreamed of a long hot soak in a bathtub but a hot bath was weeks away. Put soapy water on all those cuts and they'd sting like a hundred angry bees, so I was getting a masters degree in the art of the sponge bath. I was also walking on the edge of my feet. I looked like an apprentice Japanese geisha when I waddled into work.

My consolation was eating a fresh box of Bernachon chocolates, courtesy of Paul Denis, who knew how to find quaint shops in Paris better than the tour guides. I never thought I'd eat chocolates that rich and intense. I don't get a chance to sample Paris restaurants on my Interpol salary. I placed the beautiful gold Bernachon box in the center of my cluttered desk, using my undamaged elbows to push aside a backlog of case folders that piled up while I was on sick leave. Technically, I wasn't supposed to be in the office yet, so I spent the morning admiring each bonbon like it was a rare gem, savoring all the flavors and aftertones.

The chocolates should have been a guilt gift from Pierre Corday but that wasn't his style and he wasn't going to change. The best I got from Pierre was a sheepish look when he dropped a copy of the morning newspaper in front of me, mumbling excuses for not being able to stay. I understood why Pierre left in a hurry when I picked up the paper.

The front page headline read "Arsonist Killed in Paris Archives." The newspaper asserted Diane St. Remy was the arsonist who ambushed firefighters and murdered the occupants of an apartment building. The newspaper account was a cover story created by Vernier, a convenient fiction to hide his involvement and truth wasn't part of the article. For example, the story portrayed Pierre Corday as the hero who shot Diane and as a result, he was getting a promotion with a raise in salary. I was

sure Vernier actually gave Pierre the raise to buy Corday's silence. Reporters were told that Pierre's leg was injured in the Archives, not that Corday was wounded by a grenade exploding inside Villa Toth.

I didn't expect to find anything in the newspapers about what happened to Villa Toth. Vernier would have squelched any reports about the mansion. So I didn't look at the papers and instead scanned the Interpol database. I found a report of an old mansion on Lake Geneva burning to the ground. Local firefighters didn't know the mansion existed and they were surprised by the blaze. The cause of the fire was under investigation, but I knew why there'd been a fire at Villa Toth. Vernier had the real arsonist torch the mansion to ensure all evidence vanished. Diane may be gone for good, but the real arsonist was still on the loose, a merciless killer for hire. I wasn't happy about it. I made sure Vernier knew the arsonist was still fair game when we negotiated a truce deal with the City Commissioner. The man who'd killed dozens of firefighters and innocent victims had made #1 on Interpol's most wanted list and we were going all out to catch him.

Vernier warned me any attempt to catch the arsonist was a "mistake." I knew what the City Commissioner meant by "mistake." The truce with Vernier was a fragile thing and capturing the arsonist would set off a chain reaction linking the City Commissioner to the warehouse fire. Vernier's career would be wrecked by the scandal and he'd get revenge, meaning the City Commissioner would hire another pro hit man to eliminate me, Paul and Corday.

The reason we weren't already dead was that I had the Rudolf Hess diary tucked in a bank's safe deposit box, with my sworn statement describing Vernier's involvement in the arsons. The box would be opened and its contents examined by a judge if I was killed. I was paranoid enough that I had copies of the Hess diary and my statement in other banks scattered around Paris. In case Vernier bribed the judge, my last will and testament directed my attorney to open the safe deposit box and brief the media on the truth behind the arsons. Paul Denis and Pierre Corday had the same arrangement with their lawyers.

Vernier killing us meant the end of his political career since our attorneys would tell the press about the conspiracy behind the arsons. Even though I couldn't convict the City Commissioner, I could ruin him and he knew it. So the three of us lived together with Vernier in a fragile truce. The system worked so long as we left each other alone and nobody did anything foolish.

I was sure Vernier had visions of wiping us out and destroying all evidence. His chances of a perfect sweep weren't good. There was always a wildcard in every situation, as Vernier learned the hard way with Taylor Hansen. Still, I wasn't taking any chances.

I wasn't going to hang around with Pierre Corday, making the two of us an easy target. We couldn't work together as partners but I'd still see Pierre often. He was a major player in the Paris Interpol office. I'd seek out his advice on my cases from time to time. I didn't have a grudge against him and I'd work with Corday to solve a crime if it became necessary.

I planned on calling Paul Denis frequently to make sure he was all right, but I couldn't spend time with him either. It was too risky. I respected Paul and wished I had the chance to know him better. At least I got to talk with him several times a week, checking that we were all safe. He seemed so happy on the phone talking about his remodeling plans. I wished I had something to look forward to like Paul did, a hobby or someone special.

I opened my desk drawer and looked at my battered camera, an old graduation present that should have been discarded years ago. But it still worked, so I kept it handy, using it to freeze beautiful images. I promised myself that one day I'd paint those images, dragging my dusty easel on the apartment roof some mythical warm Sunday morning to start my real life. In the meantime, my other "real life" was calling. There were case folders stacked a foot high on my desk and I'd soon have a new partner. Somewhere along the line, there'd be another exotic case like these arsons.

In the meantime, Paris was always enchanting. I had a real hunger to sit in Place de Furstemberg and eat a croque monsieur under the lavender blooms of the paulownia trees, listening to a string quartet exploiting the perfect acoustics of the square. I looked out a dirt-streaked window, wishing I could go outside for lunch. Well, my feet would heal up soon and I'd have a somewhat normal life again, eating in cafes and shopping in my favorite places.

But I'd always have fear nagging me, wondering if Vernier had found a way to get to me. I'd spend my life looking over my shoulder to see if I was being followed. I was sure the day would come when my fragile truce with City Commissioner Vernier was swept away. The truce could end anytime. All it would take is one careless moment.

www.ingramcontent.com/pod-product-compliance
Lightning Source LLC
Chambersburg PA
CBHW062011170626

46813CB00001B/117